LONG TEXAN

Center Point
Large Print

Also by William MacLeod Raine
and available from Center Point Large Print:

Border Breed
Courage Stout
Clattering Hoofs

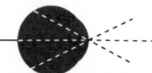

LONG TEXAN

A WESTERN DUO

WILLIAM MACLEOD
RAINE

CENTER POINT LARGE PRINT
THORNDIKE, MAINE

A Circle Ⓥ Western published by
Center Point Large Print in the year 2015 in
co-operation with Golden West Literary Agency.

First Edition
November, 2015

Printed in the United States of America
on permanent paper.
Set in 16-point Times New Roman type.

ISBN: 978-1-62899-770-5 (hardcover)
ISBN: 978-1-62899-775-0 (paperback)

Library of Congress Cataloging-in-Publication Data

Raine, William MacLeod, 1871–1954.
[Short stories. Selections]
Long Texan : a western duo / William MacLeod Raine. — First edition.
pages cm
Summary: "In two western stories set in Arizona, strong and silent
cowboys use their wits to overcome bullies while avoiding gunplay as
much as possible"—Provided by publisher.
ISBN 978-1-62899-770-5 (hardcover : alk. paper)
ISBN 978-1-62899-775-0 (pbk. : alk. paper)
1. Large type books.
   I. Raine, William MacLeod, 1871–1954. Scalisi claws leather.
   II. Raine, William MacLeod, 1871–1954. Long Texan. III. Title.
PS3535.A385A6 2015
813′.52—dc23

2015032460

LONG TEXAN

TABLE OF CONTENTS

FOREWORD
by
Vicki Piekarski

Hailed in his later years by reviewers and contemporaries alike to be the "greatest living practitioner" of the genre and the "dean of Westerns," William MacLeod Raine was born in London, England, on June 22, 1871. Although raised in London, where his father, William, Sr., was a merchant, William, Jr., spent his summers, along with his three brothers, James, Forrester, and Edgar, in the cattle country of Ayrshire with his grandparents. Following the death of his wife in 1881, William, Sr. decided to take his sons to the United States. The Raines settled on a fruit farm on the Arkansas/Texas border that had been purchased sight unseen, where William, Sr. also began raising cattle. Years later, his brand, the Circle WR, would become a hallmark on the spine or title page of the majority of William, Jr.'s Western novels. Always delicate and unable to engage in strenuous activities, the young Raine experienced a frontier existence mostly through observation, but he could write that it was his luck to be in the West "when the Man on Horseback was still king of that vast domain."

Raine attended Sarcey College in Arkansas

briefly and then Oberlin College in Ohio, receiving a Bachelor of Arts degree from the latter in 1894. He got his first taste of journalism while at Oberlin when, to help defray the costs of his education, he persuaded both the *Chicago Tribune* and the *Cincinnati Enquirer* to use him as a local correspondent. Following graduation, Raine made his way west to Seattle, where his father had relocated after a series of catastrophes in Arkansas, including the death of his son Forrester. Failing in an attempt to work as a ranch hand, William, Jr. found a job as a teacher for $36 a month in rural Seattle and then, later, as principal—for which his salary was increased to $70 a month provided he also supplied janitorial services. Years afterward he admitted to being "a rotten teacher". Craving a more adventurous profession, he finally landed a job as a reporter for the *Seattle Times*, receiving $3 a column. He tried to enlist with the First Washington Volunteers for the Philippine campaign in the Spanish-American War, but he was deemed ineligible by medical examiners who diagnosed his lingering illness as tuberculosis. The hope of improving his health was behind his decision to head for the drier air of Colorado.

Raine arrived in Denver in 1898 with $14 in his pocket. Due to his health problems, he worked intermittently for the *Denver Republican* and *The News* (the former eventually merged with the latter) and spent those times, when his condition flared up and his funds were not yet exhausted, absorbing the sun outside the north Denver boarding house that he now called home. He loved reporting but was convinced that he would have to find "some way to make a living sitting on my front porch." He began writing short stories, mostly romantic, swashbuckling tales. Although he would receive his share of rejection slips, the first story he sent out in 1899 was accepted. Titled "The Luck of Eustace Blount", it was bought by *Argosy* for $25. He soon began selling stories regularly to *McClure's*, *Ladies' Home Journal*, and *Harper's*, generating a total income his first full year of creative writing of $225. As his success as a writer improved, apparently so did his health.

His first novel, *A Daughter of Raasay: A Tale of the '45* (Stokes, 1902), first serialized in *The American Magazine* in 1901, had as its background the Jacobite rebellion. It sold four hundred copies. That same year *The American Magazine* hired Raine as a correspondent, and he traveled to Arizona Territory and rode with the Arizona Rangers. He penned articles on the Montana copper war and the Tonto Basin feud as well as of meetings with Pat Garrett and Billy Breckenridge. This was the type of life about which Raine had dreamed, and he decided to make use of the West in his fiction.

Wyoming (Dillingham, 1908) was his first

Western novel. Years later he reflected that it was "really a terrible story . . . melodramatic . . . a hash of two novelettes joined together." Notwithstanding, with the appearance of *Wyoming*, his output shifted almost exclusively to the Western genre. Ultimately it was Raine's ability to depict ranch life accurately through character detail, dialect, and topography that quickly established his reputation as a Western writer who was intimately familiar with his subject. His work appeared regularly in a number of pulp publications, and beginning with *Steve Yeager* (Houghton Mifflin, 1915), a story using Western filmmaking as a background, Raine began a forty year relationship with Houghton Mifflin that would continue through his final Western novel, *High Grass Valley* (Houghton Mifflin, 1955), which, left unfinished at the time of his death, was completed by Wayne D. Overholser. He wrote over eighty novels during the span of his career that sold over twenty million copies during his lifetime.

From the very beginning, Raine considered himself a conscientious writer, part professional and part craftsman, rather than an artist. He approached writing fiction as a business, rising early so that he could produce his requisite one thousand words per day. Once his income was sufficient, he worked in a downtown office, hammering out stories on a typewriter with two fingers and minimal revision. He rewarded himself by playing bridge in the afternoons, and was known as a notorious under-bidder. He was astute at marketing his work, implementing a practice of selling first serial rights, then book rights in the States and abroad, then reprint rights, then second serial rights to newspapers, and finally movie rights. It proved a lucrative strategy. While his income prior to 1915 had been under $5,000, that year it topped $7,500. Between 1919 and 1940, his income from magazines and book editions averaged between $20,000 and $30,000 annually.

Despite this success, Raine persisted in thinking of himself as primarily a newspaperman and throughout his writing career he was wont to set aside his Westerns to take a journalistic assignment. He was one of the few to have contributed to all five of Denver's turn-of-the-century newspapers, including contributing editorials for *The Rocky Mountain News*. His reputation led to his involvement in 1932 in setting up the first journalism course at the University of Colorado in Boulder where he also taught for five years.

Wyoming first appeared as a novelette in *The Popular Magazine*, a Street and Smith publication. As his second novel, *Ridgway of Montana* (Dillingham, 1909) serialized in *Ainslee's* as "His Little Partner", it features a somewhat contemporary setting with modernisms such as automobiles, as would others among his Western novels, such as *Tangled Trails* (Houghton Mifflin, 1921), *Sons of the Saddle* (Houghton Mifflin, 1938), and *Justice Deferred* (Houghton Mifflin, 1941). While *Wyoming* is basically a traditional story concerned with sheepman Ned Bannister's reign of terror in the Bighorn country, and a plot hinging on a case of mistaken identity, it shows Raine's proclivity to experiment with the Western story and its characters, something that would win him a wide audience over the years as he perfected his own brand of Western storytelling. Another unique aspect of *Wyoming* is Raine's focus on the story's heroine, Helen Messiter, a gutsy, intelligent schoolteacher from the East who inherits a ranch and who is the antithesis of the majority of fictional Western schoolteachers. Raine continued to portray a wide variety of unique and sympathetic heroines, the majority of whom play active rôles in the conflicts as well as supplying the romantic interest.

If Raine's heroes are in possession of fine constitutions, they also possess a great many other admirable characteristics, even if they are not completely invincible as illustrated by frequent scenes in which the hero is wounded and must spend time recuperating. Above all, youth is the hallmark of a Raine hero. It is rare in his stories to find a hero over thirty years of age; most often, they are just barely one side or the other of their majority. In looks, they are often compared to the gods, but perhaps the best description of a Raine hero occurs in the laconic economy of words found in "Last Warning" in *Short Stories* (1/10/43): "He sat lightly in the saddle, a figure to draw the eyes of men as well as women."

Beyond the physical traits, a Raine hero stands out because of his extraordinary moral character. As the hero's friend says of him to the heroine in *On the Dodge* (Houghton Mifflin, 1938): " 'It isn't what he does for you. It's what he is.' " Raine's heroes never boast; indeed, they exhibit an extraordinary "capacity for silence", particularly when it comes to their own good deeds or courageous acts. His heroes are capable of tears at times of intense sorrow as in *Gunsight Pass* (Houghton Mifflin, 1921), or at times of extreme joy as in *The Sheriff's Son* (Houghton Mifflin, 1918), an unusual occurrence in Western novels written during the first half of the 20th Century.

The focus of a Raine Western is the destiny or character of a *settled* frontier that still lacks the safeguards of established and civilized life, in which very often prior to the emergence of the hero on the scene villains have maintained an unchallenged stranglehold on the community, owning the law and oftentimes terrorizing the citizenry. While the hero is not looking for trouble, once confronted by it he is guided by a code that tells him how he must play out his hand. It is this code of the West, a set of principles as encompassing as the feudal code of chivalry, that is the most striking characteristic of Raine's West. Over the years he articulated an ever-growing body of tenets that were set forth for the reader in story after story. In his novels from the early 1920s, a particularly strong period of writing for Raine in terms of plotting and characterization, these principles are scattered throughout the narratives. Thus we learn in *Gunsight Pass* that "it is written in their code that a man must take his punishment without whining," and that a man clenches his teeth against pain "because he had been brought up in the outdoor code of the West which demands of a man that he grin and stand the guff," and that "at a time of action speech, beyond the curtest of monosyllables, was surplussage." Loyalty and trust are central to this code and the testing of these virtues between friends and among family members through periods of severe adversity is a common thread in all of Raine's Westerns. In fact, in a Raine story the highest compliment one character can pay another is that a person will "do to ride the river with." With his interest in loyalty to a moral code, it was perhaps inevitable that Raine would occasionally include members of the Northwest Mounted Police among his heroes, as in *Man-Size* (Houghton Mifflin, 1922) and the short story, "Without Fear or Favor", in *Frontier Stories* (5/28).

In *The Fighting Edge* (Houghton Mifflin, 1922), Raine perhaps best summed up the qualities that make a hero: "Courage is the basis upon which other virtues are built, the fundamental upon which he is most searchingly judged. Let a man tell the truth, stick to his pal, and fight when trouble is forced on him, and he will do to ride the river with. . . ." While courage, sometimes to the point of recklessness (particularly among his outlaw heroes), is present in the majority of Raine's heroes, some of his most gripping stories are those in which the hero lacks such fundamental courage in the beginning of the story. This plot ingredient is probably nowhere better exemplified than in *The Sheriff's Son*, which remains one of Raine's most haunting and strongly imagistic stories, first serialized as "One Who Was Afraid" in *All-Story Weekly*. A poignant prologue to the story recounts the last night five-year-old Royal Beaudry spends with his father, John Beaudry, "one of the great sheriffs of the West," who is ambushed and killed in front of his son when they arrive in town the following morning. Raine shows the reader an interior view of John's troubled soul, torn by his duties as lawman and his love for his son, when Beaudry speaks his thoughts to his sleeping child that night. " 'Son, one of these here days they're sure a-goin' to get your dad. Maybe he'll ride out of town and after a while the hawss will come gallopin' back with an empty saddle. A man can be mighty unpopular and die of old age, but not if he keeps bustin' up the plans of rampageous two-gun men, not if he shoots them up when they're full of the devil and bad whiskey. It ain't on the cyards for me to beat them to the draw every time, let alone that they'll see to it all the breaks are with them. No, sir. I reckon one of these days you're goin' to be an orphan, little son.' " Raine skillfully and sympathetically portrays Royal's battles with his demon, cowardice. In contrast *Justice Deferred*, a reworking of the same plotline in which the hero, who also witnesses his father's murder twenty years earlier, is Royal's antithesis, only awaiting the death of his mother so that he can finally avenge that cold-blooded killing.

Raine's villains are a mixed group, from the visionary empire builders of *The Yukon Trail* (Houghton Mifflin, 1917), a story with a sub-theme about conservation in Alaska, to the greed-driven empire builders in *Ridgway of Montana*. Generally Raine's villains have such an insatiable appetite for land or power or money that even when they appear to be respectable and law-abiding, the laws are of their own making. Russell Mosely of *Trail's End* (Houghton Mifflin, 1940) epitomizes the breed: "He had no sense of moral values. He could see nothing except what was to his own advantage. When he thought of right and wrong, he twisted the meanings of the words to suit himself."

By his own admission, Raine concentrated on character in his Westerns. "I'm not very strong on plot. Some of my writing friends say you have to have the plot all laid out before you start. I don't see it that way. If you have it all laid out, your characters can't develop naturally as the story unfolds. Sometimes there's someone you start out as a minor character. By the time you're through, he's the major character of the book. I like to preside over it all, but to let the book do its own growing."

Although Raine's storylines may be amazingly various, if he liked an image or a turn of phrase he would frequently reuse it. In *Gunsight Pass* there is the image of the heroine "at home in the kitchen. She was making pies energetically. The sleeves of her dress are rolled up to her elbows and there is a dab of flour on her temple where she had brushed back a rebellious wisp of hair." Almost this exact description of a woman in the kitchen can be found elsewhere, including in *Rutledge Trails the Ace of Spades* (Doubleday, Doran, 1930). A description of men pouring out of a bar as "seeds are squirted out of a pressed lemon" can be found in at least four novels including *Bonanza* (Doubleday, Page, 1926) and *On the Dodge*. In *The Sheriff's Son*, a character comments " 'Guns are going out, . . . and little red school houses are coming in.' " Thirteen years later in his exceptional short story, "Doan Whispers" in *Short Stories* (10/25/31), this same remark is echoed nearly verbatim. Words to the effect of "I once knew a man who lived to be one hundred minding his own business" is a common adage used by at least one of Raine's characters in a number of novels.

Notwithstanding the impressive and consistent output of two books a year over a forty-year period, the progression of Raine's work as a writer showed continuous and inspired development. Perhaps his most skilled accomplishment was to have made the Western story seem infinitely adaptable and effortlessly versatile. "The best thing about a Western," he once said, "is that it can't become dated. Like Tennyson's brook it goes on forever." He might have added that they could be written anywhere. In the years after the First World War, Raine, who was head of the division in charge of syndicate features supplying longer articles to newspapers as part of the committee of public information, desired to see the world. He took time out to travel with his wife and typewriter, writing *Judge Colt* (Doubleday, Page, 1927) in Antibes and Nice and *Moran Beats Back* (Hodder and Stoughton, 1928) in Africa.

It was his intimate knowledge of the American West that provides verisimilitude to all of his stories, whether in a large sense such as the booming industries of the West or the cruelties of Nature—a flood in *Ironheart* (Houghton Mifflin, 1923), blizzards in *Ridgway of Montana* and *The Yukon Trail,* a fire in *Gunsight Pass*—or in minor details. He raised any number of social issues and everyday human problems in the course of his storytelling. His weaknesses early in his career—a reliance on foreshadowing, multiple sets of lovers, and the cliché of the weak brother—disappeared for the most part as he gained mastery at his craft. There are, of course, novels that are off the mark, but this is not surprising considering his impressive output, and they are the exceptions.

Raine's interest in historical figures and history prompted him to write four Western histories— *Famous Sheriffs and Western Outlaws* (Doubleday, 1929), *Cattle* (Doubleday, 1930) in collaboration with Will C. Barnes, *Guns of the Frontier: The Story of How Law Came to the West* (Houghton Mifflin, 1940), and *.45-Caliber Law: The Way of Life of the Frontier Peace Officer* (Row Peterson, 1941). Although they are not without factual errors, these books are considered indispensable works for researchers in the field. Historical figures were also used in some fictional pieces, including *The Bandit Trail* (Houghton Mifflin, 1949) which features Butch Cassidy, Harry Longabaugh, and Kid Curry as characters and "A Friend of Buck Hollister" in *Zane Grey's*

Western Magazine (11/47) which includes Billy the Kid. Raine tended to interweave snatches of history in his fiction whenever he could, usually by way of footnotes that covered a wide variety of topics from pronunciations, Western phrases, or even the ingredients in White River country lard to the design of a Red River cart, as well as mining terminology.

Throughout his career, reviewers commented that Raine's writing just kept getting better and better. In 1945, one critic wrote: "It'll be a sad day for us Western fans when fate decides it ain't goin' to Raine no mo'." Although he preferred socializing outside his profession, Raine was active in writers' organizations such as the Colorado Author's League. In 1953, as a charter member of the newly-formed Western Writers of America, he wrote in the first issue of WWA's *The Round-Up*: "It is my opinion that there is no more honest or competent writing in the country than that done by our group. Our fiction is far less stylized and pattern-built than that of other types which receive more consideration from the pundits who review books." In June, 1954, he was made the first honorary president of the WWA. In spite of failing health, he appeared at the awards banquet where he addressed the group by saying: "There's only one reason why we are gathered here tonight: it is because we are all engaged in recreating and recording the most vital and fascinating era of our history since the creation of our nation. . . ." He died a month later, on July 25, 1954.

Notwithstanding his achievements as a Western author, including the support of his publishers, highly laudatory reviews, and a wide readership, Raine knew well the obstacles facing a writer of Westerns and he spoke out against those obstacles, simply yet strongly, with words that are as applicable today as they were forty years ago. "A story set in our terrain ought to be judged solely on its merits as other novels are without having a black mark against it before it is even read." For all who met him, he was a gentleman of the old school, while for writers like Wayne D. Overholser, he was "a legend". Although his popularity continued for some time after his death, by the 1980s he had virtually disappeared from book racks. Yet, it is perhaps Raine's love of the West of his youth, the place and the people where there existed the "fine free feeling of man as an individual," glimmering in the pages of his books that will warrant the attention of readers for a long time to come.

The two stories in this book are "Scalisi Claws Leather", which appeared in Street & Smith's *Western Story Magazine* (1/16/32), and "Long Texan", a five-part serial (2/1/28–4/1/28) which appeared in *Adventure Magazine* and was reprinted in 1934 in *Complete Western Book*

Magazine. I would like to think Raine had as much fun writing "Scalisi Claws Leather" as one has reading it as Pete Scalisi, a gang leader from Chicago, gets his comeuppance on the Bar BQ Ranch in Arizona from waitress Rose Dunn and cowhand Jim Falconer. The code of the West by which Raine's heroes live is clearly represented in Boone Sibley in "Long Texan", when he finds himself the enemy of the toughest men in the area upon his arrival in Tough Nut, Arizona, when he protects a child and a newspaper publisher from possible death. This is the first appearance in book form of both stories as originally published.

Scalisi Claws Leather

Mr. Scalisi looked over the breakfast menu card sourly. His swarthy face wore the dissatisfied expression of one not at peace with his world.

He had not slept well. In Arizona it seemed to be a quaint custom to go to bed at night. Where he came from, the great city woke to life only after a million lights flung out their blazing challenge to the darkness. When at last his day ended, the clang and roar of the streets were music lulling him to the placid slumber of an honest gangster. The stillness that pressed in on him here made him want to scream, as though he were being buried in a great coffin a thousand miles away from anyone.

After he had snarled out his order, he leaned back and waited impatiently, his fingertips drumming on the table, his black beady eyes wandering around the dining room. The eyes came to rest on a waitress, the one who had charge of the rear corner tables on the south. His bold gaze traveled up and down her slender trimness and approved. There was a quality shy and sweet about her fresh youth, not usual in the women he knew. He watched her whenever she was in the room.

On his way out he stopped for a moment at the office to buy cigarettes.

"Have me changed to a table near the back on the sunny side," he told the clerk.

"Yes, Mister Peters."

"What's the name of the blonde waitress with the pink cheeks?"

"Her name is Rose Dunn."

The clerk spoke with awe in his voice. He knew that Peters was an alias. This man was the notorious Pete Scalisi, the gang leader who made millions yearly defying the law, who condemned his enemies to death with five words spoken out of the corner of his thin-lipped mouth.

Mr. Scalisi walked to the corral. Three young men in high-heeled boots and wide-brimmed hats were roping a wild colt that had to be broken to the saddle. Half a dozen guests of the dude ranch, most of them young men and girls, also in cow-boy boots and big hats, sat on the corral fence and watched the show. One of the girls caught sight of the newcomer and whispered to the youth beside her. This was observed by Mr. Scalisi with satisfaction.

For reasons urgent, Pete Scalisi had come to Arizona incognito. Entirely in the way of business, it had been necessary for him to put three of the North Side gang "on the spot." To show he had no hard feelings, he had attended the funeral with four armed guards, after contributing costly floral tributes.

His overtures had been neglected. The Villanos

were Sicilians and had exhibited a narrow-minded bitterness. Two of Scalisi's men took the one-way ride, and Pete himself was marked for death. This was disturbing. Pete liked to play at being a superman, but it was unnerving to find his foes attempting the same rôle.

Within a month or two Pete intended to slip back to the big city where he would make the necessary arrangements for Joe and Mike Villano to be rubbed out by a machine-gun volley from an armored car. Then everything would be OK. He would be once more the big boss, and a stream of gold would again flow in to him.

But, although Pete had come to hide from vengeance, it was characteristic of him that he had to betray his own secret. His vanity was greater than his fear. He bragged, in hints. He made a present to the hotel clerk of the book a news-paper man had written about him, *Pete Scalisi, Napoleon of Gangsters*. Within forty hours of his arrival at the Bar BQ guest ranch, every corral dog on the place was aware of the identity of the new dude who called himself Peters.

The ropers saddled and blindfolded the pony. One of them, a lithe, broad-shouldered young fellow, swung to the back of the animal. As soon as his feet had found the stirrups, the blind was slipped from the eyes of the bronco and the horse released. Instantly the three-year-old swept into cyclonic action.

The battle was magnificent. The young range horse pitched wildly, went sun-fishing, whirled in the air, and fought savagely to dislodge the human clothespin clamped to his back.

One of the girls on the fence swung her cowboy hat and shouted encouragement. "Ride him, Jim! Stick to him." The dudes joined in a chorus of applause. Scalisi said nothing. His eyes foliated the movements of the infuriated animal until it had been ridden to a standstill.

"Bully for you, Jim!" the enthusiastic girl cried. "That's riding, boy."

Jim slipped from the saddle and smiled at her. Scalisi laughed satirically. The young rider looked at him, a little surprised.

"A Chicago cop could ride that rocking horse," Pete said with a sneer.

All present looked at Scalisi and nobody said anything. In that silence he turned and strutted back to the house.

Why he had spoken as he had, Pete did not know, unless it was because he was in a bad humor and because it always annoyed him not to be the center of attention. In his home city, wherever he went, men observed him with stealthy, awed glances. The newspapers recorded his movements as British journals do those of the Prince of Wales. To come to a hick ranch in the sticks and to find that people were more interested in the performance of a bronco peeler than in the great Scalisi was irritating. It was absurd, the extravagant way these girls admired this Jim Falconer merely because he could ride a horse.

The incident at the corral was of a piece with the rest of Pete's behavior. His superiority took the offensive form of jeering at the West and all its products. This was a desolate country. The inhabitants were boobs. Anyone living in it was buried alive.

Since the other guests were distant, even though very civil, Pete's contemptuous comments were offered chiefly to the employees of the Bar BQ. In spite of his lavish tips, he was cordially detested by them. To use the old phrase of the cow country, they walked around him whenever they could.

Sometimes they could not escape him. Jim Falconer was the chief victim. He had been selected as a guide by Scalisi on his riding trips into the hills, not because the gang leader liked him, but because he could gratify his resentment against the young cowpuncher by sneering at all of the things that made up his life.

Scalisi was not a good rider. He was an incurable tenderfoot and could be taken into a tangle of hills and lost hopelessly a mile or two from the ranch house. He made a virtue of his limitations.

"You're a hundred years behind the times," he said scornfully. "Fellow, I've got two planes and five autos for my personal use. Back home I wouldn't be caught dead on a horse."

Jim said—"No, sir."—in a voice gentle but expressionless. His inscrutable gray eyes regarded the distant hills.

One of Scalisi's complaints against him was that he never made conversation. In words of one syllable he answered questions. "Yes, it is," he would say, or "We turn to the right here."

"Are all Arizonans such dumb eggs?" Pete once asked him in exasperation. "Why don't you take a trip to Chicago or New York and get on to yourself?"

Falconer had been to both cities but he did not say so. Mr. Scalisi would have been surprised at the things he thought but did not say. He was a reservoir of unvoiced criticism, though his exceedingly grave, respectful manner conveyed no hint of it.

"All this stuff I've heard about the West is bunk," Pete informed him. "Take these badmen they're always writing up. They were false alarms. If I had this Billy the Kid in my town for about a week, I'd make him eat out of my hand or I'd blast him out of the way."

Automatically Jim said: "Yes, sir."

In the dining room Scalisi devoted as much time to Rose Dunn as he did to eating. He always dressed for dinner, and in the course of three days appeared in six different suits for breakfast and luncheon. Never very sure of herself, Rose was flustered by the cold, impudent stare of the man. She felt his black beady eyes stabbing at her. Though she rarely looked at him, she was intensely aware of him. His dark hair, brushed with brilliantine, lay back, slick and shining. He was a slender young man, handsome in a shallow, obvious way, but what impressed her was not his good looks but the quality in his swarthy appearance that made him sinister and dangerous.

It was at luncheon that he left the $100 bill beside his plate as a tip for her. The girl caught him before he had left the dining room.

"You've made a mistake, sir," she said, and tried to hand the bill to him.

He stared into her soft-brown eyes. "So I have." From his pocket he drew a fat roll, selected another $100 bill, caught her hand in his, and crumpled the second bill beside the first, closing her fingers on it. Before Rose could recover from her embarrassed astonishment, he was gone.

She took the bills at once to the manager of the guest ranch, who, in turn, went directly with them to Scalisi.

"Rose asked me to return these, Mister Peters," he said. "She can't accept such a gift from a guest."

"Why can't she, if I want to give it to her?" demanded the gangster. "I can give any tip I please, if the service suits me. That's chicken feed for me. I've left tips that big twenty times at restaurants and night clubs in Chicago."

"This isn't Chicago," the manager explained. "Of course, I understand you meant it in kindness, but it would make Rose unhappy to take such a sum. She's a good girl, and she wouldn't think it right."

Pete did not argue the matter. He took the bills, thrust them into a pocket, and turned abruptly away. If she was so squeamish about taking money, he would give her presents.

At dinner he discovered that Rose had been transferred to another part of the room. A hard-boiled young woman with the face of a battle-axe waited on him. He scowled, much annoyed, half of a mind to insist upon the return of the pink-cheeked blonde. But he decided against this—no use alarming her. He would get what he wanted just the same, as he always did.

Pete made it a point to be the last guest to leave the dining room. He stopped to speak to Rose at the table she was brushing up. "Why did you leave my table?" he asked.

She blushed. "I . . . I was moved."

"I'll be seeing you later," he said.

It was impossible for the girl not to understand him. His attentions were as direct as the machine-gun volleys that annihilated his business competitors. "I want you," his shining eyes told her, and his words scarcely veiled the same insolent intent.

That any woman would not feel honored at his regard did not occur to Pete. Was he not an international figure? Had not the British Parliament discussed him? And the great Mussolini? He was the king of gangland and accustomed to deference from both men and women.

Rose was greatly disturbed. There was something excitably mysterious about this dark young man with the scores of neckties as garish as Rocky Mountain sunsets, with the innumerable suits he seemed always to be changing. But the excitement was terrifying rather than exhilarating. She did not want to meet in any personal relationship a man who had the reputation of having sent a score of others to their deaths.

She did not trust him. There was not a corral dog at the ranch with which she would not have felt safe at night in the hills fifty miles from anyone else. In one of those corral dogs, Jim Falconer, she had a special interest, so much so that she wore on the proper finger a gold ring with a small diamond set in it. These long-bodied, quiet-spoken sons of the range she knew and understood. But this gangster, who looked through her with glittering opaque eyes and cut his words out of the corner of a slitted mouth, was an unknown and an alarming quantity.

Scalisi waited for her until she was through with

her work that evening and joined her in the moonlight. Rose turned to smile a welcome and gave a startled little cry at recognition of him. He was not the man she had been expecting to meet.

"Here we are, kid," he said to her.

He had her cut off from the house. She moved a little faster, in the direction of the windmill that fed the cattle trough with water. It was clicking now, in the evening breeze.

"What's your hurry, Rose? We've got all night. That's your name, ain't it . . . Rose?"

She felt her heart fluttering against her ribs like a caged bird. "Yes, sir. Please, I'm not allowed to walk with the guests."

"You're allowed to walk with this guest. What I say goes. See?"

"Yes, sir, but . . ."

"Listen, kid. You're going to be my girl. Get me? I've fallen for you. That's your luck. You'll wear diamonds and ermine wraps."

Rose had little experience to guide her. His assurance frightened the girl. "I don't want to wear diamonds and . . . those other things," she said in a small voice, and held up her left hand to show him the ring.

He took her fingers in his and looked at the cheap little stone. "D'you call that a diamond?" he asked contemptuously. From his own hand he slipped the five-carat stone he always wore. "Throw away that chip of nothing and slip this rock in the place of it. I'll fill your little fist full of sparklers if you want 'em. That's the kind of guy Pete Scalisi is."

"I told you I didn't want your diamonds!" she cried, and pushed the ring into his coat pocket.

She turned to leave. He caught her by the arm, drew her close, and kissed her on the eyes and mouth and throat with a ruthlessness that outraged her. With a cry of fear she pushed him away.

An arm leached out of the darkness and caught Mr. Scalisi by the coat collar. It jerked him violently backward and, before he could get his balance again, propelled him toward the clicking windmill. He tried to twist free but only succeeded in strangling himself. The fingers knuckling into the back of his neck were like iron knobs at the end of a steel bar. When he reached for his automatic, a swift turn of the wrist made him scream with pain as he dropped the weapon.

He was snatched from the ground and plunged into the cattle trough. His hand and feet thrashed in a struggle to escape, but he was helpless as a child in the grips that held him. Half a dozen times his head was soused under the water before he was dragged from the trough and flung aside.

Pete gathered himself to his feet and glared at Jim Falconer. The gangster was sobbing with rage. He dripped like a dog just out of the water.

"I'll get you, fellow. I'll take you for a ride sure," he said, showing his teeth in a most unmistakable snarl.

Jim was dropping the automatic into his coat pocket. "Better run along and get into one of the other fifty-seven varieties of suits you own," the cowpuncher advised cheerfully. "You don't know how like a wet dish rag you look."

Scalisi departed, cursing venomously. A minute later one of the ranch guests saw him vanishing into his quarters. She gave a gasp of surprise at sight of the immaculate gangster covered with green scum from the trough.

With awed admiration Rose looked at her lover and murmured: "Oh, Jim." His swift efficiency seemed to her remarkable.

Jim grinned, a trifle embarrassed and ashamed at his own impetuosity. "I don't reckon the Bar BQ pays me to bathe its guests," he said.

Rose giggled. "He did look so like a drowned rat." She added a question. "What did he mean about taking you for a ride?"

"Just talking foolishness," Jim said briefly.

He understood the sinister significance of the gang phrase, but he did not think it necessary to worry Rose by translating its meaning to her. That he was in danger, he knew. He had wounded unpardonably Scalisi's vanity. The man would never rest until he had evened the score. Moreover, the gang leader would try to see that his victim did not have a chance when the hour of reckoning came.

Jim was not afraid of him. The gangster was a rat, and he would have to be watched. But one did not fear rodents, even though they had sharp teeth. One took care not to give them a chance to bite. It did not matter to the young cowpuncher that Scalisi had contrived the murder of two or three dozen other criminals. He was in the West now. If they clashed, it would be man to man, unless he gave the gangster a chance to ambush him. About that Jim intended to be very careful. He was not going to sit in a lit room or walk out from one into the darkness of the night.

When Jim returned to his room, he opened a suitcase and took from it a .38 Colt revolver. This he cleaned and loaded. He had not the least intention of killing Scalisi, but he certainly did not intend to be killed by him if he could help it.

As he went about his work next day, Jim moved warily. He had that acute sense of hearing possessed by many men who have lived their lives in the open. Nobody could approach him without his being aware of it. The steel-gray eyes in his brown face were quiet and undisturbed, but they were very watchful.

Yet Jim expected no open attack. Scalisi was shrewd, in his rat-like way. He knew he was not at home. A cold-blooded killing in Arizona is called murder, and usually it is punished as such.

The other guests at the Bar BQ saw nothing of Scalisi the day after the episode of the trough. He had his meals served in his own rooms. Before he reappeared, Jim had been assigned to work preparing a camp in the hills for some of the dudes who wanted to sleep outdoors.

Young Falconer was busy setting up tents when he caught sight of someone skulking in the rocks above him. He gave no evidence of having seen anyone, but moved leisurely across the clearing to his saddle horse. Before he reached it, his plan of campaign was worked out. If Scalisi had set out to trail him down, he would give the man a run for his money. With no haste Jim turned into a draw leading to a gorge. He picked a snaky course up the slope among the boulders. It was rough going, and his cow pony took the steep grade like a cat, the muscles of its legs standing out as it clambered from rock to rock.

Jim did not look around, but the faint ringing of a horse's hoof on a stone told him that he was being followed. He grinned sardonically. Good enough. If he only knew it, Mr. Scalisi was setting out on a hard ride.

The gorge rose abruptly. It twisted so often that each short stretch looked as though it led directly to the summit. More than once Jim stopped, behind a bend, to make sure his pursuer had not quit.

Scalisi was jubilant. He had this fellow now,

alone in the hills. They would find his body someday, but nobody in the world could prove that he had shot him. Pete did not like this business of going up a rock wall on horseback, but, if another man could do it, he could. He liked it still less when the rock cleft narrowed into a chimney filled with boulders and rubble slides. If his horse stumbled, if it fell on him . . .

But the dude wrangler had gone up the trough and so could he. These mountain ponies, he had heard, were very sure-footed. His mount was a rangy, long-legged sorrel. It took the incline by dashes, reaching for footholds, slithering down, and snatching at new grips for its hoofs. There were moments when Pete's heart jumped to his mouth with a sudden fear.

Halfway up the chimney, the sorrel stopped for a rest, breathing hard. Scalisi looked up at what was ahead of him and shuddered. No horse could do it. The thing was not possible. The animal would slip on the rubble and its rider would be crushed to death. Pete took a glance down the stretch up which he had come. At sight of that almost sheer wall, the blood in his veins thinned to water. He could not go back. Merely to look at the descent made him dizzy. The longer he looked, the worse it seemed. The night life to which he was accustomed had not tuned his nerves to face such a job. The roof of his mouth went dry. The heart died under his ribs. He

41

slipped from the saddle, his legs trembling beneath him. Pete shut his eyes to fight down the panic rising within him. He opened them suddenly, letting out a shriek of pain. The sorrel had turned its head and taken a nip at his arm.

From the boulders above appeared Jim Falconer's head. "Someone down there?" he asked, as though surprised.

"This horse bit me!" Scalisi cried.

"It won't hurt him. Old Geronimo could eat locoweed and not get sick," Jim said gravely. To himself the young fellow chuckled.

He was wondering who had given the gangster Geronimo to ride. The sorrel had a jolting trot that jarred the spine like the thump of a pile driver, a racking road gait that wearied the hardiest rider. One of the corral dogs, no doubt, was paying a debt to Mr. Scalisi for his courteous manners.

"Is it much farther to the top?" Pete asked.

"Quite a way. Coming up to have a look at the scenery?"

Pete's eyes traveled up the dizzy height. "I'm feeling sick today. I . . . I think I'll go back."

"No chance. This is a one-way ride," Jim told him blandly.

Scalisi felt the cold feet of mice running up and down his back. A one-way ride! Did the fellow know what he was talking about? Were his words a prophecy—or perhaps a threat?

"I can't make it," the Chicago man said, his

throat like a limekiln. "It's like the wall of a house."

Jim let him do the worrying. "Hang on to the horn and let old Geronimo scrabble up. If he keeps his footing, you'll be OK."

"But if he slips . . ."

"Better not think of that. It's a long way down. Just grab the apple for a strangle hold."

"The apple?" Pete repeated in a small husky voice.

"The saddle horn. Well, I'll be moseying along now. I'll see you later."

"Wait!" implored Scalisi. "I'm stuck here. Can't get either up or down. Don't leave me."

"You'll have to send for one of those planes you were telling me about, looks like," Jim suggested. "Unless you're aiming to roost there permanent."

"I'll give you a hundred dollars to get me up . . . five hundred."

"Couldn't use your money, sir." Jim disposed his long length comfortably on a flat rock and lit a cigarette.

"A thousand."

"An Arizona hick wouldn't know what to do with all that mazuma."

Scalisi realized he was to get no help from the cowboy. He climbed to the saddle, flung one frightened look into the gulf of space below, and clucked weakly to the sorrel. Geronimo took the rocks with a rush, fighting the way up with straining muscles. Once the horse went to its knees, heaved up again to its feet, and clambered to the ledge above.

Shaken with terror, the gang leader slid to the ground and leaned against the saddle. Through a haze the cowpuncher's cheerful voice drifted to him.

"Now, all you'll have to do is trail along this ledge for a quarter of a mile or so. We'll hope Geronimo won't act up."

"Act up?"

"Make out he's scared to travel on a narrow ledge so high up. If he does, I reckon you'll show him who's boss. Look out, or he'll take another bite. That's one of his crazy ways."

Scalisi removed himself hastily from the vicinity of the horse.

"Treat him rough, the way you would Billy the Kid," advised the dude wrangler. "He'll eat out of your hand then, I expect."

Pete viewed sickly the ledge along which he must travel with this man-eating brute. He couldn't do it, and said so. Always heights had made him dizzy.

"Please yourself," Jim said casually, and he started along the path.

"I'll walk," Pete said desperately.

He followed Geronimo. The ledge was scarcely two feet wide. On one side rose a rock wall, the precipice fell away from his feet from the other.

The frightened man crept along the path, a panic in his bosom. His swarthy face was green. Tiny beads of perspiration stood out on his forehead. He had an insane impulse to hurl himself from the trail into space. It seemed to him that the rock was leaning out and pressing him to the edge.

"I'll never make it," he whined, giving up.

Jim did not turn around. He disappeared around a bend. Ten minutes later the tenderfoot crawled around the turn and gave a deep breath of relief. The path broadened, angling up a slight incline to the summit. The climbers were in a little park of pines that seemed to be the top of the world. Through the trees the sun poured, making a dappled carpet of the mossy turf upon which Scalisi limply sank.

"Were you heading for anywhere in particular, Mister Peters?" Jim asked sardonically, looking down at the spent man.

Scalisi remembered why he had come. His nerves were too shaken for that business yet, but it would be just as well to get his bearings.

"In what direction is the ranch from here?" he asked.

"I'm wondering that myself," the dude herder said.

"Don't you know the way back?"

"I know one way back," Jim said, "but I don't reckon you want to take that."

"You mean we're lost?"

"You know how these dog-gone' hills are," Jim replied. "Likely we'll be able to find our way out somehow."

The cowpuncher put his horse to a lope across the park. Pete caught the bridle of his horse and pulled himself with difficulty to the saddle. For Geronimo was already in motion, reaching out into a gait that might, by courtesy, be called a trot. The rider's feet could not find the stirrups. Clinging wildly to the saddle horn, Scalisi went up and down like a sack of meal. His stomach plowed into the pommel. From side to side he bounced. He was sure his spine was being driven together like an accordion. The pain from the contact of his raw thighs with the leather flogged through him fiercely.

Afraid he would fall off, Scalisi clung like John Gilpin, made famous in the comic ballad by William Cowper. All the organs inside of Pete churned wildly. In vain he tried to stop the hard-mouthed beast on which he was astride. Geronimo had the bit in his teeth and was going, lickety-split, to catch his stable mate, paying not the least attention to the biped bouncing on his back.

Pete called to the cowpuncher to stop. Jim held his mount to a steady lope until he reached the farther lip of the park. Here he drew up and turned in the saddle, waiting for Geronimo to jolt to a halt.

46

"Did I hear you say something, Mister Peters?" he asked gravely.

There was not a flicker of mirth in his eyes as he looked at the disheveled gang leader. Scalisi's hat was gone. His long black hair hung lankly in front of his eyes. The jaunty insolence that did not take the trouble to mask a quality, dangerous and sinister, had been wiped out. He looked like a whipped schoolboy instead of the man of destiny he liked to think himself.

Impotently he glared at Jim. "You knew I wasn't ready to start," he complained. "When I get back, I'll find out at the office whether you're hired to make it hard for the guests."

Jim grinned. "Going to tell teacher, are you?"

Scalisi gave way to a fury of weak anger. He used scabrous epithets, applying them to Jim, to Geronimo, to the ranch, and to Arizona at large.

Not until he had used up his vocabulary and exhausted his verbal energy did the ranch hand speak. "You'll feel better now," he drawled. "A naughty kid always does after he's stomped his foot."

Pete's right hand slid into the pocket of his coat. The cold, steely eyes of the Arizonan were fastened on him.

"Don't you," Jim advised very quietly. "Don't you make a mistake."

He rode close to the gangster and held out a

brown strong hand. "Gimme that popgun," he sternly ordered.

Scalisi hesitated. He might do the job—now. Why not? Nobody could ever prove he had done it. Just one touch of the finger would be enough. He stared out of a green, strained face into that easy, sardonic smile. In a fraction of a second he could blast the life out of the lithe, graceful figure and send it buckling down into the moss. But he found he couldn't do it. He had not the nerve. His impulse to kill had not back of it the cold will to make his flaccid muscles function. He was afraid.

From his pocket he drew an automatic with trembling fingers and passed it to Falconer.

All day they rode, apparently trying to find a way down out of the sea of hills surrounding them. They explored gulches, tried blind pockets, pushed into draws that led nowhere. The black head of Scalisi drooped lower and lower. Every joint ached. The flesh, in contact with the saddle leather, was like raw beef. Never had he been so exhausted. He wanted to lie down and not get up again for days.

The stars were out before Jim gave up and let him rest. He lay down on the ground and groaned. To his other discomforts cold and hunger were added.

"Aren't you going to build a fire?" he asked the dude wrangler querulously.

"Just used my last match," Jim mentioned calmly, puffing at a cigarette.

Pete found that he had forgotten to transfer his lighter to the riding clothes he wore. He discovered this just as his companion trod out the glow on his cigarette stub.

Jim chose a large flat boulder instead of spongy moss as a sleeping ground. "This is what they call a Tucson bed," he explained cheerfully. "A fellow uses his backbone for a mattress. Think we'd better not roost in the moss. A hydrophobia skunk or a rattler might cuddle up to get warm."

"What's a hydrophobia skunk?" Scalisi asked miserably.

"A breed of skunk that's mad. I'll bet more cowpunchers have been planted in the cold, cold ground from skunk bites than from any other cause, unless it might be from rattlesnake bites when they were camping at night."

Jim dwelt on the subject at length. Apparently most of the friends of Jim's youth had gone to early graves from the virus of these pests.

The night grew steadily colder. This was nothing in the young life of the Arizonan. He had bucked blizzards and was as tough as cactus. But Scalisi suffered. He felt the cold go to his vitals. The hard rock bruised his flesh. He was hungry and stiff and sore. In his soft upholstered life he had never spent a night in the open a mile and a half above sea level. Moreover, he was afraid. Jim had said that rattlers often crept under blankets and nestled on the chests of sleepers for warmth. Pete's ears, tuned to nervous alertness, heard curious crepitations in the vast silence. He imagined he could hear the slithering of a snake and the movements of animals in the brush.

It seemed to him the night would never end. Toward morning he dropped into troubled sleep. He awoke in a panic of terror, screaming to Falconer to get up.

"For Pete's sake, what's ailing you?" asked the wrangler.

A weird, unearthly shriek interrupted him, a most blood-chilling sound.

Scalisi caught at his arm. He was trembling. "There it is again."

"A cougar hunting for its breakfast," Jim said. "Probably looking for some nice tender man-meat."

"Let's get our horses and go," Pete suggested.

"When it's daylight," the native amended.

As soon as it was light, Jim went to get the picketed animals. He returned without them.

"The bronc's have pulled their picket pins and lit out," he explained.

"And left us here . . . lost . . . on foot?" Scalisi wailed.

"You've said it." By way of consolation Jim added: " 'Course, in two, three days Mister Lewis

50

will send out search parties for us and maybe they might . . ."

"I'll be dead by then," Scalisi interrupted. He broke down and wept. This was the last straw.

All morning they wandered among the hilltops, Scalisi dragging wearily behind. His new riding boots pinched his feet until every step was a torment. Shortly after noon he flung himself down and gave up. He absolutely refused to take another step.

Jim looked at the bedraggled wreck and grinned, then bowlegged it to the edge of a ridge, just above them. He gave a shout.

"Dog my cats, if the ranch isn't right below us under the bluff."

Painfully Pete got to his feet and limped to him. There, not half a mile distant, was the windmill of the Bar BQ, shining in the sun.

"I'll bet it's been there all the time!" Jim exclaimed happily.

Scalisi looked at him, black eyes full of suspicion. He knew then, beyond a doubt, that the cowpuncher had known the way home all the time.

Twenty minutes later Jim reached the office of the Bar BQ. Mr. Scalisi was plodding along fifty yards behind him. Half a dozen guests were sitting on the porch.

The manager came out, took one look at the limping gangster, and then one at Falconer.

"What have you been doing to him?" he asked.

Jim registered injured innocence. "Not a thing. I just took him for a little ride and we got lost." He reached into a pocket for a cigarette and a match.

Scalisi dragged himself to the porch and sat down heavily on the floor. "You said you didn't have a match," he accused weakly.

"I must have forgot to look in that pocket," Jim confessed.

The exhausted man gave him one poisonous look. There was no fight left in him. He was beaten.

"So you got lost," the manager said to the dude wrangler. "After taking parties into these hills for two years?"

Jim gave him a warm smile. "Dumb of me," he admitted. From his pocket he took the gangster's automatic and handed it to its owner. "A little souvenir of our ride, Mister Scalisi. You want to remember that little boys hadn't ought to fool with guns."

Pete staggered to his rooms. After three days in bed he entrained for the big city where a man need fear nothing but the occasional rattle of a machine-gun.

Long Texan

I

Tough Nut lay in a coma of sunshine. Apache Street was almost deserted. A hound crossed the dusty road, leisurely pursued by a three-year-old child giving orders in a piping voice.

"Turn here, Tarlo, dod-done you."

Carlo went his way, magnificently oblivious of the infant. Drooping horses waited patiently at the hitch racks in front of the saloons. A grocery clerk came out of a store and from a watering can sprinkled the hot ground in front.

A four-mule team came down the street. The fine yellow dust of travel lay thick on the canvas covering the load. The muleskinner, Boone Sibley, was a stranger to Arizona. He had come to Cochise County from New Mexico by way of the San Simon Valley. Already he was pleased with Tough Nut. It sat on the top of the world. A roll of hills and valleys fell away on either side to the shining mountains, to the Mules and the Whetstones, the Dragoons and the Huachucas. The miles of cholla and greasewood and mesquite in that panorama of space were telescoped to a minimum in the clear, untempered light of the champagne atmosphere.

The adobe town was clean. The road of disintegrated granite gave evidence of municipal pride. Tough Nut belied its name, its evil reputation. So Boone Sibley decided. It was a nice town, and peaceful as old age. He was glad he had come. His arms and his long lithe body stretched in a yawn of indolent well-being. Soon he would hit the hay. For thirty hours he had not slept. Grub first, then sleep. Yes, a real nice, quiet town. That woman now going into the butcher shop with the baby in her arms. . . .

A shot shattered the stillness. Through the swing doors of a saloon burst a man. He was small, past the prime of life. As he ran, odd sounds came from his throat. They were not yelps or shouts, nor were they moans, rather a combination of all three. The awkwardness of his flight would have been comical but for the terror written on his pale face.

A big man, revolver in hand, tore through the doors in pursuit. Another shot ripped the silence. The little man staggered, stumbled, and went down just beside the wagon. With swift strides the gunman moved toward him. The eyes in his bearded face blazed.

Boone Sibley lived by the code of the West. This was a private difficulty. Therefore, none of his business. He started to slide from the far side of the wagon in order to use it as a bulwark between him and stray bullets.

Started to do so, but changed his mind. The hound had come around the tail of the wagon, and hard on its heels the three-year-old. The bearded man, intent on the kill, did not see the youngster. His weapon jerked up, covering the victim.

The muleskinner swung his whip swiftly, expertly. He could pick a fly from the ear of the off leader. Now the lash snaked out, twined itself around the wrist of the big man, and sent the revolver flying. Yet another moment, and one hundred and ninety pounds of bone and muscle had descended upon the killer from the sky. The fellow went down as though hurled into the earth by a pile driver. He lay motionlessly, the breath driven out of his body by the shock of the assault.

Lean-loined and agile, Boone was up like a cat. He scooped up the revolver from the ground and whirled, his back against the front wheel of the wagon. For out of the saloon had come men, four or five of them. They had drawn guns—at least, two of them had—and they were moving toward the scene of action. Out of the tail of his eye Boone saw the little man, dragging one leg, vanish behind the wagon.

The bearded man sat up, one side of his face covered with dust. He was still dazed, but anger and annoyance were rising in him. He glared at Boone, ferocious as a tiger with its claws cut. His .44 gone, he was momentarily helpless.

"Who in Mexico are you?" he roared.

The mulewhacker answered not the question but the issue: "The kid. You didn't see it."

"What kid?"

"With the dog. In the line of your fire." Boone's words were directed toward the bearded man, his eyes and his attention toward the newcomers.

They were big, rangy men, hard-eyed and leathery. They wore long drooping moustaches after the fashion of the period.

One of them spoke harshly, with authority. Beneath the black moustache he had a stiff imperial. His mouth was straight and thin-lipped. "That's right, Curt. You didn't see the kid."

The bearded man rose and took two long steps toward Boone. "Gimme that gun," he demanded.

The young teamster had lived all of his twenty-three years on the frontier where emergencies must be met by instant decision. Already he knew that the man with the imperial was a leader. The breadth of his shoulders, the depth of his chest, the poised confidence of manner were certificates of strength. He alone had not yet drawn a weapon.

"I'll give it to you, sir," Boone replied. "Your friend is some annoyed yet, I expect, and this way seems more sensible."

Holding the revolver by the long barrel, he handed it to the man selected.

"I'll take that gun, Whip," its owner said roughly.

"Don't burn up the road, Curt," his friend answered. "This young pilgrim is right. You might have hit the kid. He didn't aim to jump you but to save the little fellow. I reckon you'll have to leave him go this time."

"Leave him go? After he lit on me all spraddled out? Gun or no gun, I'll sure take him to a cleaning." Curt moved toward Boone, a trifle heavily. He was a full-bodied man, physically more like the grizzly than the panther. He stopped in front of the teamster.

Young Sibley looked at him quietly, steadily. "I'm not looking for trouble, sir," he said. "Sorry I had to drag on you on account of the kid. I figured you wouldn't want to hurt the little fellow."

"I aim to work you over proper," the bearded man announced. "I don't need no gun."

Boone's revolver was on the wagon seat. This was just as well. He was debarred from using it, both because his antagonist was unarmed and because the man's friends would instantly have shot him down if he had drawn a weapon. A crowd was beginning to gather. He heard comments and prophecies.

"Curt will sure eat up this pilgrim."

"Y'betcha! If Mister Muleskinner allows he's the venomous kypoote, he's due to get unroostered *pronto*."

The bearded man lashed out at his intended victim. Boone ducked, drove a left to the fellow's cheek, and danced out of range. Curt roared with anger, put down his head, and charged.

His heavy arms swung like flails, savagely, wildly, with great power behind the blows. The younger man, lithe as a wildcat, alert to forestall each movement, smothered some of these swings, blocked others, dodged the rest. His timing, his judgment of distance were perfect. He jolted the bearded man with two slashing lefts and a short-arm uppercut, side-stepped the ensuing rush, and with a powerful right, all the driving power of his weight back of it, landed flush on the chin at precisely the right instant. Caught off balance, the big man went down like a pole-axed steer.

He went down and he stayed down. His body half rolled over in the dust. He made a spasmodic effort to rise, one of his hands clawing the ground for a hold. Then he relaxed and seemed to fall into himself.

For a moment nobody spoke, nobody moved. Curt French had the reputation of being the best bit of fighting machinery in the new camp. In the current parlance, he could whip his weight in wildcats. So it had been said, and he had given proof in plenty of his prowess. And now an unknown muleskinner, probably a greener who hailed from some whistling post in the desert, had laid him out expertly, with a minimum of effort, and there was not a scratch on the young chap's face to show that he had been in a fight.

An enthusiastic miner slapped his hat against

the leg of a dusty pair of trousers. "Never saw the beat of it. Short an' sweet. Sews Curt up in a sack, an' when he's good an' ready, bing goes the sockdolager, an' Curt turns up his toes to the daisies."

"Say, you ain't Paddy Ryan, are you?" demanded an admiring bartender.

The man who had been called Whip pushed forward and spoke curtly. "What's your name, young fellow? And where d'you hail from?"

The teamster met his heavy frown steadily. "Boone Sibley. I'm from Texas."

"Well, Texas man, I'm offerin' you advice free *gratis*. Drive on an' keep right on going. Tucson is a good town. So's Phoenix."

"What's the matter with this town?"

"Not healthy."

"For me, you mean?"

"For you."

The eyes of the two clashed, those of Boone hard and cold as chilled steel, his opponent's dark and menacing, deep-socketed in a grim, harsh face. It was a drawn battle.

The older man added explanation to his last answer. "For anyone who has done to Curt French what you've done."

"Meaning there will be a gun play?" Boone asked quietly.

"Don't put words in my mouth, young fellow," the other said stiffly. "Leave it as it lays. Light

61

out. Make tracks. Vamoose, if you don't understand the others."

Boone did not say he would take this advice.
He did not say he would not. "I'm sure a heap
obliged to you," he murmured with the little
drawl that might or might not conceal irony. His
glance went around the circle of faces, some
curious, some hostile, some frankly admiring. It
dropped to the man he had vanquished and took
in the fact that the fellow was beginning to stir.
Then, unhurriedly, he turned his back, put a foot
on the hub of the wheel, and climbed back into
the wagon.

"Gidap!" he clucked to the mules.

The long whip snaked out. The tugs straightened
as the mules leaned forward. The wagon went
crunching down the street.

II

A man called on Boone that evening at the Dallas House. He gave his name as Mack Riley. A youngish man, weather-beaten and tanned, his face had written on it marks of the Emerald Isle. He spoke as a Westerner does, with only a trace of accent.

"I come from Mister Turley," he explained. "He wants to see you. Reckon he feels some obligated to you."

"Never heard of him," Boone answered.

"He's the fellow you kept Curt French from killin' today. Curt got him in the leg, so he couldn't come himself. He asked would you come to see him."

"What's he want?"

"I dunno. He's kinda mysterious . . . lives under his own hat, as you might say. It's not far. He stays in a shack back of the Buffalo Corral."

"What was the trouble between him and this Curt French?"

"Somethin' he put in the paper. He's editor of the *Gold Pocket*. Say, young fellow, I saw the show you put on. You certainly were sailin'. You been educated all 'round, up and down, over, under, and between. Either that or else you had luck."

"I expect I was lucky. Tell me about this Curt French, him and his friends, too."

Across Riley's map-of-Ireland face there flitted an expression as though he had put on a mask. "What about 'em?" he asked warily.

"Anything about 'em . . . or all about 'em. I didn't quite *sabe* the game."

"Meanin' just what?" asked Riley cautiously.

"I got an impression . . . maybe there's nothing to it . . . that this Curt and the man he called Whip and two, three others were kinda in cahoots."

Riley said nothing, in a manner that implied he could say a great deal if he chose.

Watching him, Boone continued: "When this Whip fellow told me to throw the bud into my leaders and keep traveling, I reckoned he was talking for his gang as well as for French."

"Me, if I thought so, I'd sure take his advice," Riley said in a voice studiously colorless.

"Why?" asked Boone bluntly. "Is this Whip a bad crowd?"

"You'll never get me to say so, young fellow. I told you what I'd do. That's enough."

"You've said too much or too little, Mister Riley."

"I've said all I aim to say."

"Those other blackbirds that had their guns out, who were they?"

"One was Russ Quinn, brother of Whip. The other was Sing Elder."

"Kinda hang together, do they . . . them and this French fellow?" Sibley asked.

"You might say they were friends."

"Got any business?"

"Right now I'm swampin' for Dave Reynolds at the Buffalo."

"I was speaking of these other gents . . . the Quinns and Elder and French."

"Oh, them! Whip owns the Occidental. Biggest gamblin' house in town. Sing runs a game for him. They're cousins. Russ is shotgun messenger for the express company."

"And Mister French?"

"Curt? Well, I dunno. He bucks the tiger consid'rable. Once in a while he's look-out at the Occidental."

"A tinhorn?"

"I'm not usin' that word about him. Not none. And if I was you I wouldn't either, stranger. You're a likely young fellow, and you're sure a jim-dandy with your dukes. You'd do fine in Tucson likely. It's a right lively town, and the road there is in first-class shape."

"Tucson certainly gets good recommendations from you gentlemen in Tough Nut," Boone said drily. "Any of you ever try that road your own selves?"

Riley gave up, his patience exhausted. "All right. You're the doctor. Maybe you know best. Maybe nobody is aimin' to hang your hide on the

65

corral fence anyhow. I thought, you bein' only a stranger and not knowin', I'd see could I do anything for you. More fool me. You know your own business, likely."

"I'm much obliged, Mister Riley," the Texan said in his gentle voice. "But I reckon I'll look around a while before I move on."

"Suit yourself," the Irishman said shortly. "What about Turley?"

"I'll see him. Want I should come with you?"

"Better sift around after dark. It's the 'dobe shack just west of the corral. You can't miss it."

Boone did not wait till after dark. He saw no reason why he should. For the present, at least, he meant to stay in Tough Nut. To move about furtively, after dark, avoiding trouble that might never materialize, was not consistent with his temperament. There was no reason why these men should make difficulties for him. The affair with French had been none of his seeking. He had acted instinctively to save the child's life. Afterward he had apologized, had tried to placate the angry ruffian. His associates would probably talk him out of his resentment.

Nonetheless, Boone went prepared for trouble. In a sling under his left arm he carried a Colt .45 six-shooter, one, with a nine-inch barrel. Another, not so long, hung from his belt. He did not expect to have to use them. Still, he wanted to know that they were handy if needed. The point about trouble was that it usually jumped you suddenly when least expected.

The sun was in the west, setting in a crotch of the jagged porphyry mountains. It was still king of the desert, its rays streaming over the silvery sheen of the mesquite. Boone stood a few minutes to watch the spectacle at the end of a street that stopped abruptly at the rock rim above the valley. The dust, finer than sand, gave color to the landscape, an opal-like mist that blurred and softened garish details. Already an imperial purple filled the pockets of the hills. Soon now, that burning lake above, which fired the crags and sent streamers of pink and crimson and orange flaming across the sky, would fade slowly into the deep blue of approaching night.

Boone turned and walked with his long easy stride back to Boot Hill Street, then followed it as far as the Buffalo Corral. His eye picked up the adobe shack described to him by Riley, and two minutes later he was knocking at the door.

It was opened to him by Riley. There were in the cabin a bed, some plain furniture, and a great many books. On the bed lay the wounded man. Against the wall, chair tilted back and one run-down boot heel caught in a rung of it, lounged a curly-headed youth with the rich bloom of health in his cheeks. He was dressed as a cowboy.

Riley did the honors. "Meet Mister Turley,

67

Mister Sibley. Shake hands with Mister Rhodes."

The cowpuncher unhooked his heel, dropped the front legs of the chair to the floor, and got to his feet, all with one swift, lithe motion. "Known as Dusty Rhodes," he added by way of further introduction. "Pleased to meet you, Mister Sibley. You're right famous already in our li'l' burg."

"News to me, sir," Boone replied. He liked the appearance of this impetuous youth. An open face recommended him, and the promise of buoyant gaiety was prepossessing.

"You couldn't expect to make Curt French look like a plugged nickel without having word of it spread like a prairie fire. He's been the big wind pudding here for quite some time."

"Meaning that he's a false alarm?"

"No, sirree. He's there both ways from the ace. In strict confidence, he's a dirty flop-eared wolf . . . but I reckon he'll back his own bluffs."

The man on the bed spoke. "I have to thank you, Mister Sibley, for saving my life today." His voice held a clipped precise accent. He tugged nervously at his short, bristly moustache. Boone was to learn later that this was a habitual gesture with him. It arose from nervousness, from an inner conviction that he was quite unfitted to cope with the wild frontier life into which some malign fate had rudely thrust him.

"That's all right," young Sibley said. The subject embarrassed him, though no sign of this showed in his immobile face. "Fact is, I was thinking of the kid. Mothers hadn't ought to let their babies go mavericking off alone."

"Not much to you, perhaps, but a good deal to me," the little editor replied, referring to what was in his mind rather than to what Boone had said. A muscular spasm of reminiscent fear contorted his face for a moment. "The ruffian meant to murder me, and, but for the grace of God and your bravery, I would now be a dead man," he concluded solemnly.

"There's a right few slips between what a feller figures and what he makes out to get done. Curt aimed to bump you off like I aimed once to bring to my wickiup for keeps a li'l' lady in the San Simon, only my plans got kinda disarranged when she eloped with a bald-headed old donker who had four kids and a cow ranch. You can't always sometimes most generally tell. Lady Luck is liable to be sitting into the game," the cowboy suggested with philosophic flippancy.

"It wasn't luck this time. It was God's providence that I'm so little injured," Turley corrected. "He held the hand of the slayer because my work is not yet done. It is about that I want to see you, Mister Sibley."

Boone said nothing. Evidently the editor had some proposition to make. The Texan had a capacity for silence. He could wait while another did the talking. It was an asset in the Southwest

69

to be a man of few words, especially when those few were decisive.

"The Lord chose you as His instrument. I take it as a sign that we are to be associated."

"How?" asked Boone.

He was not favorably impressed. Turley was not his kind of man. A feeling of distaste, almost of disgust, rose in him. He had seen the editor running for his life, in a panic of raw fear, the manhood in him dissolved in quick terror. Now he was talking religious cant like a preacher. In Boone's code, inherited from his environment, the one essential virtue was courage. A man might be good. He might be bad. Without nerve he was negligible, not worth the powder to blow him up. Measured by this test, Turley failed to pass. It looked now as though he were a hypocrite, to boot.

Turley settled his shoulders nervously before he began to talk. "You are a stranger, Mister Sibley. I do not know you, nor do you know me. What I have to say will be spoken by one who has the best interest of the community at heart. I am editor of the local newspaper, the *Gold Pocket*. That paper has a duty to perform to Cochise County. It must stand for law and order, for advancing civilization. Do you agree with me?"

"I'm listening," Boone said. "You're talking."

"I take it that you have had a reasonable amount of schooling Mister Sibley, from the standpoint of the Southwest."

"Correct, sir."

"This community stands at the crossroads. It is infested by gunmen, gamblers, and criminals. These are largely outnumbered by honest citizens who stand aside and let the ruffians have their way. The *Gold Pocket* must be the organ of righteousness. It must be the center around which can rally all those who believe in law enforcement. Mister Sibley, I want to enlist you in that cause." The editor's voice had become a little shrill, oratorical with excitement.

Boone looked at him with a wooden face. Again he asked: "How?"

"As assistant to me in editing the paper."

The Texan's answer was immediate. "No, thank you."

"Don't make up your mind precipitately," the editor urged. "Think it over."

"Not necessary. Your proposition doesn't interest me."

"At least leave it open. You do not have to say no today."

"I can't leave open what never was open. I'm not a politician. I don't care who is sheriff. Why come to me? I never was inside a newspaper office."

"That doesn't matter." The editor sat up, his black eyes shining. "This is a fight, Mister Sibley. I have put my hand to the plow. I can't turn back. What I need is a fearless man to back me up in my fight for good."

71

"Maybe it's your fight. It's not mine."

"It is yours as much as mine. It is every honest decent citizen's business to stand up for what is right!" he boomed.

"Dusty Rhodes to bat," announced the owner of the name genially. "What's eatin' Mister Turley is that the bridle's off this burg and she's kickin' up her heels every jump of the road. He gets all het up about it. Give us time, I say. Tough Nut is only a kid yet." He rose from the chair, stretched himself, and announced that he was going to waltz uptown to the Can-Can for grub. "It's a good two-bit restaurant, Mister Sibley. Better come along and feed your face."

"Reckon I will," assented the Texan.

"What I object to," the editor said by way of correction, "is cold-blooded murder on our city streets, and robbery under arms, and intimidation of justice, and corruption of officials. As an American citizen . . ."

"As an American citizen," interrupted Riley, "you are entitled to squawk, and you've done right considerable of it. If you had any horse sense, carryin' that pill in your leg, you'd know when to quit. If I was you, I'd sure turn my back on that plow you was so eloquentious about. I tell you straight, you ain't got a lick of sense if you don't shut your trap. I don't want to be listenin' to nice words from the preacher about you. Now I've said all I'm gonna say to you and this young fellow both. I aim to live long in the land myself, and I oncet knew a fellow got to be 'most a hundred by mindin' his own business."

"Amen!" agreed young Rhodes in his best mourners' bench voice. "Meanwhile, it's me for the Can-Can to eat one of Charlie's steaks smothered in onions."

The young men walked uptown together.

"So you reckon you don't want to be an editor," Rhodes said, by way of getting his companion's opinion.

"Funniest proposition ever put up to me," Boone responded. "How come he figured I might throw in with him? What's his game, anyhow?"

"Well, sir, that's right queer. He ain't got any game, except he thinks it's his duty to bawl out the Quinn outfit and any others ridin' crooked trails. 'Course, they'll bump him off one of these days. He knows it, too. Scared to death, the li'l' prune is, but stickin' right to the saddle."

"Why? What's the use?" asked Boone, puzzled.

Dusty looked at him, grinning slightly. "Leavin' our beautiful city tonight, Mister Sibley?"

"No, I reckon not."

"Soon?"

"Thought I'd look around a while. Were you aiming to tell me that Tucson is a right lively town where I'd probably do well?"

"No, sir. But you got your answer. You can't

see why old man Turley stays here, but you're aimin' to stay your own self."

"Not the same. First off, I haven't been objecting to the bridle being off the town."

"No," agreed the cowboy drily, "you jest jumped Curt French when he hadn't done a thing to you, and that ain't supposed to be safer than throwin' a match into a keg of powder."

"And second," interposed Sibley, "if this Curt French is sore at me . . . well, I expect I'll be present when the band begins to play. But Turley . . . he'll wilt right off the earth."

"Sure he will."

"He's got no more nerve than a brush rabbit."

"That's whatever. He's plumb scared stiff half the time."

"Then why doesn't he light out . . . cut dirt for Boston, or wherever he comes from?"

"Because he's got sand in his craw . . . guts."

"You just said . . ."

"I said the goose quills run up and down his spine every time he sees a bad man. Now I say he's the gamest bird I ever raised. You and me . . . he's got us backed off the map for sand. If I was half as scared as he is, I'd be in New Mexico by now and still travelin'. No, sir. I take off my hat to him."

"I didn't cotton to him much myself."

"You wouldn't . . . not at first. He don't know much about this border country. Came out for his health. Got all sorts of funny notions. He aims to gentle us and get us saddle broke to nice lady-like ways. Yet I'll be dog-goned if I don't like the li'l' cuss . . . and respect him. He's gonna play out his hand to a finish."

"Why doesn't he get you to back his play?" Boone asked.

Dusty suspected sarcasm in the question, but he grinned cheerfully. "Me? Why, I ain't bought any chips in this game. I'm one of these here innocent bystanders. Come to that, I do a li'l' hellin' around my own self, oncet in a while."

Boone nodded. He could believe that.

The cowboy added another reason. "And I don't aim to take up a residence in Boot Hill if I can help it. I don't claim everything's right in this town. It ain't. But nobody elected me to read the riot act to the bad actors."

"Meaning the Quinn gang?"

"I'm naming no names. Here's Charlie's place. We'll sashay in and feed us at his chuck wagon." He hung on the threshold a moment to add a word to what he had said. "But Whip and Russ ain't a bad crowd, stranger. There's a heap worse than them in this man's town."

"And French . . . have you got a gilt-edged testimonial framed up for him, too?" Boone asked.

The cowboy grinned. "Shh! Hush your fool mouth."

75

III

A thin old man, toothless, sat in the Can-Can eating a plate of flapjacks. Dusty Rhodes hailed him.

"How you makin' it, Dad?"

"Fat like a match. How's your own corporosity sagasuate?"

"I'm ridin' high, wide, and handsome."

"*Humph!* You sayin' it don't mean a thing to me. You got no ambition . . . none of you young riders. Give you a saddle, a quirt, spurs, a bronc', a forty-dollar job, an' oncet in a while God send Sunday, an' you don't ask another thing."

"Meet Mister Sibley," the cowboy said. "Mister Sibley, shake hands with Mobeetie Bill. Don't ask me what his oncet name was. All I know is he lit in Cochise three jumps ahead of a posse."

"Nothin' to that, Mister Sibley," the old man corrected. "Fact is, I skinned a jerkline string when I fust come."

"I been told he hit Texas when the Palo Duro wasn't a hole in the ground yet. No tellin' how old he is. Mebbe a hundred. You've heard the legend that you can't tell the truth oncet you drink of the waters of Hassayampa River . . . well, don't you believe anything this old Hassayampa tells you, Mister Sibley. By the way, Dad, Mister Sibley is from your own range."

"Not exactly, if you hail from the Panhandle," Boone said. "I come from the Brazos."

"Sit down, Texas man," the old-timer invited. To the slant-eyed waiter he gave orders. "Another stack of chips. An' wait on these gents, Charlie."

They sat down, ordered, ate. Casual conversation flowed on. For the most part Boone listened. Mobeetie Bill had been a buffalo hunter. He had, in his own words, "tooken the hides off'n a heap of them." Before that he had served with the Confederate Army, and prior to that with General Sam Houston. He had known the Southwest many years before barb wire had come in to tame it.

"Yes, sir, them was the days," he said reminiscently. "There was mighty few cutbacks in the herd when I fust come to Texas. Clever folks, most of 'em. 'Course, there was trouble, lots of it. If you was anyways hostile, you could always be accommodated. At El Paso there usta be a cottonwood at the head of a street where folks grew personal. They nailed their opinions of each other on it. Anse Mills posted three citizens as liars. That was sure fightin' talk then. Dallas Studinmire stuck there a list of bad men he aimed to kill *pronto* if they didn't light out sudden. He bumped off three, four to show good faith, an' the rest said 'Good bye, El Paso.' Times ain't like they was. Folks, either. Me, I'm nothin' but a stove-up old donker."

"This country is wild enough for me right now," Rhodes said. "Four of us was jumped by 'Paches last year. If it's shootin's you are pinin' for, why, I expect Tough Nut could accommodate you."

"*Humph!* Boy, you're a kid hardly outta your cradle. You brag about your Quinns an' your Curt French. Say, if they had bumped into John Wesley Hardin when he was going good . . . or even Clay Allison . . . our Texas killers would sure have made 'em climb a tree."

Boone observed that Rhodes looked around quickly to make sure nobody else had come into the restaurant. "I ain't arguin' with you, Dad. All I say is that when I meet the gents referred to, I'm always real polite." He had, even in making this innocuous remark, lowered his voice.

"Why, someone was tellin' me on the street that some pilgrim from back East beat up your Curt French this very damned day," Dad said belligerently.

"No need to shout it, Dad," the cowboy warned. "Old as you are, you might annoy Curt considerable if he heard you. In which case, he'd take it outta either you or me or both of us. But since you're on the subject, it wasn't any pilgrim from the East but this Texas brother of yours who mixed it with Curt today."

Mobeetie Bill's eyes glistened. "Son, you'll do to take along, looks like. But, boy, pack your hog-leg wherever you go, or you'll sure sleep in smoke. Hell coughed up this fellow Curt French. He's a sure enough killer, an' he trails with a bad bunch."

"You're certainly gabby today, Dad," Rhodes protested mildly. "A young fellow like you had ought to learn to keep his trap shut."

The old-timer paid no attention to the cowboy. He addressed himself to his fellow Texan. "If you're a false alarm, you better cut dirt *pronto*."

"For Tucson?" Boone asked bravely.

Dusty grinned. "Mister Sibley has been told two, three times already that Tucson is a right good town, and the wagon tracks are plain headin' that-a-way."

"Correct," agreed the old buffalo hunter. "That's good advice, Texas man, an' it don't cost a cent Mex."

"Good advice for anyone that wants to take it," amended Boone.

Mobeetie Bill looked into his cool flinty eyes. "Correct once more. Good for anyone but a fightin' fool, an' maybe for him, too. If I get this Curt French right, he'll aim to make Tough Nut hotter than Hades with the blower on for you. He'll likely get lit up with tarantula juice an' go gunnin' with a pair of six-shooters. Like enough he'll take two, three Quinns along when he starts to collect."

"Cheerful news," commented the young Texan. "He seems to be some lobo wolf."

"Prob'ly you could get a job freightin' up Prescott way, thereby throwin' two stones at one bird."

"Right now I'll throw my stones, if any, at birds in Tough Nut. For a day or two, anyhow, while I look around."

Mobeetie Bill let out a soft-pedaled version of the old Rebel yell. "You're shoutin', boy. That's the way folks talked in the good old days. Make this tinhorn climb a tree."

Rhodes spoke quickly, in a low voice: *"Chieto, compadre."*

Men passed the window of the restaurant. A moment later they came in, two of them. Instantly Boone recognized them as two of the men who had been with French at the time of his difficulty with the gambler. They took seats at a small table in a corner of the room. As they moved across the floor, the Texan saw again that they were big and rangy. An arrogant self-confidence rode their manner.

"Brad Prouty and Russ Quinn," murmured Rhodes.

The buffalo hunter bridged any possible silence the entry of the newcomers might have made. His voice flowed on as though he had been in the midst of narrative.

". . . made camp in a grove of cottonwoods on White Deer creek that night. I rec'lect I was mixin' up a batch of cush when a fellow rode up with his horse in a lather. The Cheyennes were swarmin' over the country, he claimed. They had burned his ranch, an' he had jest saved his hide. Well, sir, we headed for 'Dobe Walls an' got there right after the big fight Billy Dixon an' the other boys had there with about a thousand Injuns. That's how clost I come to being in the 'Dobe Walls battle."

"Was you in the War of Eighteen Twelve, Dad?" asked Rhodes with innocent malice.

The old man shook a fleshless fist at him. "I ain't so old but what I could take you to a cleanin' right now, boy," he boasted. "Trouble with you young sprouts is you never was wore to a frazzle with a hickory limb when you needed it most."

Dusty slapped his thigh with a brown hand. "Dawged if I don't believe you'd climb my frame for four bits," he chuckled.

"Make it two bits. Make it a plug of tobacco," Dad cackled with a toothless grin.

Quinn and Prouty ordered supper and ate. Russ, facing Boone, said something to his companion in a low voice. Prouty turned and stared at Sibley. The young Texan, apparently absorbed in what his friends were saying, endured the look without any evidence that he knew he was the object of attention.

"Curt's right. Population of this town is too promiscuous," Russ said, not troubling to lower his voice.

"That's whatever, Russ. Ought to be thinned out."

"Good thing if some emigrated. Good for the town. Good for them." Through narrowed lids, slits of eyes watched Boone. "If I was a friend of some of these pilgrims, I'd tell 'em to hive off for other parts . . . kinda ease outta the scenery, as you might say."

Making notes of these men without seeming to see them, Boone took in the lean shoulders, muscular and broad, of Russ Quinn, his close-clamped jaw, a certain cat-like litheness in the carriage of his body. Brad Prouty was heavier and shorter of build, a hairier man. His mouth was a thin, cruel line below the drooping moustache. It might be guessed that Prouty was of a sullen disposition, given to the prompt asser-tion of what he considered his rights.

"Yep, slap a saddle on a broomtail an' light out. I'd sure call that good medicine." This from Prouty.

Quinn took up the refrain: "Sometimes a guy has a li'l' luck and presses it too far. I've seen that happen several times. Don't know when to lay down a hand. Boot Hill for them right soon. Nobody's fault but their own."

Into this antiphony Boone interjected a remark, addressed apparently to Mobeetie Bill, in an even, level voice. "Yes, like I was saying, I like your town. Reckon I'll camp here a while. Lots of work, and folks seem friendly and sociable."

The old hunter strangled a snort. "Well, they are an' they ain't. Don't you bank on that good feelin' too much."

"Oh, I'll take it as it comes," Boone answered carelessly.

It occurred to Mobeetie Bill, looking at this tall, lean young man, with cool, sardonic blue-gray eyes in the sunburned face, that he was competent to look after himself.

"If you stay, it's on your own responsibility," Dusty Rhodes chipped in. The cowboy's eyes were shining. This by-play took his fancy. If the odds had not been so great, he would have been willing to take a long-shot bet on Sibley's chances.

"Well, yes," drawled Boone. "I eat and sleep and live on my own responsibility. Fact is, I've been hitting too fast a clip. I kinda want to rest a while in a nice, quiet, peaceable town like this. Two churches here already, and another heading this way, they say. Nice little schoolhouse on Prospect Street. First-class climate. Good live newspaper."

It was Russ Quinn who took up the refrain on the part of the other table. "That's right, come to think of it, nobody been buried in Boot Hill for a week. Liable to be someone soon . . . some guy who blows in and wants to show he's a bad man from Bitter Creek. Well, here's hopin'. Shove the salt this-a-way, Brad."

"So a quiet young fellow like me, trying to get along, looking for no trouble and expecting none, had ought to do well here," Boone went on placidly.

What Dusty Rhodes thought was: *You darned old horn toad, you sure have got sand in your craw.* What he said was: "I can get you a job on a ranch in the Chiricahuas, above the San Simon, forty dollars per if you're a top hand with a rope."

"Maybe I'll take you up later. No rush. I reckon the cows will calve in the spring, same as usual," Boone said nonchalantly.

"I'll be rockin' along that-a-way in a day or two. Like to have your company," Rhodes insisted.

"Oh, well, we'll see."

Dusty Rhodes paid the bill, saying that it was his treat. His guests reached for their hats and sauntered out.

Russ Quinn spoke a word as the cowboy was leaving. Rhodes turned and went back to the table. A minute later he joined Sibley and the old buffalo hunter outside.

"What'd he want?" asked Mobeetie Bill.

"Wanted I should get this here darn' fool pilgrim outta the neighborhood before Curt qualified him for his private graveyard."

"Kind of him," Boone said with mild sarcasm.

Rhodes had his own point of view. "Russ is no

crazy killer. 'Course, he'll gun a guy if he has to, but he's not lookin' for a chance. I reckon he'd like to see you light out for your own sake."

They walked along the roaring street. Already it was filled with lusty, good-natured life. Men jostled each other as they crowded in and out of the gambling halls. Sunburned cowboys, sallow miners, cold-eyed tinhorns, dusty freighters, and prosperous merchants were out for amusement. Inside the variety halls and the saloons, gaudily dressed women drank with the customers and offered their smiles to prospective clients. But, outside, none of the weaker sex showed themselves on Apache Street. Rich man, poor man, beggar man, thief, they crowded one another impartially in democratic simplicity. One was as good as another. All were embryonic millionaires, sure that the blind goddess luck would strike them soon.

Whatever else it was, Tough Nut was a men's town.

IV

Boone Sibley was not looking for trouble, but he was warily ready for it. He and his companions wandered through Jefford's and the Golden Eagle. They took a flyer at the wheel in Dolan's Palace. They watched a stud game running at the Last Chance.

More than one man recognized Boone and out of the corner of his mouth murmured something to his nearest neighbor. The Texan's face was impassive, his manner indifferent. He seemed to be negligently at ease. But his cool eyes carried to him all the information they could gather. They searched out the personnel of every crowd. When swing doors were pushed open, they were aware of who entered. Each gambler's face was noted and dismissed.

His business was to show himself in public, briefly, at several places, to put at rest any question of his being in hiding. This was not bravado. It was an insurance policy, by no means bulletproof, against attack, for if Curt French suspected that Boone was afraid of him, he would certainly begin burning powder when they met.

The Texan did not invite a challenge. He stayed away from the Occidental, where French was most likely to be found. A visit to Whip Quinn's place at present would be considered in the nature of a defiance, and Boone had no desire to stir up the wild animals. There was always a possibility, though from what he heard about French he judged it slight, that if he did not meet the man too soon the fellow's simmering wrath might not explode. The Quinns might talk him out of an attempt at reprisal.

It was still early, as Tough Nut judged time, when Boone went back to his room at the Dallas House. He rolled and smoked a cigarette meditatively. Certainly it was hard luck that within five minutes of his arrival in town he had made an enemy of a bad *hombre* like Curt French and had fallen tentatively into disfavor with the Quinns. They would be a hard combination to buck against. He could not run away. That was not consistent with his code. But he would stand back and sidestep trouble, unless it was forced on him.

He went to bed and was asleep within five minutes.

Sunlight was streaming into the room when he awoke. He dressed, breakfasted, and walked the quiet streets as he went about his business of feeding the team and disposing of the supplies he had brought to the camp. French was a night owl, as gamblers are, and the chances were that he would not be seen till afternoon. Nonetheless, Boone went cautiously. The fellow might surprise him.

Noon passed. The sun moved westward and sank lower. Twice Boone saw some of the Quinn crowd. Once Whip and Prouty, at a distance, came down Apache Street and disappeared into the Occidental. Later, he passed Russ and another big dark man standing on a street corner. Someone spoke to the second man, calling him Sing.

Russ looked bleakly at Boone. "Still here?" he said.

"Still here," Boone answered curtly.

Just before supper time Dusty Rhodes came to Boone with news. "I saw Doc Peters a li'l' while ago. Whatcha think? Curt is down with the measles."

"Measles?"

"Yep." The cowboy grinned. "Got 'em bad. He's in bed and liable to stay there three, four days. Kinda funny, a big elephant like Curt gettin' a kid disease like the measles."

For Boone this was good news, unless it was a trap to throw him off his guard.

"What kind of a fellow is this Doc Peters? Stands in with the Quinn gang, does he?"

"No, sir. He's a good doctor . . . educated 'way up, and he's straight as a string. Anyone will tell you he's a good citizen."

"Find out from him how sick French is, will you?"

"Bet your boots. Say, what about that Chiricahua

proposition we was talkin' about. No use stickin' around waitin' for French to get well enough to bump you off. I'm for bein' accommodatin', but there's sure a limit."

"I'll throw in with you if you'll wait two or three days."

Dusty hesitated. "Looky here, fellow, I like your style. But let's git down to cases. The Quinns are our friends . . . us fellows up in the hills. Kinda mutual give and take. 'Nough said. I can't plumb throw 'em down. I'm figurin' to get you outta town before the earthquake."

"Suits me fine," agreed Boone, smiling. "But I've got business here for a couple days. After that, I'm with you."

"You don't figure on havin' a rumpus with any of the Quinns?" the cowboy asked cautiously.

"No, not unless some of 'em ride me."

"All right," Dusty conceded reluctantly. "But why wait two days? You want to show you ain't scared, I reckon."

"That's about it. Just like a kid," Boone admitted. But he knew that his reason ran deeper than vanity. He was staying a reasonable time partly out of self-respect, partly because he knew that a man in trouble is always safer if he puts on a bold front.

Dusty took occasion to drop around to the Occidental for a word with its owner. He found Whip Quinn making measurements with a carpenter for an addition of an ell at the rear of the house to enlarge its capacity.

The cowpuncher had come for a definite purpose, but he stood around rather awkwardly, trying to find a way to make what he was about to say sound casual.

Whip anticipated him. "Hear you've found a new friend, Dusty," he said.

The cowboy met the hard stare of the gambler. "Looks that-a-way," he admitted, somewhat disconcerted. "I kinda like the guy. It was about him I wanted to speak to you."

"I'm listenin'," Whip said briefly.

"Sibley is not lookin' for trouble. It was sorta wished on him."

"I was there at the time. Not necessary to explain it to me."

"That's right," agreed Rhodes. "Well, all I wanted to say was that he's leavin' for the hills right soon."

"When?"

"In a day or so. He's got some business to finish."

"Did he ask you to tell me that?"

"No-o, he didn't."

"Well, if he's not huntin' trouble, he'd better light out before Curt is around again. You can tell him that from me."

The cowboy did not carry this message. He was afraid it might have the opposite of the desired effect. Sibley would not let himself be run out of town or driven out by fear of consequences.

• • •

Boone sold his team and bought a cow pony. His saddle he had brought with him in the wagon. When at last the two were fairly on the road, Dusty took a deep breath of relief. He was reckless enough himself and had come out of more than one scrape during which guns had blazed. But he liked this Texan, and he was convinced that if Boone stayed in town, it would be only a few days until Curt French would force the issue and the Quinns would be drawn in. Under which circumstances his new friend would not have a rabbit's chance.

They rode through the grama grass into the golden dawn of the desert. Before them were the jig-saw mountains, bare and brown. In that uncertain light they had a curious *papier-mâché* effect, as though they had been built for stage scenery.

The riders descended into a valley blue and pink with alfileria. The season was spring. There had been plenty of winter rain, and the country bloomed. The brilliant flowers of the cacti were all about them; the prickly pear and the ocotillo in scarlet bloom, the saguaro great candelabra lit, as it were, with yellow flame. Here and there in the chaparral were florescent buckthorn and manzanita.

They came upon a pair of burros picketed out, and close to them the camp of a pair of prospectors. The old fellows were typical desert rats, unshaven, ragged, and dust-grimed.

Young Rhodes gave a shout. "Look who we've jumped this glad mornin' . . . old Toughfoot Bozeman and Hassayampa Pete. What do you-all gravel scratchers figure on findin' down in the flats here?"

The eyes of one of the old-timers twinkled. " 'Lowed to run acrost a stray jackass or two, maybe."

His partner took the question more seriously. "We been in the Chiricahuas lookin' around. Nothin' there. We're headin' for the Dragoons. You better quit hellin' around and go to prospectin' your own self, young fellow."

"Meet Mister Sibley, from Texas, gents. No, I ain't got the patience to spend all my time diggin' graveyards for my hopes. Me, I'll stick to cows."

"Your own or someone else's?" Pete asked innocently. Then, lest this sounded too pointed, he added: "You young galoots got jest about brains enough to head off a steer hightailin' acrost the desert. Well, go to it, boy. I'll buy you a ranch when we've done made our strike."

The two young men left the prospectors packing their outfit.

"We'll get outta the flats soon," Dusty promised.

Beyond the valley they climbed into the foot-hills and jogged along for hours, gradually working higher as the trail wound in and out of arroyos and small cañons. On the sleepy shoulder of a ridge spur they unsaddled to rest their horses.

Dusty shot a rattlesnake. "First I've seen this year," he said. "Almost stepped on it as I come 'round that niggerhead."

They lay down and chatted disjointedly. Their talk was of the common subject that interested Arizona. They mentioned the rains and the good grass and how fat cattle were. They wondered whether the Apaches would soon break out again. Both of them knew that Cochise County was the home of scores of rustlers who were engaged in running stock across the border from Mexico. But that was a subject best not discussed by strangers, and these two young men were scarcely more than that. All that Boone knew of his companion was that he seemed a friendly, likable youth. No doubt he was a wild buckaroo. Left an orphan at an early age, he had scrambled up without training or family traditions. What his reaction toward honesty might be, Boone did not know. But the Texan noted that Dusty gave no details of his manner of life. He did not name his employer—if he had one—nor did he say anything of a ranch and brand of his own.

There were few cattle ranches and these as yet not well stocked. The Mexican line was close, and beyond it were the *haciendas* of *señores* rich in land and cattle. It was an easy though a risky undertaking to slip across to Sonora, round up a bunch of cows, and drive them into Arizona in the dark of the moon. The ranchers on the San Pedro and the Sulphur Springs valley asked few questions as to length of ownership. They "bought at a whack-up" and were glad to stock their range at a low price. If the local market was glutted, the rustlers hid the cattle in small mountain parks, changed the brands, and drove a herd to some of the government posts that needed beef for the Indians on reservations.

The two young men resaddled and took up again the trail for the uplands. They were now in a rough country. The arroyos had become gulches, the hills mountains. The cholla and paloverde had given place to scrub pine and juniper. The riders followed a tortuous path. They climbed stiff shale ascents and dropped down precipitous pitches.

To them drifted the sound of a shot, faint and far.

"Box Cañon over that-a-way," explained Dusty. "Back of it the McLennon Ranch."

Another shot came to them, and after it the popping of four or five more explosions, much as though someone were setting off firecrackers.

The riders drew up to listen. For a few moments there was silence, then again another cracker went *pop!* Presently, like a muffled echo of it, a duller report reached their ears.

Dusty looked at his companion. "Trouble, sounds like. Rifles and six-shooters both. We better head that-a-way."

The Texan nodded. Neither of them said anything about the need for caution, but instinctively they left the draw they were ascending and put their horses to the steep hillside. Both wanted to see as soon as possible those who were shooting. There was a good deal less chance of riding into a trap from a hilltop than from a gulch.

While they were still climbing to the ridge, other shots sounded. These were louder than the others. Boone judged that the riflemen were moving rapidly nearer. Oddly enough, both men knew that what they heard was not the exuberance of youth making a noise to express itself. This firing meant battle, the spit of deadly bullets, the sinister whistle of death screaming on its way. How they knew it, neither could have told. Perhaps by some sixth sense given to those who tread wild and dangerous trails.

From the summit they looked down on a hill pocket of mesquite terminating in a rocky wall. Three men lay crouched in the brush behind such shelter as they could find. Fifty yards in front of them was another. His body lay huddled, face down, where he had fallen.

The men were trapped. That was clear enough. But even from the height where Boone stood, it took him some seconds to find any of the assailants. They, too, had taken such cover as the draw afforded. Presently the sun glinted on the barrel of a rifle, though no man was visible behind it. A puff of smoke some distance to the right showed him where another squatted. His eyes picked out a third behind the trunk of a twisted mesquite. There were others, of course, hidden in the chaparral. In the distance a bunch of cattle could be seen grazing.

"Our boys!" Dusty cried, his voice shrill from excitement. "They've got one of 'em."

Already he was sliding from the saddle, rifle in hand. Boone followed his example and took refuge behind a low broad oak. But the Texan did not imitate him in his next move. For Dusty, from behind another live oak, took careful aim and fired at the man hidden back of the twisted mesquite.

The man jumped up and ran for the shelter of a wash. Boone made a discovery. He was a Mexican in tight trousers and big sombrero.

There was quick, excited speech. A second man broke for the wash, and a bullet sang past him as he scudded for safety. Then Boone saw two men moving cautiously through the brush. They, too, were heading for the wash. All of them were Mexicans.

"We've got 'em runnin'!" Dusty shouted to those below.

A moment later a compact group of men, on horseback, clambered out of the wash, on the far side, and rode away at a gallop. They broke formation, scattered, and circled the cattle. Dusty let out an exultant: "Hiyi!"

V

Except as to details, the situation explained itself to Boone. It told its own story without words. These cowboys in the hill pocket below were rustlers. They had driven this bunch of cattle across the line and had almost reached safety. But for once the Mexican *vaqueros* had outgeneraled them. They had pursued, cut off the cowboys, killed one of them, and recaptured their stock. Already the victors were hustling the tired herd along the back trail.

The arrival of Dusty Rhodes had been opportune. It was his shot from the bluff that had startled the attackers. They had settled down to wipe out the rustlers, but the sound of reinforcements had frightened them. They were in the enemy's country and might in turn be caught in a trap. Hence, their immediate withdrawal.

Boone counted seven of the *vaqueros*, and he was not sure that he had not missed one or two. They had ridden bunched, and after they had spread to gather the herd, the riders were so mixed with the cattle that it was not easy to distinguish them.

There was a puff of smoke, and an instant later the sound of a shot. Boone could see now that someone had ridden out to a little spur almost in

97

front of the moving mass of animals. One of the Mexicans had fired at him. Too late the man turned to escape. A second shot brought down his horse. He picked himself up and ran for a clump of firs. Bullets popped at him as he fled along the spur. He was a slim, lithe young fellow, and he ran fast.

One of the *vaqueros* spurred his horse forward to cut off the retreat.

"They've got him!" Dusty cried in excitement. "They've sure got him. What a fool trick to show himself!"

The runner stopped, cut off from the timber. He dragged out a revolver and fired. He had aimed at the Mexican who barred his flight.

The sequel was surprising. From his horse the *vaquero* leaped and swept his sombrero almost to the ground in a raffish bow. What he said was indistinguishable, but there was apparently an exchange of words. Another rider cantered up. The first *vaquero* led his horse toward the cornered man. There was more talk. The Mexicans urged something at which the other demurred. With a swift gesture, one of them snatched the weapon from their captive. Reluctantly, so it seemed, the latter drew nearer the bronco. His foot found the stirrup, and with one lithe motion he was astride the horse of the second rider, sitting behind the *vaquero*.

"They're takin' him along," Dusty said. "Why,

by golly? How come they didn't pump him full of lead and leave him lay?"

Before he had finished speaking, he knew why. The hat of the prisoner had fallen off when the horse had gone down. Now, as the *vaquero* gave his mount the spur, a flag of red hair streamed out in the breeze. The captive was a woman—more than that, a young and lissome one.

"Who is she?" asked Boone.

"Tilatha McLennon, I reckon. We better move down to where the other boys are at."

They found a break in the bluff where their horses could pick a way down by sliding rather than walking.

The men below were grouped around the one who had been killed. A pockmarked man turned to Dusty as he approached.

"They done got Bill. Lucky for us you drifted along, prob'ly. The greasers got scared and lit out."

Dusty looked down with awe at the dead rustler. He had known him for a year and more as a gay and carefree boy. "Sure tough," he said, his voice grave. He swallowed a lump in his throat before he went on. "Meet Mister Boone Sibley, boys. This is Sandy Joe. Shake hands with Tom Tracy and Sid Edwards."

The invitation to shake hands was a figurative and not a literal one. They wasted no time in formalities, but fell at once into a discussion of ways and means. All of them had seen the Mexicans pick up the girl. She must, of course, be rescued. They did not need to argue about that. The question was how.

"They'll head through Box Cañon. That's where they laid for us and jumped us," Edwards said. "They can't follow that bunch of cows and make their getaway. We got time enough." He was a squat, heavy-set man with bowed legs, the oldest of the party. By common consent, he took command. "Can't stop to bury Bill now. Have to wait for that. Sandy, you light out for the McLennon place and pass the word to Hugh about his sister. Tell him to bring whoever is handy and meet us at Galeyville. He'll come hotfoot. The rest of us will trail these birds till we're through the cañon."

Boone fell in between Edwards and Dusty Rhodes.

"We'll need fresh horses," Dusty said. "We been on ours all day, and yours look plumb wore out."

"Pick up plenty at Galeyville," Edwards said. "Two or three of us will stay right behind the greasers whilst the rest round up horses for the outfit."

"Question is, can we get at 'em to settle their hash before night." Dusty looked at the westering sun. "We don't want to leave Tilatha with 'em all night. She'd sure think we was a nice lot of cautious guys. Hadn't we better bust right into the bunch and give 'em billy-be-damned?"

100

"No sense to that," said Edwards. "They won't hurt Miss Tilatha any, I don't reckon. They collected her as a kinda hostage, likely."

"I don't care what they collected her for," Dusty snapped out. "You can bet your boots they ain't a-goin' to keep her as long as I'm sound enough to tote a gun."

"Hold your horses, boy. Who is figurin' on them keepin' her? But tell me how we can take her away without pumpin' lead right near where she's at. No, we gotta use strategy."

"Beats me what Tilatha was doing there, anyhow," Dusty went on. "How come she was on that dog-gone' ridge right then, and why for did she ride out so's they could see her?"

"Humph!" This contribution came from the man called Tom Tracy. He was a hard-faced citizen with shifty eyes and a mean, thin-lipped mouth. The tone of the exclamation seemed to suggest a good deal that might as well be left unsaid.

"What you gruntin' at, Tom?" challenged Dusty.

The other cowboy drawled his answer out insultingly. "Thought you claimed to know that gal right well. She's liable to be any place any time, particularly if it's where she hadn't ought to be."

Indignantly Dusty denied it. "She's a right fine young lady. 'Course, she clicks her heels some.

101

Why shouldn't she when she's the prettiest thing in Cochise? Me, I like a gal whose eyes flash . . . one who has got a will of her own."

"I've seen guys before that liked to be tromped down like a doormat," jeered Tracy.

Edwards interfered. He did not like the man's manner. In the hill country of the frontier, it was not customary to speak of women except with respect. "That'll be enough, Tom," he said with finality.

Boone guessed that there was something personal back of this interchange between Dusty and Tom Tracy. It was possible they had clashed about the young lady, or, for that matter, on some other subject. Tracy's fling at her might have been made merely to irritate young Rhodes.

The Texan rode beside the cowboys with a mental reservation. He would go as far as any man to rescue an American woman captured by Mexicans, and that meant to the limit of endurance, as long as he could ride or stand or fight. That was not any distinction in the borderland. It was in the code, was expected of every man. But there was another aspect to the situation. These men, with the possible exception of Rhodes, at least, were rustlers caught in the act. If the question came to issue, he would make it clear that he was joining them to help rescue the young lady and not to get back the cattle.

Boone was no prig. He held the ideas of his

class in those times regarding rustling stock from the Mexicans. In the first place, he had been brought up, like most Texans, to hate Mexico and the Mexicans. The days of the Lone Star state's fight for freedom were too near to forget. One of his great-uncles had been with Ewen Cameron on his fatal expedition, had drawn a black bean when life and death had been in the balance, and had died with a score of his companions in front of Santa Anna's firing squad. Boone had met old men who remembered the Alamo. A score of incidents in his own time had kept green the bitter memories of earlier times, in many of which no doubt the Texans had been aggressors.

But young Boone Sibley came of honest pioneer stock. His father had been a God-fearing man and had taught him the difference between right and wrong. Yet, in practical application of this teaching, Boone found himself just now in some doubt. Running cattle across the border, with the risk of a desperate fight thrown in, was not plain stealing. It had at least some of the elements of high adventure, and it might be excused, even though not justified, on the ground that it was despoiling the enemy.

All that Boone was sure of just now was that he must go slowly. He had no intention of letting himself be driven by force of circumstance into a position that would make him an unwilling rustler. He knew that most of the wild young cowboys engaged in lifting cattle were not criminals at heart. They had drifted into lawlessness out of good fellowship or carelessness, or to meet a temporary shortage of funds. But Boone was no drifter. He walked the way of the strong. When he did wrong, it would not be because of weakness but by reason of deliberate choice.

They rode fast, though their horses were tired. It was well enough to assure themselves that the Mexicans dared not injure their captive, but all of them had heard stories that made their blood surge. That these stories might not be true did not affect their feeling, since they believed anything of Mexicans. They were prejudiced beyond hope of change.

After an hour of riding, Edwards drew up. "We'll head for Galeyville, Tom and me," he said. "Dusty, you and Mister Sibley better stay by the trail. Don't get too close to these fellows. The idea is jest to keep tab on them. We'll start soon as we can and ride for the foot of the round top north of Nigger Bill's claim. Ought to reach there soon after dark. You join us there, Dusty, and guide us back to where you left Mister Sibley. After that we'll figure out some way to surprise the greasers."

The herd trail had been dropping down from the mountains through rolling hills toward the flatlands. The two young men rode through mesquite thickets to open slopes of bear grass, spiked yucca, and tufts of Spanish bayonet. In front of them, a mile and more away, moved a cloud of yellow dust. It drifted leftward in the wind, and when Boone and his friend topped a rise, they could look down on a moving mass, closely bunched as is a herd of cattle driven hard. At this distance it was impossible to distinguish horse from cow, but somewhere among those crawling dots was one that represented the figure of a girl whose heart was heavy with dread.

The sun went down. The hot sands of the desert began to cool, though the fine dust still rose from the hoofs of the horses and settled upon the faces of the riders, into their nostrils and baked throats, upon every wrinkle of hat and shirt and boot.

Behind Sugar Loaf Peak the sky was a splash of brilliant hues slashed above the horizon line by the master painter. From moment to moment it changed. The scarlet and the crimson grew less vivid, died away. Violet became purple as the darkness descended over the land. With the coming of night the harshness of the desert softened. Garish details were blotted out. It was as though a magic wand had touched the land to beauty.

The wind freshened. Clouds drifted across the sky. In the air was a hint of coming rain. There would be no moon, perhaps no starlight.

"Reckon I better be hittin' the trail for that

round top back of Nigger Bill's," Dusty said. "I don't want to hold back the boys any. You stick right here till we get back. ¡*Adiós*!"

Dusty vanished into the night. Before he had gone five yards, he was a blur, no more distinct than one of the ironwoods that surrounded them. A moment more, and his position could be told only by the creaking of the saddle and the *clop-clop* of the horse's hoofs beating rhythmically in the sand.

Boone delayed only to be sure that Dusty was gone. He had no intention of staying there to wait for the cowboys. Presently he was guiding his horse through the chaparral in the wake of the herd. The Texan rode with a purpose. He had conceived a plan, one that at first thought seemed wild and harebrained. But its boldness, its very danger, might make for success. Failure would prove disastrous, but that was true of most hazardous enterprises.

He had no confidence in the wisdom of any scheme the cowboys might devise. If they succeeded in rescuing Miss McLennon, it would be only after a fierce battle and much bloodshed. Boone meant to play a lone hand and trust to a more subtle attack. Both the darkness and the nature of the country favored him. The terrain was rough and the vegetation thick.

The Texan rode as fast as he could wind in and out among the brush. What he had to do must be done quickly, for fear the clouds be brushed aside by the wind and let the starlight through.

There drifted back to him the lowing of the cattle. He knew cows. As he drew closer, he could tell by the bawling that they were thirsty as well as spent and weary.

VI

Boone knew he must have luck to succeed. But he knew, too, that by shrewdness and audacity a man sometimes makes his own luck. If he could plan carefully . . .

He drew closer to the herd, watching for a chance. The steady, insistent bawling, the stringing out of the cattle, made him think that they were drawing close to water. Experience told him that the *vaqueros* would be strung out as lead, flank, and tail riders.

What he had to determine was at which position Miss McLennon rode and how well she was guarded. He drew closer to the right flank and presently brought his horse alongside the longhorns. Just in front of him a rider moved.

The *vaquero* called to another riding on the point to look out for the cutbank. He spoke, of course, in Spanish.

The cattle bunched. Evidently they had reached a deep arroyo, and the leaders were hesitating on the edge. Boone pulled his hat low. A bandanna handkerchief covered his face from the bridge of the nose down, ostensibly to protect him from the dust. He put his horse to a canter and swung back of the herd.

A *vaquero*, turning back a straying cow, shouted

a question at him. Had they come to water? Without stopping, Boone called back an answer. He could speak Spanish like a native Mexican.

The Texan passed within five yards of one of the drag drivers, who mistook him in the darkness for one of his companions. By this time Boone knew that Miss McLennon must be with some of the men on the left flank or point. So far his luck had stood up fine.

The bunching of the cattle was fortunate for Boone. The two swing men were close in, urging the beasts on the outskirts forward to bring pressure on those in front. Unnoticed, the Texan rode past them.

Excitement drummed in Boone's veins. The young woman was directly in front of him, not more than seven or eight yards away. She was still riding behind one of the Mexicans. A second *vaquero* rode on the left.

Boone staked all he had on one card. "Head them up the arroyo, not down!" he called.

It is the instinct of a Mexican peon to take orders first and question them later, if at all. The *vaquero* beside the girl put his horse to a jog trot and slithered down into the arroyo to turn the cattle.

Next moment Boone ranged up beside the horse carrying double. He pushed in between it and the cattle. The unsuspecting Mexican turned to speak to him and at the same instant the

Texan's deft fingers withdrew the man's revolver from its pocket on the chaps.

The *vaquero*'s startled eyes stared at him. Out of nowhere an *americano* had suddenly appeared and disarmed him. His own weapon was pressed against his ribs. In another moment bullets would be tearing out his vitals. Terror held him dumb.

Boone's cool voice, in good understandable Spanish, gave quiet directions. "Turn to the left into the chaparral. Easy now. Don't you make a break and I'll not hurt you."

The man gasped. He took little stock in the promise, but the gun barrel pressing against his ribs was a mighty persuader. He swung his mount slowly to the left and rode into the brush. Boone kept pace with him, step for step. They wound in and out, skirting mesquite and cholla and prickly pear. For a hundred yards Boone held to that even pace, without another word being spoken.

Then he gave another order. "Get out of that saddle slowly. On this side. Stand right there with your hands up. Now move forward exactly like I tell you. Keep to the right of that cholla. Head for the big mesquite . . . now to the left. No, stay in the open."

He gave no directions to the girl. It was not necessary. She had slipped at once into the saddle left vacant and was riding beside him. He remembered afterward, though he did not think of it at the time, that she had not spoken a word, had not made a sound from first to last. What she looked like, he had not the least idea. His whole attention was concentrated, and had been from the moment he had first seen him, on the Mexican walking in front of them. The man might have another weapon concealed on him. Boone was taking no chances.

They came to a place where two mesquites grew, one on either side. A narrow path ran between them. The Mexican passed through the opening, then ducked sharply to the right. There was a sound as of a rabbit scuttling into the brush. Boone pushed the branches of the mesquites aside as his horse plunged forward. He stood and watched the prisoner escape.

The young woman spoke. "He got away."

"Yes," the Texan agreed.

She noticed that he made no attempt to follow the man, did not take a shot at the bushes through which he was diving. Her guess was that the man beside her did not want to call attention to their presence by a shot.

"We'd better drift," he said. "Follow me close."

It struck her as odd that he paid no particular attention to her. She was not sure that he had even looked at her. He appeared to think she was just a necessary part of the scenery.

The night became vocal with shouts. "He's letting 'em know," Boone said evenly.

His companion observed that he did not quicken his pace. He held his horse to a walk as he led the way through the mesquite. For hours she had been anxious and frightened. Now she wanted to call out to him to hurry, that if they did not run, the Mexicans would come swarming on them like bees. She had controlled herself before the *vaqueros*, knowing that it would be a mistake to let them know how much afraid she was. Though her fears had choked her, she had given no sign, fighting back the panic in her bosom. The reaction of weakness was now on her.

"Won't they find us?" she asked in a small voice.

"No chance," he said over his shoulder, without stopping. "They won't even look for us, I reckon. They don't know where they're at. Might be a dozen cowboys trailing them instead of just me. Right now they're bunched together expecting an attack. It would look like suicide for them to start combing the brush for us."

There was reassurance in his quiet, steady voice, poise in the flat-backed figure clamped to the saddle. Whoever he might be, she knew that he was a man unafraid and one very sure of himself. They were following a crooked trail on account of the rough terrain and the heavy growth of mesquite and cactus, but she knew they were traveling as directly as possible to some given point he had in mind. Not once did he hesitate.

"Where are we going?" she asked.

"To your friends. We're to meet up back here a ways."

They were climbing a stony slope where there was little vegetation except some catclaw and scrub paloverde. He fell back beside her.

"Did they send you to get me?"

"No, ma'am. They had other notions. While they were away rounding up help, I played a lone hand."

The scudding clouds, driven by the wind, no longer hid the stars just overhead. For the first time their eyes met, and for a long moment held fast. She had an odd feeling that she was plunging fathoms deep into the cold steel-gray depths of his. When she reached the surface again, it was to take a deep breath of recovery. *What kind of man was this?* she asked herself. Not like others she had known. It came to her that she was not going to like him, that there would be a clash of battle between them, and with this went as accompaniment the flash of fear. She was used to victory, but a sure instinct told her she would get little profit of this man.

"Who are you?"

It was a question that had been in her mind from the first. Now she flung it at him like a challenge.

"My name is Sibley," he answered with the little drawl he had inherited.

"From Texas?" she asked.

"From Texas."

"Just got into this country?"

"Just got in, ma'am."

In his soft answer there was, she thought, a faint flavor of irony. She resented it. The repetition of her words, some hint of hidden mirth, the cool detachment of him stung her pride. He was treating her almost as though she were a child. He had saved her, and he made it a matter of no importance. If he stayed in the hills, he would find out that Tilatha McLennon could be scornful of men to her heart's content, that when she snapped her fingers, half a dozen would come running.

"I've met Texas men . . . and heard of others," she said, and somehow contrived to make of the remark an offence, even though she hated herself for it.

Boone smiled, not at her, but at the stars. She found, for the first of many times, that he had an irritating capacity for silence. What she meant was clear enough. A good many of the riff-raff from Texas, wild young hellions ready for any deviltry, had drifted into Arizona and New Mexico. This was notorious. They had been used as *warriors,* to employ the local name, in the Lincoln County war where Billy the Kid achieved notoriety. They were floating in and out of every frontier town in the Southwest. Dozens of them were now rustling for a living in Cochise. Why did he not speak up and resent her insinuation so that she could apologize with a smile that mocked her words? That would satisfy her a little.

Yet, even while she felt the stir of antagonism, deep within her flowed a current of gratitude. What the intentions of the Mexicans had been she did not know. Perhaps they had taken her along merely as a hostage, to protect them against attack. But their view toward her might have changed. Racial hatred might have stirred their inflammable passions. And he had saved her, without a blow, without the firing of a shot, by the coolest audacity and daring. She wanted to pour out to him her thanks, to let him know how much she admired him. It was all she could do to keep from breaking down and sobbing out her relief. If he had been less flinty, less indifferent, she could have told him what was in her heart. Once she tried.

"I . . . I want . . . if you hadn't come . . ." Her voice faltered.

He waved her emotion aside as a matter of no importance. "The boys would have been around after a while, don't you reckon? And the *vaqueros* wouldn't have harmed you none. Once they had reached the line, they would have turned you loose."

His manner froze her. He had thrust her gratitude back on her almost carelessly, almost

115

insultingly. It was hateful of him, she felt, to put her in such a position immediately after having rescued her. She bit her lip to keep back the quick tears.

After that they rode in silence. Once or twice they stopped to listen. He knew that they were close to the place where Dusty Rhodes had left him.

Presently he stopped. "We'll wait here," he said.

"What for? Why can't we go on to the ranch? Or toward Galeyville? We'd likely meet them."

"And more likely not. No, we'll stay here."

He was right, of course, and she knew it. Nonetheless, she rebelled at his easy assurance, his assumption that any decision he made would be final. What right had he to step into her life and take charge of it, even for a little while? And on the heel of that thought, with swift repentance, came another. If he had not taken charge of it, she would still be riding the heavy-hearted trail to Sonora.

They waited, once more in silence, until out of the darkness came sounds of horses' hoofs striking stones, the jingle of bits, the voices of men.

VII

The voices were raised in debate. "If you ask me," one of them urged, "I'd say stampede the herd and get the greasers on the run. They'll drop Miss Tilatha quick enough then."

"*Humph!* How d'you know they will? They'd prob'ly all light out for the line hell-a-mile and leave their stock. Then where would we be at in the darkness? My notion is to lay for these guys and bushwhack 'em."

"How about makin' them a proposition to keep the stock, if they'll turn over Tilatha to us? Kinda flag of truce business."

One of the men raised a shout. "You there, Sibley?"

"Here!" Boone called back.

As the men rode up, the young woman moved forward.

Dusty gave a gasp of astonishment. "Hugh!" the girl cried out to her brother.

A big man, broad shouldered and raw-boned, flung himself from a horse and ran toward her. "Tilatha!" he shouted. Then: "Where'd you come from? How'd you get away from the greasers?"

"Mister Sibley took me from them."

"Took you? How took you?"

"Just rode up and got me."

They stared at her and at the young man sitting at negligent ease on his horse, a little way back from the group. For an hour they had been discussing how to rescue this girl without endangering her life, and already it had been done.

"How rode up and got you?" asked Dusty.

"Why, rode up . . . acted like he was one of 'em, spoke Mex to 'em, and made my guard ride off into the brush with me."

"Made him?" Hugh repeated.

"With a gun poked into his ribs. Then he let the guard go back and brought me here."

"But, hell's bells! How many of the *vaqueros* were there?"

"Eight."

"Eight!" echoed Dusty. "And he rode up and took you away from eight fightin' greasers?"

"Not exactly." It was Boone's cool drawl speaking for the first time. "I reckoned some would be on the point, some on the flank, and some pushing along the drag. All I had to do was to locate the lady, surprise the gent or gents in charge, and persuade him or them to let her come back with me."

"That was all, eh? And if they got a good look at you, why they'd pump a pint of lead into you. Fine."

"It was right dark, Dusty."

"Was it any darker for them than it was for you?"

"I was looking for them and they weren't looking for me. A big difference. Then, too, they were busy getting the cattle down to water. I passed three or four on the jump, and not one took a second look at me. That's the way I figured it might be."

"Didn't you figure it might be another way?" Dusty asked. "I'd go quite some way for a friend of mine's sister, but . . ."

"I had the drop on the fellow with Miss McLennon," Boone interrupted. "He wasn't any more dangerous than a brush rabbit."

"Well, you take the cake, brother. You sure go through from hell to breakfast. Me, I ain't got the nerve to jump eight guys all armed and on the prod. I'd be scared my days wouldn't be long in the land, as Parson Brown usta say."

Someone laughed, not pleasantly.

Without turning his head, Dusty snapped out a question. "Somethin' on your mind, Tom?"

"Why, I was thinkin' I would admire for to see you . . . or your friend there . . . pullin' off this grandstand play. I expect it would be right amusin'." Tom Tracy's voice carried a jeer.

"Yes? Meanin' what?"

"Oh, nothin'. Just a private notion of my own."

"Mebbe a fellow sometimes had better close herd his private notions," Dusty said to the world at large.

The blustering answer of Tracy came promptly:

119

"Say, fellow, anyone that tries to ride me is liable to go to sleep in smoke."

Hugh McLennon cut in curtly: "That'll do, Tom. Nobody cares a plugged dime what you think. Me, I'm indebted to Mister Sibley right consid'rable. He can hang his hat up at the ranch long as he's a mind to. What next, gents? I aim to cut dirt back to the ranch with my sister. Anyone heading that-a-way?"

There was a moment's silence. Sid Edwards broke it.

"Do we let these greasers get off scotfree after they done killed poor Bill?"

"Better send 'em a vote of thanks," Tracy suggested.

The subject was one that could not be discussed before all of those present without dangerous admissions. The cowboys had been rustling cattle belonging to the Mexicans at the time of the attack that had resulted in the death of Bill. Since he had been shot down in fair fight, there was no need of avenging his death. But Hugh McLennon and those who thought with him could not raise this point before the stranger Sibley or before the young woman.

"Dusty, you ride on a ways with Mister Sibley and Tilatha," advised Hugh. "I got to cinch this saddle tighter."

"A nod is as good as a wink to a blind horse, Hugh," his friend murmured.

The three rode toward the hills, a man on each side of Miss McLennon. The stars were out, and for the first time Boone got a good look at the girl. She was wearing plain leather chaps and a dust-brown shirt. The sun had browned her face to a coffee tint. She rode with the straight back and the easy saddle of long experience. So far she was externally a product of her environment. But out of question she was an individual of a very specialized variety. Through the tan burned the rich bloom of youth. The skin was as finely textured as satin. Beneath long lashes incredibly live eyes gleamed insolence or passion or sulkiness. For one moment he had seen them flash gifts of love to her brother. He guessed she was an untamed little devil, ruling her slaves with a rod of iron. That temperament would go with her red hair.

In the darkness he smiled. Boone was impervious to the charms of women. Their moods did not disturb him. He lived his life among men.

Dusty was the first to speak. "You got that coyote Tracy, didn't you, Sibley? Got what he meant? That's his way, always hintin' and hintin'."

"It doesn't matter what he says or thinks," the girl said impatiently. "Hugh is right about that. Why do you quarrel with him, Dusty?"

"I get sore at him. For instance . . . just now . . .

what did he mean? That Sibley here had some kind of stand-in with the greasers?"

"He's a jealous cur . . . doesn't like anyone to get a good word except himself. You oughtn't to pay any attention to him," she reproved.

"He's got no license to ride me," the cowboy protested.

"Just pay no attention to him," she advised virtuously.

Dusty looked at her and grinned. He was thinking that it depended on whose steer was gored. Tilatha McLennon would not for a moment let Tom Tracy or any other man run over her without putting him in his place.

Horses cantered toward them. Out of the darkness rode Hugh McLennon and a nester named Charles Brown.

"Where are the others?" the young woman asked sharply.

"They're heading for Galeyville," her brother said after a moment's pause.

She pulled up her horse and listened. The far faint sound of horses' hoofs could be heard. "They're not, either. They're not going that way."

"All right. If you know already so dog-gone' well, why do you ask?" her brother said impatiently. "It's none of your business anyhow, is it?"

"They've gone south," she charged.

"South or north, do you care?"

He caught the rein of her horse and started it. Though she pulled the rein from his hand, she let her mount move forward beside his. The other three fell in behind. Boone could hear fragments of what she and Hugh said to each other.

"I know where they've gone," she flung at her brother.

"Not your business . . . or mine."

". . . own fault . . . get killed someday."

"Shut your mouth, girl."

The men behind dropped farther back. This seemed to be a family quarrel.

Charles Brown chuckled. "She sure hasn't got red hair for nothing. Miss Tilatha is a right up-an'-comin' young lady."

To draw out information Boone asked a careless question of Dusty. "Just the two of 'em in the family now?"

"That's whatever. Old man McLennon died year before last. Got thrown by a wild horse."

"They're mighty friendly folks, too," Brown said. "Think a lot of each other, Hugh an' Miss Tilatha do."

The girl's voice came back to them, lifted rebelliously. "I had a right to ride out and find out who was driving them, didn't I? It's a free country, isn't it?"

Dusty laughed with relish. "They sure enough do, Sibley. Her bark is worse than her bite. She don't mean a thing by it."

Boone made no comment. Come to think about it, he might have safely predicted that she would be a tempery woman with that flaming hair of hers.

They came, by steep trails which circled hills and plunged into gulches, to a mountain park watered by a stream twisting across the meadow. Here the current was deep and swift close to the bank, there it widened and grew shallow, with riffles foaming down.

"Trout here, looks like," Boone commented.

"Y'betcha!" Dusty agreed with enthusiasm.

The horses splashed through and climbed a slope leading to the house. The riders dismounted.

"Show Mister Sibley the bunkhouse, Dusty," said McLennon. "Soon as you've washed up, come up to the house for supper."

"Be there *pronto*," promised Dusty. "I could eat a government mail sack, let alone Tilatha's cornbread."

To Boone, while the Texan was combing his hair, Dusty stopped drying his face to prophesy: "This ain't any fair test, because she's got to knock together some grub in a hurry, but I'll bet my boots you say it's the best supper you've had in a month. Tilatha has got the world beat as a cook."

Forty minutes later Boone was willing to agree with Dusty. He couldn't remember when he had tasted anything so good.

VIII

Dusty, doing his full duty by the wheat cakes at breakfast, announced that he had to see a fellow in the hills but that he would be back the next day.

"If you're not pushin' on your reins, Sibley, why don't you stick around the ranch today?" he suggested. "We'll ride in to Galeyville tomorrow. . . . I could do with another stack of flapjacks, Tilatha."

"Don't hurry Mister Sibley, Dusty. He's hardly rested his saddle yet," Hugh McLennon said. "This is his headquarters while he's up here."

Boone made the proper acknowledgement of this hospitable offer.

Tilatha's eyes were on Boone. The Texan thought he had never seen a woman so vivid and so unaware of her own beauty. Her sleeves were rolled to the elbows of her well-molded arms. It was easy to understand why the cowboys paid court diffidently to this young queen, so free, so untamed, so rhythmic in her movements.

Later in the day, while he was fishing the creek, Tilatha wandered down to ask him what luck he was having. With the mannish clothes of yesterday replaced by a simple print frock that was very becoming, she had also discarded her willfulness and impatience. She was smiling and friendly, without any touch of sexual coquetry.

"Are you as good a fisherman as you are a rescuer?" she asked.

He pointed to his string and smiled.

"There ought to be one in that riffle just above there," she suggested. "Usually there is."

"There was. I got him."

He made a cast toward the opposite bank. A trout struck, but did not take the hook. As Tilatha watched this tall brown man, observed the muscles in his long, flat back, and saw with what light ease he handled himself, she thought she had never seen a human being so well proportioned. The movements of the body seemed to express him. There was no dissipation of energy, no waste of force in the poised rhythm.

He hooked a trout, and while he was landing it, she did not speak.

"That's a nice one. . . . Dusty Rhodes says you had a run-in with the Quinns."

Before he answered, he took care of his catch. "Dusty is a right pleasant old lady," he murmured. "Yes, he sure gets my vote for head of the sewing circle."

"Why shouldn't he tell me? It's common talk for everybody in Cochise."

"Matter of fact, I didn't have any run-in with the Quinns."

"With Curt French, then. It's the same thing.

And Whip Quinn did serve notice on you, didn't he?"

"He recommended Tucson."

"I wouldn't start trouble with them. They're dangerous."

"You have it wrong. I'm noways hostile to the Quinns. If there is no trouble till I start it . . ."

"They're fighting men . . . killers. That's the reputation they brought here. So is that Curt French. He's bad. You can't help admiring Russ Quinn and his brother, but French . . ."

"I reckon the Quinns are more friendly killers," he said in his gentle, derisive drawl. "Maybe they don't kill you so hard or so rough as Curt."

"They're men," she came back quickly. "Whip and Russ may meet trouble more than halfway, but they don't go hunting it."

"Friends of yours?" he asked.

Beneath the tan in her cheeks the quick color ran. "They are kind of friendly to Hugh and to lots of the men in the hills."

Boone wondered what was the basis of this friendliness. Why any relationship at all? The Quinns were townsmen, parasites who lived from the pickings of a rich mining camp. What interest had they in cattle, which was the only occupation of the cowboys? And of what benefit would it be to the rustlers and cattlemen to have an understanding with these gamblers whose influence was so potent in Tough Nut? Perhaps it was politics. It was said that Whip wanted to be sheriff, which was a very lucrative fee office. He might be only playing up to the cowboys for their votes. Bob Hardy was deputy United States marshal, and one of Whip's loyal henchmen. The brothers might be trying to get control of the party machine in the county.

The young woman went on, her voice a little anxious: "Don't have trouble with them. Their enemies have bad luck. They are too strong a combination."

"That seems to be a general opinion," he said drily, "I'm not bucking the combination. If they lay off me, that's all I ask."

"I think they will. I'll speak to Russ," she replied.

Instantly he flung back curt refusal of her aid. "Don't you, unless you want to make trouble. There's nothing to this, likely. But if they want to run on me, why, that's between them and me. You're not in it, you or any other woman."

Again the color flooded her face. She stared at him, her eyes hot with resentment. Her desire had been to do him a service, and his answer had been like a slap in the face. In effect, he had told her to mind her own business. Her stormy gaze challenged for a long moment his steel-cold eyes. She wanted to pour out furious words pell-mell. Instead, she turned on her heel and walked like an outraged queen to the house.

Boone watched her, a grim little smile on his

lips. *That'll hold her, I reckon. No use arguing or explaining. She'd have her own way, anyhow. Now she'll keep still. I'd look fine hiding behind a girl's skirts, wouldn't I?* His thoughts flowed on: *She'd ask Russ to let me off, would she? I expect she figures she's got a right good stand-in with Russ. Well, I can see where one Quinn has a mighty fine reason for tying up with one Chiricahua cattleman.*

An hour later Boone returned to the house. Hugh was on the porch sorting out some horseshoes. Every ranch in those days had its own blacksmith shop.

The cowman looked up. "Nice string of trout. Better leave 'em in the kitchen."

Boone walked in. Tilatha was baking pie. There was a dab of flour on one temple where she had brushed back her rebellious hair with the back of a hand.

"Where'll I put the fish, Miss Tilatha?" the Texan asked evenly. His manner ignored the fact that he had so lately managed to get himself out of her good graces.

She looked at him explosively. He was not sure whether she was going to say nothing or a great deal. Unexpectedly, after a tense pause, she surprised him.

"In that pan of water," she said, almost as though she grudged the words. He did as she had told him, then sauntered out to the porch.

"You might as well hear it now as later," Hugh told him. "Two of the boys got shot up last night."

This was not unexpected. It had been an easy guess that Edwards had led the cowboys in pursuit of the Mexican *vaqueros*.

"Killed?" asked Boone.

"No. They'll make the grade. Sandy Joe and Tom Tracy." McLennon hesitated before he continued. "I'm not offerin' advice, you understand, but personally I don't know anything about it. Least said, soonest mended, as the fellow says."

There was a flicker of sardonic mirth in Boone's eyes. If this was not advice, he did not know it when he met it. But he intended to follow it and did not resent the suggestion.

"I've got notions along that line myself," Boone agreed. "Most generally I keep my trap shut when in doubt."

"I figured you that-a-way. Fact is, in Cochise right now a man has got to be some blind. I notice the officers are. Prob'ly there's more going on than they can ride herd on. Fact is, a fellow has to take conditions as he finds them. When I buy a longhorn bunch, I got no way of knowin' whether they come up the San Simon with their tails draggin'. 'Course, I take reasonable precautions as to previous ownership."

A rider had come into the park and was dropping down from the rim to the meadow. As the ranchman talked, Boone watched the stranger idly. The horseman splashed through the creek and moved up the slope to the house. He was a big man tanned to bronzed health by wind and sun.

Boone's eyes were no longer indifferent. They had narrowed slightly when they recognized Russ Quinn. Otherwise there was no change in the Texan. He sat on the porch at negligent ease.

Quinn swung from the saddle with a casual: "'Lo, Hugh! How are cases?" He stood there, the bridle still in his hand, looking at Boone. Evidently he was surprised.

"Meet Mister Sibley, Russ," the ranchman said.

"Why, I've met the gent, Hugh," he said, his manner conveying more than his words. "Down at Tough Nut." His manner dismissed the Texan as unimportant. "Got kinda tired ridin' the stage and come up for a coupla days."

"Fine. Long as you like."

"Anything new?"

"No-o, I reckon not. How about down your way?"

"Stage robbed yesterday near Bisbee. They killed Buck Galway."

"Buck was the messenger?"

"Yep. Never got a chance for his white alley. The fellow cut loose on him before he hollered to stop."

"How many hold-ups?"

"Two. Masked, of course." Quinn looked at the Texan deliberately from head to foot. "One of 'em a tall, well-built fellow on a sorrel." He added presently: "With a kind of Texas drawl."

"You might be describing me and my horse," Boone said in his low voice, meeting the look of the other.

"Didn't happen to be down Bisbee way yesterday about ten a.m. in the mornin', did you?" Quinn asked insolently.

"No, I didn't. Did you?"

Russ laughed hardily. "You got a come-back, fellow. I wasn't askin' did you hold up the stage. Thought mebbe you might have met the birds that did."

"Not that I know of. I've met undesirable characters off and on lately, though."

"Well, so have I," Quinn said, and turned his back on the Texan and spoke in a low voice to McLennon.

Boone rose and strolled over to the stable.

"When did that fellow show up, Hugh?" asked Quinn.

"About sundown yesterday. Don't get off on the wrong foot, Russ. He didn't hold up the stage."

"How you know he didn't?"

"He's not that kind. Anyhow, he was with Dusty all day."

"With Dusty, eh? A middle-size cowboy wearin'

chaps and a brown shirt." The last was apparently a quotation.

"Now, look here, Russ. If you're implyin' that Dusty was in that hold-up . . ."

"I'm not. I'm just mentionin' a coincidence. I don't presume he rode a bay horse."

"He did. I reckon there ain't more'n several thousand bay horses in Cochise. I ride one myself. Maybe I did it."

"We lost the tracks, but they were headin' this way."

"How far back?"

"A long way. I don't claim I tracked them here."

Hugh shook his head. "No, sir, you're sure barkin' up the wrong tree, Russ. Lemme tell you about that man Sibley."

Quinn dropped the reins to the ground and sat down on the porch. "Shoot your story," he said. "I'm listenin'."

The ranchman told what he knew of the Texan, both as boy and man. "I never saw a gamer fellow or one I'd rather have to back my play," he added by way of comment.

"I ain't denyin' he's got guts. It took guts to stand up to Curt French. That's not got a thing to do with it," Quinn replied.

"It has, too. No game man would have shot down Buck Galway when there wasn't any need of it. Either a killer or a coward did that."

"How do you know this Sibley isn't a killer?"

"He don't look like one."

"That's just what he does, Hugh. Think up the killers you've met. Aren't most of 'em quiet, soft-spoken, gray-eyed birds that look as though they were never lookin' for trouble?"

"I've seen that kind."

"The most dangerous kind. See what this fellow did to Curt French . . . knocked him cold and walked off without a scratch on him."

"The way I heard that was . . ."

Quinn waved the explanation aside. "I'm not blamin' him. He can put up a reasonable story about bein' in the right. That ain't what I'm drivin' at. The point is there's trouble wherever these fellows are. It just drifts their way, looks like. They may claim they're not to blame. Anyhow, it happens."

"Lookin' at this thing fair and square, Russ, you'll have to admit a fellow doesn't have to be a trouble hunter to get into a ruckus with Curt. He's a sure enough bully. You'll have to admit that."

"His parlor manners ain't lady-like, if that's what you mean."

"Me, I like this Texan, personally."

"Me, I don't, personally."

McLennon smiled. "Well, every fellow I don't like isn't necessarily a stage robber. I reckon that goes with you, too."

"I haven't claimed he is. All I say is, I wouldn't put it past him, and there's circumstantial evidence against him."

"Look here, Russ. I know Dusty right well. He's a good boy, take him by and large. If he'd helped murder Buck Galway in cold blood, he wouldn't've sat here joshin' this mornin' like he didn't have a care in the world. No, sir. You better get this fool notion outta your head."

"Dusty might of been an innocent bystander at the killin'. There's a difference between holdin' up a stage and shootin' down without reason a man who hasn't hurt you any and who doesn't have to be killed."

Still arguing, they moved toward the stable with Quinn's horse.

IX

Dusty watched Russ Quinn saddle the two horses. The cowboy sat on the porch with his back against a post, legs stretched at full length. On his face was a look of disgust. His companion guessed it was due to jealousy.

"That fellow sure has ridden close herd on Tilatha all day. First off, when I drifted in, she was fishin' and Russ fixin' her lines like she couldn't do it well as he can. Now he's aimin' to go ridin' with her. They seem to be havin' a right nice time. If a girl liked that big black kind of guy, she'd call him good-lookin', don't you reckon?"

"I reckon."

"Nothin' to me, of course, but shucks . . . he's no kind of man for her to encourage."

"Is she encouragin' him?" Boone was amused at his friend's naïve complaint.

"What else would you call it? Actin' like he's the only man on earth. She'd ought to know any of the Quinns are bad medicine for any girl. She does know it, too."

"Maybe that's why she likes to be with him," the Texan said indolently. "Nice tame good men don't go so strong with women, I notice."

"Saddlin' that pinto for her now. *Humph!* There he goes helpin' her on so tender, and, by cripes,

136

I've seen her swing on that bronc' without ever touchin' the stirrups."

"Prob'ly a handsome bad man wasn't beauing her right then," Boone suggested.

"What I say is you never can tell about a woman," Dusty said, "not when it comes to a man. They don't use their judgment, looks like. I'd sure hate to see Tilatha marry Russ Quinn. He's got his good points, but he'd sure ruin her life. He's one of these here masterful devils, and that wouldn't suit Tilatha."

"Wouldn't it?"

"Not by a jug full. She wants to rule the roost her own self. He'd break her spirit like he would a wild horse. That's the Quinn of it. Rule or ruin. Likely he's got her fooled into thinkin' she can twist him round her li'l' finger."

"They're sure a good-looking couple on horseback. . . . Hugh is calling you, Dusty."

The cowboy bowlegged his way to the corral. For ten minutes he engaged in conversation with the ranch owner, after which he returned to the house.

"Helluva note," he said to Boone, apparently not sure whether to be annoyed or amused. "Hugh says the stage was robbed near Bisbee day before yesterday and they are claimin' we did it, you and me."

"Got that far, have they? I had a notion that was coming."

"You knew about it?"

"Only what Russ Quinn said. He hadn't got farther than insinuations yesterday."

"Well, I don't know as he claims we did it, out and out. But he sure enough describes us and our horses. Hugh told him he was crazy with the heat, but I noticed he was glad to have me tell him there is nothin' to it. I've been some wild, and with a cowboy most generally you can't tell. He's liable to go bad unexpected after a spree. Worst of it is they killed Buck Galway, the shotgun messenger."

"You're unfortunate in your friends, Dusty," the Texan drawled. "The Quinns would like to hang this on me, if they could. It's a convenient excuse to drive me outta the country."

"I reckon I'm drug in because I was with you. Well, don't you worry about me, Boone . . . if the Quinns ride me too hard, my six-shooter will be smokin' right beside yours."

The other man shook his head. "Don't talk that-a-way, Dusty. We're law-abidin' citizens, and we don't aim to go gun-fannin' like a pair of crooks. First off, we'll ride into Galeyville and see what talk there is, if any."

"Then what?"

"If there's a serious charge against me, I'm going back to Tough Nut to face it down."

"Would that be wise, do you reckon? If the Quinns are fixin' to hang this on you, they'll have evidence, you can bet your boots. And Buck was popular. No tellin' how far a drunken crowd might go if it was worked up. The only alibi we got is somewheres up in the Dragoons. We might be gosh-awful dead before we could dig up our witnesses."

"A fellow has to take chances when his good name is at stake. That's my platform. You don't need to take my view of it."

Dusty flushed. "If you go, I will, too."

They saddled and took the road for Galeyville. The wagon tracks ran plain before them. Half a mile from the house Dusty drew up. He pointed to the marks of horses' hoofs deflecting from the road to follow a bridle path.

"They're takin' the high-line trail," he said gloomily.

"He's showin' good judgment. Don't tell me, Dusty, you'd stick to the main traveled road if you had such good company."

They held to the wagon tracks, though the cowboy looked up at the pine-clad slope regretfully. To ride the high trails in dappled sunshine, with the blue sky back of the green trees, the lady of one's choice beside one is an enchanting experience; to know that another man is riding them under the same conditions not so exhilarating.

"We'll beat 'em to town by an hour," Dusty predicted mournfully.

It developed that he was more or less a true prophet.

Galeyville was a one-street adobe town. Chiefly it consisted of saloons, gambling houses, one-room mud huts, and two or three shaft houses with gray dumps drooping from them like great beards. There were a couple of general stores, too.

The two riders tied up at a hitch rack and went into one of the saloons. Eight or nine men, evidently cowboys, were in the place. Four were playing stud poker. Two were having a drink at the bar. One lay on a bench, asleep.

" 'Lo, Dusty!" someone called. "When did you-all get back?"

Boone noticed that the eyes of all present, except those of the sleeping man, turned curiously upon him. And more than curiously. There was in their regard a wary intentness. They had heard about him. That was clear. What had they heard? About his brush with French? About the rescue of Miss McLennon? No doubt. But had they heard, too, that he was charged with stage robbery and the murder of the shotgun messenger?

"Meet Mister Boone Sibley." Thus Dusty, in a sweeping introduction to all present.

The Texan nodded to two or three of those nearest and moved to the bar. He knew that the eyes still watched him, but no evidence that he knew it reached the cowboys. He was at ease, unconcerned, indifferent. He drank, watched the stud game for a few minutes, sauntered out.

Dusty stayed. His friend had murmured a suggestion.

"Find out what they know."

Boone moved across the street to one of the stores. There were three or four men inside. One was inquiring for mail, another trying on a pair of boots. But at his entrance business was suspended. Again he was the focus of all their regard. These men, too, had heard of a stranger answering his description. They, too, watched him with a fasci-nation, respectful but ominous.

In cattle land news flies on the wings of the wind. It is swept, with incredible swiftness, to the remotest ranch and the loneliest cow camp. It happened that Boone was the central figure of three startling episodes. He had whipped Curt French. He had rescued the McLennon girl from eight armed Mexicans. He had robbed a stage and killed Buck Galway. That this last was not true did not matter. An accused man is guilty in popular opinion till proved innocent.

These recent adventures were reason enough for the attention given him. Yet Boone was not entirely satisfied with his explanation. It did not cover the whole ground, he felt. The absorption of their interest in him held an eagerness almost wolf-like. The glitter in the eyes of some of these men suggested that they were crouched for the pounce. Why? Even if he were an outlaw, what personal attraction had he for them?

To pass time, he was buying a pocket knife. His manner was easy and unconcerned. Apparently he gave his whole attention to examining the quality of the steel. Yet all his senses were keyed to alertness. He was aware of a man coming into the store, and knew a moment later that the person was Dusty. Without turning his head, he became conscious that the cowboy was striding fast, that he was moved by excitement.

"Let's get outta here *pronto*," whispered Dusty in the ear of his friend. The young man's voice was rough and hoarse.

"I'll take this one," Boone said casually. "What's the tariff?"

"Six bits," the clerk said. He showed excitement, too. His face had the shine and the pallor of the consumptive, but a red spot burned in each cheek.

Boone did not hurry. He paid for the knife and sauntered down the aisle toward the door, the center of still fixed observation. Once outside, Dusty almost dragged him down the steps to what protection there was near the adobe wall of the store.

"We got to light out!" the cowboy exploded. "There's a reward for us . . . three thousand for you, five hundred for me."

A reward? Boone understood now what the glittering eyes had been telling him. The emotions shining out of the faces of some of these men had been greed and the lust to strike, tempered by the uncertainty of fear.

"Dead or alive?" asked Boone evenly. His question struck at the very heart of the matter. If he was worth as much dead as alive, they very likely would not risk an attempt to capture him. A shot from the window of some saloon might drop him at any moment.

"Dead or alive, either one," Dusty answered. "Jim Barkalow got in from Tough Nut an hour ago with the news. Listen, Boone. They don't want me, none of the boys. It's you they're after. Well, we got to hustle. They're talkin' it over . . . what they had best do. I'll kinda saunter up and get the horses."

Boone shook his head. "Too late, Dusty."

An eruption of men had poured out of the saloon in front of which the two mounts were tied. Also, the Texan noted, a man and a woman, riding down the street, had reached the spot. The man was Russ Quinn, his companion Miss McLennon. Quinn swung from the saddle and joined the other men.

"Some of the boys were talkin' up for you, account of what you did for Tilatha," Dusty explained. "Listen, Boone, I'll go try and talk 'em out of any notions they got."

"You're not in this, Dusty. Like you say, it's me they want. I'll play a lone hand."

A shot sounded. A bullet struck the adobe wall behind Boone and sent dirt flying.

"That come from lower down the street!" Dusty cried in excitement.

"This town will be a hornet's nest in three minutes. Get back into the store, Dusty," Boone ordered.

"No, by golly. Not without you." Another bullet struck the wall. "We gotta go, Boone." As he spoke, Dusty crossed in front of his friend, intending to duck around the corner of the store.

At the same moment came the crack of a revolver. Boone caught sight of a face, almost directly opposite them, lifted above a window sill.

Dusty turned to his friend, a look almost of incredulity on his face. "I'm hit, dog-gone it," he said petulantly, catching at Boone to steady himself.

The hinge of one knee shut up like a knife blade. Boone caught him, dragged him up the store steps, and left him just inside the door.

Yet another moment and the Texan was again outside. Even as he leaped from the steps, he saw that the group of cowboys from the saloon above were moving down—Russ Quinn a few yards in advance of them, a bald-headed man with a rifle was peering out of a doorway at him seventy-five yards below, and two others were crouched behind cottonwoods a little back from the road. He was cut off from his horse. Both ends of the street were blocked.

Viciously bullets spat at him. One took a splinter from the window frame close to his head. Others scattered dirt from the soft adobe wall. He zig-zagged across the street and plunged into the first open doorway he saw.

X

What Dusty had said was true. Tilatha had been more kind than usual to Russ Quinn. It was as though some inner excitement drove her to him. She was cherishing resentment against another man, but she would have denied that that had anything to do with it.

She loved to ride. There was something that stimulated her interest in the dark personality of Quinn. Was it necessary to give herself any other reason why she rode to Galeyville with him? After they took the upper trail, they rode in silence until it broadened sufficiently for Quinn to join her, knee-to-knee.

"No, you're wrong, Russ," she said in her decisive way, pursuing their previous conversation. "I don't believe it at all. He's not that kind. Mind, I don't like a hair of his head. He's so insultingly . . ."—she stopped to search for a word, then, for want of a more definite one, spat out—"superior. He thinks a woman should sit in the corner and sew. A detestable man!"

"Then what makes you so sure he didn't rob the stage?"

"Because . . . he doesn't look like one of that kind. He isn't one."

"Can you tell a stage robber by the color of his hair, girl? Do you reckon a hold-up man looks different from anyone else?"

"I could tell my brother isn't one, couldn't I?" she flung out.

"All right. Name some fellow that does look like one," he persisted with a view to making her position untenable. Somehow it annoyed him that she should defend this fellow Sibley against him. He wanted to drive her to admit that he was right.

Tilatha was a little irritated herself. She did not have to accept his opinions ready-made. "Well, your friend, Curt French, looks like he might be one," she said, not without malice.

He turned dark eyes on her, frowning. "I wouldn't say that if I was you, even if I was funnin'."

"I'm not funning," she replied with spirit. "You asked me what I thought a hold-up man might look like and I told you. And why shouldn't I say it about Curt French if you do about Mister Sibley?"

Quinn was not looking for a quarrel with her. He laughed a little sourly. "Have it your own way, girl. All I meant was that Curt . . ."

". . . might come in and beat my head off if he heard," she cut in. "Like he did to this Mister Sibley."

"You get the last word, Tilatha," he said

147

ruefully. Then added: "Women sure take the cake. You claim you don't like this pilgrim Sibley, but you stick up for him through hell and high water, beggin' your pardon."

"I don't, either." She cast in her mind for a simile. The one she found was not very apropos, but it was the best at hand. "I don't like Benedict Arnold, but I don't have to believe that he tried to poison George Washington, do I?"

"You win."

"After what he did for me, I ought to like this Boone Sibley, but he gets my back up so. I suppose I'm ungrateful."

"Oh, well, leave him lay. No use worryin' about him. One of these days, if he stays around here promiscuous, Curt will make him step high as a blind dog in a stubble field. . . . It's been a thousand years since I saw you, Tilatha. Last week I tried to make it out here, but I couldn't cut it. A gold shipment goin' out, and the company wanted me to take it."

"You get tired of town, I reckon. At least I soon do. The wild cherry blossoms are lovely, aren't they?"

"No, I don't get tired of town," he answered. "And I didn't come to see wild cherry blossoms but a wild rose with thorns. I aim to pluck it one of these days. Right soon it'll be, too."

She did not look at him. Her gaze was on the trail ahead, but she knew his bold, dark eyes were on her, filled with passionate and possessive desire. It did not just now suit her to challenge his assurance.

"The thorns might prick you," she said lightly.

"Who cares? I wouldn't have my rose without the thorns." He opened his big brown hand and closed it tightly. The back of his fingers were covered with short black hair. There was something almost cruel in the strength of the gesture. "I'll crush 'em . . . the thorns . . . till there's no sting left in 'em."

Her smile was not quite true. "Don't you think you might crush the rose, too?" she asked.

But she did not wait for an answer. They had come to an open plateau on a hilltop, and she put her horse to a canter.

One of these days she would have to make up her mind about this dark Quinn. He was a strong man, positive, assertive. It was his boast that he always got what he wanted. Well developed in him were the primal virtues of the frontier. No man without these could hope to marry Tilatha McLennon, for she was of the outdoors, what the wind and the sun and pioneering ancestors had made her. But she knew a score of men who possessed courage and energy, were faithful to their friends. More than these she demanded of the man who was to be her mate.

As yet there was some barrier between her and Russ Quinn. Her heart had not been swept toward him on a tide of emotion. More than once she had wondered why. He was stronger than she, and she wanted for her husband a dominant man, even though she did not know it. When she thought of him, little doubts crept into her musings. She was not sure about the inner quality of the man. He could be hard and ruthless. He had killed, more than once, she had heard. This was bad, but not of itself fatal to his chances if he had slain from imperative need. What she must find out beyond question was the nature of the real Russ Quinn. Was he evil in his heart? She did not know, and the very uncertainty made her push him away for the time, at least. Before she gave her life into his keeping or that of any man, she must be very sure of him.

Therefore she evaded the issue during the ride, not once only, but several times. By the light turn of a phrase, by the touch of a spur to her pony's side, by a sudden exclamation at sight of a flowering ocotillo, she deflected his attention until they reached Galeyville.

He was not naturally a patient man, this dark, dangerous wooer. But he had all the self-confidence in the world. The girl was interested in him. He knew that. She was a little afraid of him. That did not displease him; he had seen more than once how it kindled a woman's feeling for him. She would think about him when he was not present, and her emotions would quicken. If it suited her to play for time . . . well, he could afford to wait.

They rode into Galeyville quite unaware that the next hour or two would decide for all time who was to be the captain of her heart.

At a road gait they jogged up the dusty street.

Out of the Silver Dollar saloon men poured like pips squirted from a lemon.

"There's something wrong!" Tilatha cried.

Her companion did not answer. He swung from the saddle and joined the excited group.

Someone flung at him an explanation: "It's the road agent that killed Buck Galway."

A shot rang out.

Tilatha's eyes swept down the road, even as another revolver sounded. Two men were standing in front of Pete Andrews's store, and it was at these the shots were being fired. One of the men was Dusty Rhodes, the other Boone Sibley.

XI

Tilatha sat her horse, petrified by horror, while the guns blazed at their target. Neither Rhodes nor Sibley had his six-shooter out. She wanted to scream a useless warning to them, but the vocal chords in her throat were frozen. Why didn't they run? Why did they stand . . . ?

The girl found her voice in a cry of despair. Dusty had gone down. She saw his friend stoop, pick him up, and carry the body into the store. Then, to her terror, Sibley was back again on the steps, the guns once more roaring at him.

Through lanes of fire he darted across the street. Every instant she expected to see him plunge to the ground, shot through and through. But his foes were too many and too hurried. They hampered one another. They flung their bullets wildly at their victim. He reached Sanford's store and vanished within.

"Got away," someone gulped out with an oath.

"Like a streak of cat before a bulldog!" another cried.

Russ Quinn took charge of the attack. "Bart, you take four, five of the boys and see he don't get out the back way. If he shows up, plug him. Van, you hold the other end of the street. See your boys ain't too brash. This fellow is a killer. I'll handle this end. We've got him. All we got to do is smoke him out."

The girl's heart sank. They were going to kill him like a cornered rat. She must do something —stop this murder. What could she do?

From the front door of the store Sanford and his clerk came hurriedly. "He's locked himself in," the proprietor said. "You fellows want to be careful. There's all kinds of guns there."

Tilatha slipped from her mount and ran to Quinn. "You can't do this!" she cried. "You can't do it. He's the wrong man!"

Russ Quinn turned to her, listening while he brought his mind back to understand what she wanted. He stood there impatiently, his slightly bowed legs set apart, a big, black purposeful man with a Colt .45 in one hand. Then, silently, with a sweep of an arm, he brushed her aside. This was not women's business.

Tilatha caught at the sleeve of another man. "He didn't kill Buck Galway!" she cried. "He isn't the man!"

"Didn't, eh? Bet your boots he did. The poster's tacked up in the saloon . . . name, description, horse, everything. And three thousand reward, dead or alive. We've got the right bird."

"No, no, Jim. Stop to think. This man saved me from the Mexicans day before yesterday, just a little while after the hold-up."

"About ten hours after," the cowboy corrected.

153

"Sure. Why wouldn't he? Makin' a bluff to cover his tracks. Likely he was in cahoots with the greasers. You said your own self he didn't have to fire a shot."

She turned to another man, a young fellow who was an admirer from a distance. She had seen him watching her at dances.

"You won't let 'em do this awful thing, will you, Ted? It's all wrong."

He was embarrassed and distressed. "Nothin' I could do," he said. "I'd help you if I could, but they're hell-bent on going through. You can see for yourself how it is, Miss Tilatha."

"Go to the ranch for my brother. Ride fast," she begged.

He did not want to go. She saw that. But still less did he wish to refuse. "All right," he said reluctantly. "But it won't do any good. He'll not get here in time."

"He may, if you hurry." The cowboy swung to a saddle and rode out of town. For the first time in her life Tilatha felt quite helpless. As child and young woman, she had gone her self-willed way. Early she had discovered that she could get what she wanted by clamorous insistence. That had been when she was still a long-legged brat with a wild tangle of red hair. Later she changed her tactics, having gained in worldly wisdom. It was not necessary to get into a temper to win out, not if one happened to be the prettiest girl in Cochise

County. A smiling suggestion would usually do. If that failed, a flash of imperious will.

But this situation had got beyond her. The deference these young fellows had paid her was gone. She had been pushed out of their minds by the thrill of the manhunt. In their voices she could hear the rough snarl of the wolf pack. It frightened her to learn that her opinion and her desire counted for nothing with them. She was only a woman, and it was a man's world.

The attackers were at a disadvantage in one respect. They could not set fire to the building and smoke out their victim. The property was too valuable. To storm the store would probably entail heavy loss, since he was well armed and would fight to the finish.

"We'll snipe him," Quinn announced. "But, first off, I'll have a talk with him and give him a chance to surrender." He asked Tilatha for her handkerchief to use as a white flag.

She gave it to him. "I'll go along," she said eagerly. "Maybe he'll listen to me."

"You'll stay right here," the shotgun messenger told her curtly.

As Quinn moved forward, he shouted to the beleaguered man. "Say, fellow, I come for a pow-wow!" He thrust his weapon into its holster.

"Don't make any mistake," the Texan advised him, his drawling voice cool and even. "This scatter-gun shoots all over Arizona."

In spite of Russ Quinn's command, Tilatha had slipped forward at his heels. She could see Boone Sibley at the window, a sawed-off shotgun in his hands. He was surrounded, caught in a trap, with no chance for escape. A hundred foes were clamoring for his blood. But never had she seen a man who looked more to be master of his fate. In the grim face, with its tight, straight-lipped mouth and its cold steady eyes, there was no least flicker of panic.

"Fellow, you're bucked out," Quinn said arrogantly. "We got you right. But I'm givin' you a chance to surrender before we start shootin' you up."

"And if I surrender, I'd be shot trying to escape on the way to Tough Nut. Much obliged. I reckon not. When I give myself up, it will be to a sheriff with a warrant for my arrest. I'll make another proposition. Leave me go, and I'll ride in to Tough Nut and surrender."

"You got a consid'rable nerve, Texas man. How do I know you wouldn't light out for the line?"

"How do I know if I surrender, I won't be shot down, anyhow?"

"I'm givin' you my word."

"I was giving you mine."

"Hell, we got you, fellow. I'm offerin' terms, not you." Quinn's voice held the hard rasp of impatience.

"I wonder if you've got me, Mister Quinn. I'm well fixed to send a few of your friends to Kingdom Come first, anyhow. And listen. You wished this on me. If I kill, I'm driven to it. I'm an American citizen attacked by a mob."

"You're the outlaw who killed Buck Galway, that's who you are!" the dark man cried angrily. "And we're 'lowin' to collect your hide *pronto*. You claim you're a bull rattler, eh? Watch us stomp you out."

Tilatha spoke pleadingly. Her confidence was gone. "If I rode along with you to Tough Nut would you surrender, Mister Sibley?"

"No, ma'am, I would not," he answered curtly.

The sharp angry bark of a pistol rang out. Instantly the sawed-off shotgun swept up in an arc and boomed. A man crouched at a window of the Andrews store collapsed with a groan.

Quinn backed away. "Stay behind me, girl. What you here for, anyhow? Step lively. I'd beat the head off that fool who shot, if he hadn't already got his."

The battle was on. Snipers from the cover of windows, walls, and street corners centered their fire on the store. The glass of the front was shattered. Tilatha could hear those in the rear pouring in their bullets. Occasionally the trapped man's guns flamed out defiance. The heart died in her bosom. This could not last long. Some of these random shots would reach their mark.

She looked despairingly up the road. There was no sign of her brother, nor could there be for an hour. And what could Hugh do with this blood-mad mob? Her eyes took in a landscape all color, light, and air. The atmosphere was a rose-tinted haze. Lakes of lilac filled the mountain pockets, but the peaks had form without depth, an opalescence devoid of substance. Soon it would be night, and the desert would take on the softness laid on it by Nature's magic wand. Yet here, in this raw, ugly adobe village, the passions of men flung lances of death, forgetful of all the loveliness of life.

There must be some way to save him, if she could only think of it. She caught her hands together and looked up, perhaps to fling a prayer into the sky, and in that moment saw a gleam of hope. If they did not kill him in the meantime, if some of them did not think of it first, if it could be done unnoticed, there was perhaps a chance for him to escape.

She prayed for darkness, that she might set about her preparations.

XII

Inside the store, Boone built what defenses he could. Sacks of grain, piled against the lower window panes, reduced the area of attack. Barrels of nails helped to barricade the doors against the chance of being battered down. He could hear the spatter of bullets against the adobe walls, and could see the splinters they made as they tore through the doors. Looking out through his peepholes, he could count his attackers gathering.

"They're coming like buzzards to a water hole in the spring," he said aloud. As he saw it, night was his only chance. If he could survive until darkness fell, he might somehow contrive to slip away. In this frontier store he found plenty of ammunition and weapons, and he did not hesitate to avail himself of them. Through front and rear windows he fired a good many shots, but they were not intended to kill or even wound. If his foes came to close quarters with him, it would have to be different. Already he had dropped one man with a load of buckshot. That was enough for the present. A bullet struck his left hand in the fleshy part just above the little finger. He tied up the wound with a handkerchief taken from stock.

Even during the battle, Boone found time once or twice to wonder what was back of this whole thing. He understood the attack. It was born of impulses easily comprehended, fusing into emotions of anger and greed. But why had the Quinns singled him out so instantly as the outlaw? Why had they instigated so big a reward as $3,000 *dead or alive?* No doubt the reward had come from the express company over the signature of the sheriff, but Boone did not doubt that the Quinns had urged it. And dead or alive. Did they prefer to have him brought in dead rather than alive? If so, why? The Quinns had nothing serious against him. It was ridiculous to suppose that they were hounding him to his death merely because he had thrashed Curt French. The motive was not sufficient. Then what potent reason urged them?

The answer came like a flash of light. The Quinns were diverting suspicion. They were covering the tracks of the real robbers by throwing the blame upon him and Dusty Rhodes. There could be no other explanation. They had either robbed the Bisbee stage themselves, or else they knew who had.

Crouched between two dry-goods boxes, Boone listened to the spitting of the bullets as darkness fell. The fusillade had died down for the time. Only an occasional shot sounded. Were his enemies massing for a rush? He rose to find out. As he did so, a tapping came from above. Revolver ready, he looked up to the skylight.

"Mister Sibley," a low voice whispered.

"Who is it?" he asked.

"Me. Tilatha McLennon. My pony is waiting beside the Silver Dollar. You can cross by the roofs and drop down." The girl's voice was tremulous with fear. "Oh, hurry, hurry!"

His thoughts moved in lightning flashes. Swiftly he caught up a Mexican sombrero and a serape from a shelf. A moment later he stood on one of the counters, stepped upon some sacks of flour, and pushed his head through the skylight. He lay beside the girl on the roof.

"Crawl along the roofs," she whispered. "You'll have to jump across to the Silver Dollar roof, then lower yourself on the other side. What's that?" She caught her hands in a gesture of terror.

There was a sound of crashing timber below, accompanied by fierce and savage voices.

"They're breaking in," he said urgently.

Twice he had rejected harshly her mediation, once within the hour. He did not refuse her help now. She had brought him his one chance for life. He accepted it instantly. But he did not creep along the roofs as she had suggested. He slipped the serape over his head and donned the sombrero, then ran from roof to roof. They were flat. Then someone caught sight of him and shouted. Tilatha's heart stopped as she saw him leap across to the Silver Dollar, stoop, and swing down from the roof.

"It's a Mexican!" someone yelled. Then: "No, by cripes, it's the killer!"

A shot sounded, another, three or four in quick succession. There came the swift drumming of hoofs. He had gotten away.

Cautiously a man's head and shoulders came through the skylight.

"Don't shoot!" the girl cried.

"Tilatha McLennon!" a surprised voice ejaculated.

A moment later Sid Edwards stood beside her on the roof.

"What you doin' here?" he asked.

"Helping Mister Sibley get away," she answered.

His jaw dropped. "Good Lord, girl! You might've got shot. How'd you get up here?"

"By the cottonwood tree over there."

Another man's head and shoulders showed, this time those of Russ Quinn. "Is he here, Sid?"

"Gone. Miss Tilatha's here."

Quinn ripped out an oath. In three sentences the situation was explained to him. He relieved his feelings in harsh and unflattering words as he stood close to her, his sinewy fingers pressing into the flesh of her wrists.

She did not hear him. Her mind was with the man flying through the night. She had seen a bloodstained cloth around his hand. *Is he badly wounded? Had he been hit again in the rush to escape? Had he escaped only to die of his hurts in the desert?*

XIII

Swiftly Boone went from roof to roof, crouching as he ran. He leaped across to the one that covered the Silver Dollar and, from the far side, looked down. A man, revolver in hand, stood near the wall just below him. Twenty yards away, beneath a cottonwood, was a saddled pony.

The Texan did not take time to reason out his best course. Sure instinct guided him. He dropped from the roof upon the man below who went down as though a hod of bricks had fallen on him.

As Boone clambered to his feet, he heard someone shout a warning. A gun barked in the darkness. The hunted man had no time for caution, none for retaliation. One wasted second might blot out his chance for escape. With long strides he scudded for the cottonwood. More guns sounded. Voices were lifted, shrill with excitement.

He caught at the bridle rein of the horse and vaulted to the saddle. One pressure of the knee was enough. He was astride a peg pony. It swung in its tracks and was off. "Scratch gravel, you Billy boy," he murmured, his heart exultant. For already he was out of range. In the night they would never find him unless some pursuer stumbled on him by chance. Grimly he smiled.

163

Already no doubt they were blaming one another bitterly for their failure to get him. He could imagine Russ Quinn's chagrin and humiliation. The man had been outlucked by his victim, outwitted by the girl he expected to marry. Unless Boone misread greatly his temperament, Quinn would take his setback as a personal affront.

Boone owed his escape wholly to Tilatha McLennon. Except for her interference, he would have been shot to death during the assault on the store. He recognized that fully. She had risked her life to save him. This did not hurt his pride. He exulted in it. If he had known in advance and could have prevented it, he would never have let her do it. Plainly enough he had told her to mind her own business. Her answer had been to plan his escape and to venture into the fire zone to save him. He would not soon forget the sight of her on the roof—fear-filled eyes shining with excitement, tremulous voice urging him to hurry, a young thing of unconscious grace whose slender throat carried the lovely head gallantly as the stem does a rose.

It was odd, this lift of the spirit, even though he had evaded the sharp menace of immediate death. A fugitive, he was riding from pursuit, already wounded, flying from danger into danger. That he was up to his neck in trouble, he knew. His only chance, any prudent man would say,

164

was to head for Mexico and get across the line. There was in him some stubborn strain that would not let him do that. His intention was to ride to Tough Nut and face down his foes. Without a trial, without waiting for the defense, public opinion had voted him guilty. If his enemies would give him time, he might reverse that verdict. A forlorn hope, he knew. It took no wisdom to perceive that they would strike hard and soon.

He rode through the night, following no trail but heading toward Tough Nut. A tenderfoot would soon have become lost in the maze of hills, but Boone had lived almost entirely in the open. The stars guided him, the general roll of the land told him which way lay the plains. A small stream confirmed his judgment.

At the creek he stopped to wash and bind his wounded hand. *My luck sure stood up fine that time,* he thought to himself as he re-knotted the handkerchief with the fingers of one hand and his teeth. *I reckon they spilled a couple hundred bullets at me. Never did see a burg get het up so sudden and so unanimous.* Naturally at this point his thoughts reverted once more to the young woman who had starred in his rescue. They continued to dwell with her as he jogged on down the creek. He had not even had time to say: "Much obliged." Did she think he was ungrateful? Maybe so, considering how he had previously repulsed so curtly her offers of assistance.

A gray light sifted into the sky. Dawn broke. It would not do to ride into Tough Nut in open daylight. There were arrangements to be made before he surrendered. He drew aside into the thick chaparral and unsaddled. He picketed the cow pony and let it graze on alfilaria. Boone had shot two quail at a water hole. He dressed and cooked them, then stamped out the fire. The birds served him for breakfast.

Under the shade of a mesquite he slept, woke, and slept again, wearing the day away until after the sun had set. He had, as most riders of the plains have, a capacity for patience. He did not fret at the slow hours, nor did he let himself worry about the future. What would be would be.

As darkness began to fall, he saddled and again took up the road for town. When he reached Tough Nut, he did not enter by way of Apache Street, nor did he put up Billy at the Buffalo Corral. Publicity was just now the last thing he wanted. He followed a burro trail that wound up an arroyo to a cabin on the outskirts of town. Not far from the cabin he dismounted and crept forward. There was a light in the shack, but before he announced himself, he wanted to know whether the owner of the place was alone. When he raised his head and looked through the window, his first glance told him there was only one person in the one room house. Boone went to the door and knocked.

Mobeetie Bill opened to him. The old-timer's eyes could hardly credit what they saw. "Dog my skin, son, is it sure enough you?" he asked. "Come right in an' make yourself to home,"

"I'll look after my horse first," Boone said. He unsaddled the cow pony and slipped the bridle from its head. Within a day or two he knew that the animal would be back at the McLennon Ranch. "You tell your mistress that I'm right much obliged for the loan of you, Billy," the young man said aloud.

When Boone returned to the house, carrying saddle and bridle, he found that the old Texan had been busy. He was tacking a newspaper over the window.

"I reckon you've heard the news . . . some of it," Boone said. "I'm not figuring on imposing on you, not too much, anyhow. I've got no claim on you and . . ."

"You have, too. You're from Texas, ain't you? And you can call me Dad."

"A heap of scalawags are from Texas, Dad. Well, I sure would like to talk things over with you if you've got no objections."

"You're gonna stay right here with me tonight. Had any supper?"

Boone had not. His host knocked together a hurried meal.

Before Boone washed his face, he asked the old Texan the question that was heavily on his mind. "Have you heard about Dusty? Was he shot up bad?"

"In the laig. The boys will look after him all right. He's got friends aplenty. They say he's at the McLennon Ranch."

The young man drew a deep breath of relief. "I was worried about him. The fellow that shot him was aiming at me. Dusty crossed in front of me right then. That boy will sure do to ride the river with."

"A kinda nice kid. I'm glad it wasn't any worse." There was a gleam of sly humor in the old fellow's eyes. "He won't be stove up long. When he gets afoot again, they can bring him in an' hang him nice."

"Don't, Dad. You make my neck ache," Boone answered with a rueful grin.

Mobeetie Bill emptied the contents of the frying pan into a plate. "Come an' get it, son," he said.

Not till after Boone had finished did either of them mention what was in both their minds. The old man's eyes were shining with excitement. "Son, you've certainly done stood this town on its head. All kinds of stories are floatin' through the gamblin' halls. I reckon I'll know what's what quickest if you make oration whilst I listen. Hop to it, boy."

Boone told the story of what had occurred since he had left Tough Nut two days since. More than once the former buffalo hunter's toothless grin applauded him.

"Didn't have a thing to do with the Bisbee stage hold-up?" Mobeetie Bill asked.

"Not a thing. Something queer about that, Dad. Why wish it on me so immediate?"

The old fellow wrinkled his forehead, nodding his head slowly. "What I'd like to know, too. Someone's mighty anxious to settle on a hold-up man real quick, looks like. Why? What was the dog-gone' hurry?"

"You tell me, Dad. I know what I think, but I want to check up."

"You think the same I do. The guys that did it were scared someone would strike the right trail, so they picked on you an' started folks lookin' for you. Funny the hold-ups were ridin' horses same color as yours an' Dusty."

"Unless they picked horses that color because they knew the ones we were riding," Boone suggested.

"*Humph!* Say, boy, that might be, too. I reckon I'll be right busy askin' a few questions tomorrow, or even tonight."

"I hoped you would."

"What about that wounded hand? You got to have a doctor."

"How about Doctor Peters? Is he a good doctor?"

"Why, he's a right good doctor, they say. But he might figure it his duty to tell the sheriff where you're at. He's got his own notions, Doc Peters has."

"I'll risk him. He doctored Curt French for the measles, didn't he?"

Mobeetie Bill was puzzled. He did not quite see what this had to do with it, but he could see by Boone's manner that there was some connection.

"Why, I dunno, did he? Want I should get Doc Peters here right away?"

"I hate to trouble you, Dad. If you don't want to mix up in this, I'll find him myself."

The old man exploded. "You leave me lay, boy! I'll do like I dog-gone please! I was totin' a gun before these Quinns were outta the cradle, an' don't aim to git off'n the earth for the whole passel of 'em."

Boone smiled. "All right, Dad. It's your say-so. Only ask your questions careful. Don't get into a rumpus with these killers."

"*Humph!* You're a nice fellow to be givin' advice like that," Mobeetie Bill grunted. "I been hearin' about all your goin's on in the hills. Beats me how you read your title clear to talk that-a-way now."

"One thing kind of led to another, but I sure wasn't looking for all the trouble that piled up on me. How much of a haul did the hold-ups get?"

"The express company ain't give out the figures, but I heard more'n twelve thousand," Mobeetie Bill said, and put on his coat and started on his errand.

Boone called after him: "Better not tell the doctor yet who his patient is!"

"I been thinkin' that my own self," the old man replied.

XIV

Dr. Peters was a tall, thin man, very dignified. He wore an imperial but no moustache. As to clothing, he was fastidious. Shrewd eyes under grizzled brows took in the Texan keenly. Apparently the doctor was a man of few words. After the briefest greeting, he removed his coat, folded it neatly, washed his hands, and examined the wound. He asked only one question.

"How long ago did this happen?" Boone told him. Then the doctor dressed the torn flesh, washed his hands a second time, and resumed his coat. He stood frowning down at his patient.

"How much?" asked Boone.

"No fee," answered the physician. "I regret to say, Mister Sibley, that I find it my duty to report your presence in town to the authorities."

"You know me, then?"

"You were pointed out to me on the street some days ago."

"Fair enough, Doctor. You wouldn't want to take a fee from your patient and then sell him for three thousand pieces of silver, would you?"

The doctor flushed angrily. "I do not take blood money, sir, nor do I shield criminals."

"Meaning me?" Boone asked, his voice low and even.

"I won't bandy words with you, young man. But I give you fair warning that I must notify the sheriff."

"You're playing fair, Doctor. I expect you think I'll light out. Well, they'll find me here. What do you reckon I came back to town for?"

"I don't know, unless you're mad."

"Which I'm not." Boone leaned forward, an elbow on the table, his gaze plunging into the black eyes of the physician. "How far would you go, Doctor, to clear your good name if it was attacked unjustly?"

The young man could see this sink in. He had given the doctor a jolt straight from the shoulder. It chanced that Dr. Joel Peters was an honorable man who very much valued his good repute.

"You mean you didn't rob the Bisbee stage and kill Buck Galway?"

"That's just what I mean. Dusty Rhodes and I weren't within forty miles of the place when it happened. Don't know Dusty, do you, Doctor?"

"I've seen him."

"And you think he's a wild young buckaroo ready for anything? Not for cold-blooded murder, Doctor."

"I understand the descriptions fit you both, even to the horses you were riding."

"Too closely. Someone kind of touched up the descriptions, I reckon. Someone left tracks, maybe, and wanted it hung on someone else real *pronto*."

173

For a moment Dr. Peters was silent. "Young man, if you've got anything to say, I think you'd better say it without riddles. You have someone in mind, I take it," he said quietly.

"Correct, sir. But let me ask a question, first. Curt French was your patient. He had the measles. Did you call on him that day? If so, when?"

Dr. Peters cast back to remember. "In the evening. He sent word to me not to disturb him in the morning because he wanted to sleep till afternoon."

"I'll bet he did his sleeping on horseback, Doctor."

"Are you telling me that French robbed the stage?"

"Not for sure. I don't know yet, but I'm going to find out if I live long enough. Let's say he did, though, French and one of his friends. We'll say the friend's last name was . . . well, call him Quinn. Though I wouldn't swear to it . . . might be Prouty, say. We won't give him a first name yet. Let's suppose there was a slip-up some-where, and they were worried for fear it might be laid to them. What would they do if they happened to know another man they could put it on, one they didn't like, anyhow?"

"As I understand it, this is all guesswork on your part."

"Mostly. I saw they must have a reason for jumping on me so sudden and so hard. Why three thousand dollars, dead or alive, before I have a chance to prove I didn't do it? Why put a name to the robbers only on suspicion? Isn't that some unusual, Doctor?"

Peters tugged at his imperial. "Yes, it is. And the size of the reward. It surprised me. Why, too, such a difference in the price to be paid for you and for Rhodes?"

"Don't you reckon maybe they preferred me dead to alive? If I was dead, probably not many questions would be asked . . . but alive, I might be some inconvenient if I had a good alibi."

"You might, since you are the kind of a man you are." The doctor's eyes took in the lithe, muscular build of the man, the easy poised alertness of his stance. They passed to the face, cut as it were out of granite, lit by cold gray eyes, steady and hard as steel. There was intrepid force in him, either for good or for evil. Peters prided himself on being a judge of character. Sibley might be a killer, but he had the unshaken nerves that would keep him from fool murder when there was no necessity to slay. The shooting of Buck Galway had been wanton. It had been done, Peters believed, either by a man in drink or by one in panic. "What do you expect to do here, Mister Sibley? Do you know that your life isn't worth a jackstraw if your enemies stir up the town against you?" he asked.

"I could guess that after the rehearsal they put

on at Galeyville. I've got to take my chances. I'm here to give myself up to the sheriff, but I aim to round up what evidence I can first. Mobeetie Bill is out now, kind of putting a few casual questions for me. Let me ask you one, Doctor. Do the Quinns and their friends own this town? Can they put over anything they like, no matter how raw?"

The doctor considered this before he answered. "Yes and no. They are bold ruffians. I've known them to disregard the opinion of the better part of the community. But Whip, who is their leader, plays a wary game. He usually moves under cover of the law. It would not be good for business to outrage public sentiment."

"And how about the sheriff? Is he a Quinn man?"

"No, he isn't. It's a fee office and worth a lot of money. Whip Quinn wanted it, but the governor appointed Brady. I don't think the feeling between the sheriff and the Quinns is friendly, though there has been no open break. My judgment is that Brady is an honest man."

"But he offers three thousand dollars' reward for a man dead or alive before the man has been proved guilty."

"If you knew Brady you could understand that. He's slow . . . rather thick-headed, in fact. The express company offers the reward through the sheriff's office. Dugan probably talked him into that. Dugan is the local manager of the express company, and he is a great admirer of the Quinns . . . Whip in particular."

There was a knock on the door, a loud rap, and, after a pause, two softer ones. "Mobeetie Bill," said Boone. He opened the door to the old man.

"Well, Doc, how's your patient?" the old-timer asked. "I done told that fool boy he deserves to have his head shot off instead of his hand if he monkeys with unloaded six-shooters."

"Doctor Peters knows who I am, Dad," explained Boone. "How did you come out?"

The ex-buffalo hunter glanced at the doctor, then looked at Sibley. He understood that he was to tell what he had found out. "Curt French an' Sing Elder rode outta town right after you boys, maybe a half hour later. They rode horses the same color as you an' Dusty. Curt had been drinkin' some an' had a bottle with him. I got it from Mack Riley, who is swampin' for Reynolds down at the Buffalo Corral. Mack says they didn't git back whilst he was on duty. They said they were deputies for Bob Hardy on official business, which was private an' not to be discussed. Curt did most of the talkin', seems. About the time I'd got that much outta Mack, he suspicions somethin' an' shuts his trap. Mack ain't lookin' for any trouble."

"You got a lot more from him than I expected you would. We're on the right track, looks like. Much obliged, Dad."

The old man grinned his toothless smile. "You don't owe me a thing, Texas man. It would be a pleasure to help hog-tie Mister Curt French with evidence he did this."

"I expect Curt did the killing. They say he's a terror when he's drunk. Sullen and mean. What do you think, Doctor?"

Doc Peters did not commit himself. "I think you had better go slow, Mister Sibley. Your enemies are likely to move with deadly swiftness if they discover you are here and on their trail. My advice is to send for Mister Turley and give him the facts. The *Gold Pocket* has much influence with the sober citizens of Tough Nut. If it endorses you, a counter sentiment will be started in your favor."

"That's sure enough good medicine," Mobeetie Bill agreed. "I'll see Turley tonight."

"I'll drop in on him," the doctor promised. "I think what I have to say might have weight with him."

Boone made a stipulation. "Tell him not to do or say anything that might get him into trouble with the Quinns. He's not a fighting man and ought to be careful."

"He's a fighting man, though not with guns," the doctor corrected. "I'll carry your message, but he will do what he thinks right regardless of personal consequences."

Bag in hand, the doctor departed.

XV

Doc Peters found Thomas Turley setting the story of the Galeyville fight. His wound had been slight, and already he was back at the office. The two men were friends and cronies, so the editor merely motioned his visitor to a chair covered with newspapers. He did not feel it necessary to desist from work.

They were alone, both the pressman and the editor's assistant having finished for the night. Dr. Peters lit a pipe, strolled up and down the office, then sat down.

"Just got back from a visit to a patient," he said presently.

"If someone is sick, that is probably a story," Turley said.

"Even if he has been shot?" asked Peters, a twinkle in his eyes.

Turley stopped to look at him. "Someone else been shot?"

"Not someone else." Casually the doctor added: "Have you written the Galeyville fight story?"

"Just setting it now."

"I can give you a line to add to it. It is that Mister Boone Sibley is paying a short visit to Tough Nut."

"What?" Turley stared at his friend.

The doctor nodded confirmation of his news. "As the guest of our esteemed fellow citizen, Mobeetie Bill," he appended by way of footnote.

"What is he doing back here again?"

"Came to give himself up to the sheriff."

"Claims he is innocent, I suppose?"

"Claims to be . . . and I think is."

"Tell me all about it, Joel," the editor said.

Doc Peters told the story briefly, without ornamentation. Much of it Turley already knew, for the accounts of Miss McLennon's rescue and of the subsequent Galeyville battle had been brought to him by several parties. The new angle to it was Boone Sibley's point of view and the discovery made by Mobeetie Bill.

The editor thumped his fist down on a table. "I never was satisfied with the story given out. I don't know why, but I had a feeling inside facts were being held back. Then, too, I know young Rhodes. He is wild, but there is a long jump between that and cold-blooded murder."

"You met Sibley. How did he impress you, Thomas?"

"Of course, I was predisposed in his favor," the editor said in his clipped precise way. "Naturally one would be in the case of one who has saved one's life. But I watched this young man. He is strong and reserved. He knows his own mind and goes his own way. That rescue of the McLennon girl . . . I'd expect that sort of thing from him. But I wouldn't expect him to hold up a stage and murder a decent man like Buck Galway."

"Nor I. It would not be in character . . . at least as I read the man. He's a fighting Texan, but I think he would fight fair."

The eyes of the editor were shining. "Joel, I'm coming out flat-footed for him. Read tomorrow's paper. I'll say editorially that the *Gold Pocket* believes he is being persecuted and that he is an innocent man."

"Go slow, Thomas," advised his friend. "Don't make any references that point to the Quinns. Be very careful."

The door of the office opened, and two men walked in. They were Whip Quinn and Deputy U.S. Marshal Bob Hardy.

"Feelin' all right again, Mister Turley, after Curt's fool gun play? I expect Doc here has fixed you up good," Whip said genially.

"I am very much improved, thank you," the editor said stiffly.

"Fine. Glad to hear it. I certainly read Curt the riot act for his foolishness. I told him he'd ought to apologize, but you know Curt. At heart one of Nature's noblemen, but gnarly as an old apple tree."

"I know him," Turley said drily, without editorial comment.

"Well, I'm glad you're up and about again

practically good as new. All's well that ends that-a-way, as the old sayin' goes. We got to take men as we find 'em, I suppose. Curt is a little too generous with his lead pills once in a while."

The editor had nothing to say in words, but his silence was eloquent. Presently he would find out the object of this call. He knew that Quinn had not come because of any social impulse.

Bob Hardy, impatient of diplomacy, came bluntly to the issue of the day. "You've been shoutin' for law an' order, Turley. Now you got a chance to come out flat and denounce this fellow Sibley. We're expectin' the *Gold Pocket* to be there both ways from the ace."

Whip put the matter more smoothly. "Like you say, Mister Turley, this town and county has to stop lawlessness. A killing here or there . . . well, that's to be expected. But robbin' stages and shootin' shotgun messengers hurts the town. I reckon Sibley is safe in Mexico by now, but it won't hurt to hand him one of your well-known editorial scorchers. Show other outlaws where we're at, for one thing."

Turley gathered his courage for the stand he must take. His slender body grew rigid, his throat dry. "I . . . I don't believe Sibley is an out-law, Mister Quinn. We're not after the right man."

"What!" Whip Quinn flashed his hard eyes on the editor. "Not the right man? Do you claim to have some information we haven't got? If so, spit it out."

"No information." Turley swallowed a lump in his throat and went on timidly: "But I know Dusty Rhodes. He is not that kind of young man."

"We'll go easy on Dusty. This Sibley led him into it."

"But did he? I can't think so. I feel . . ."

Bob Hardy broke in roughly: "It don't matter what you feel. We've made up our minds. This fellow did it. It goes as it lays."

Once more the other found a more diplomatic way to apply pressure. "You don't want to let your personal gratitude to this killer stand in the way of the town's good, Mister Turley. I was on the ground with the marshal here, after the crime. We looked into the evidence. It pointed straight to Sibley. Why did he resist arrest at Galeyville? Why did he shoot Jim Barkalow there? Why did he light out after he got away? Where's he at now?"

Turley tugged nervously at his mustache. He felt that he was being driven toward disaster, but if he let himself be bullied into submission, he would always despise himself.

"Probably he lost his head at Galeyville. They were shooting at him. He had no chance to surrender. He was fighting for his life."

"He did, too, have a chance to give up. Russ

put it up to him, and he come back by takin' a shot at him. If your paper stands back of this Texas wolf, Turley . . ."

Bob Hardy did not finish his sentence, but the black look that went with it was a threat, a savage and ruthless one. The editor felt his stomach muscles let go, as though his vitals had become cold lead. His heart died within him.

"Bob is right," the other man agreed, his mouth tightening grimly. "You can't throw down this town because you're thick with this bad man, Sibley. Not for a minute, you can't."

"It's not only my personal gratitude, Mister Quinn. If I thought he was guilty, the *Gold Pocket* would certainly say so. But I can't feel that he is."

For the first time Dr. Peters spoke. "Nor I," he said quietly.

"Are you in this, Doc?" Bob Hardy asked roughly.

"Who do you think did it, Doctor?" Whip asked, dangerously suave.

"Haven't the least idea. Might have been some cowboys from the hills. Might have been someone from Bisbee."

"It was two fellows from right damned here. One was this Texas warrior, Sibley, the other was Dusty Rhodes." The older man looked hard at the editor. "Don't make any mistake, Turley. Get this in your paper correct."

184

"It will be true as I see it," the newspaper man said. He was white as a sheet, but he looked straight at Quinn.

"If I was you, I'd see it right. This town won't stand for you aidin' and abettin' an outlaw like Sibley," warned Whip.

"You'll shoot off your mouth oncet too often," Bob added harshly. "We're plumb tired of you runnin' on us. Me, I've had aplenty."

"Don't make a mistake, Turley," Whip advised once more, a dark warning in his voice. "Like Bob says, you've been on the prod with us aplenty."

With which the men turned and left the office.

XVI

Quinn and Hardy left behind them in the office of the *Gold Pocket* two men wretchedly down-hearted. Neither spoke for a few moments. Each of them knew that an ultimatum had been served, that there was danger ahead if Turley opposed the killers.

"They have their necks bowed, Thomas," Doc Peters said ruefully.

The editor nodded, swallowing hard. His lips were gray, his face bloodless.

"You've got no proof that Sibley is innocent. Better drop it. That is what he says himself . . . Sibley, I mean. He told me to tell you to keep out of this," the doctor continued.

"I can't," said Turley miserably. "These ruffians must not dictate the policy of this paper. I'm a coward, God knows, but . . . I've got to draw the line somewhere. I can't take orders from them . . . not and call myself a man."

The doctor spoke to his friend, his voice very gentle. "Thomas, you are not called upon to . . . to do this thing for a town that wouldn't even understand why you did it. These ruffians have an argument reason can't oppose. You are not in Massachusetts. The six-shooter is mightier than the pen out here. I advise you to make no

186

editorial comment whatever about this business."

"And this is free America, Joel," the harassed man said bitterly. "To save my skin, I'm to kowtow to these scoundrels. I won't do it."

"Why raise the point of Sibley's innocence, since you have no evidence of it? At least wait . . . see what developments occur."

"I must talk with him . . . tonight."

"Shall I bring Sibley around to see you?" Doc Peters asked.

"I wish you would. I'd like to hear what he has to say."

"I've been wondering if it would not be a good thing to sound out Sheriff Brady. We do not need to tell him at first that Sibley is here, only that we have reason to think he may not be guilty of the stage robbery."

"Perhaps you are right. I've got to line up what strength we have if I'm going to stand out against the Quinns. The sheriff would be reasonable, though he won't come out definitely on our side. But let me talk with Sibley first."

Half an hour later Turley answered a knock on the door to let in Dr. Peters, Mobeetie Bill, and Boone Sibley.

"This is a council of war, gentlemen, to decide the best policy to pursue," Doc Peters announced. "Shall I talk, Thomas, or will you?"

"Go ahead," Turley said.

Out of the ensuing conference came two

decisions. The first was made by Turley: he would go through with the editorial policy of criticizing the attempt to find Sibley guilty before he had been tried. The second came from Sibley: Sheriff Brady was to be brought to the house and all the facts laid before him.

Mobeetie Bill found the sheriff playing poker at Dolan's Palace. Brady was winning, and he viewed sourly the old man's invitation to take a walk with him. The old-timer was insistent, and to get rid of him the sheriff left his chips to hold the seat and followed the Texan out of the house.

"Dad-gum your old hide, what's it all about?" the officer asked, not unamiably. He had not wanted to leave the table, but now that he had come, he was in no hurry. The game would go on all night and perhaps all the ensuing day.

"I said for you to take a walk with me, Brady. We ain't took it yet."

"Mostly I do my walking in a saddle, Dad. What in Mexico has got in your old coconut? Is it officially you want me?"

"You're liable to find out when we get there. What's eatin' you, anyhow? Won't anyone steal your measly li'l' stack of chips."

"You're sure mysterious tonight, Dad, and you the gabbiest galoot that ever come a-running outta Texas ahead of a sheriff. I recollect oncet finding a buffalo skull on the old Chisum trail. It

188

had wrote on it . . . 'Talked to death by Mobeetie Bill.' They had stuck it up for a marker on the poor pilgrim's grave."

Turley admitted the two men to the room where the others were waiting. The sheriff glanced around carelessly.

"Hello, Doc. How's every little thing? This old donkey dragged me away from a poker game. Were you figuring on starting one here?"

"Not exactly. Sheriff, shake hands with Mister Boone Sibley."

The smile vanished from Brady's wrinkled brown face like the light from a blown candle. The starch of wariness ran through him instantly and tensed his figure. He waited silently, watching the young Texan with steady, appraising eyes.

"Don't drop jokes like that around, Doc. They're liable to go off and hurt someone," he warned.

The sheriff had spoken to the doctor, but his gaze did not for an instant release Sibley.

Boone nodded his head. "No joke at all, Sheriff, I'm the man you want."

"Who took you? How come you're here?"

"Nobody took me. I came to surrender myself because I hear I'm wanted."

The officer stared at him, dumb with amazement. His mind grappled with the situation and could find no light. If this was the bandit

Sibley, what crazy scheme had brought him straight to the vengeance awaiting him?

"Surrender yourself?" the sheriff repeated at last.

"Yes. To clear my name. To prove I didn't do it."

"Not hold up the stage?"

"And to find out . . . if I can . . . who did do it?"

"You got me whipped," the sheriff said. "Why, you damn' fool, you've been identified practically. You haven't got a dead man's chance."

"Who identified me, Sheriff?" Boone asked.

"One of the hold-ups was about the size of Dusty Rhodes, and he wore chaps and a brown shirt like they claim Dusty was wearing when he left here. He was on a bay horse."

"You ever wear a brown shirt and ride a bay horse, Sheriff?"

"Might have done so, but not last Tuesday. The other hold-up, the one that did the killing, was taller than his friend. He rode a sorrel."

"As I did," Boone added. "Bay and sorrel are right frequent colors for horses. I know two other fellows left here Tuesday morning mounted that-a-way."

"Who?" asked Brady.

"Coming to that soon. Isn't that kinda slim identification, Sheriff, for a reward of three thousand, dead or alive?"

"Whip Quinn and Bob Hardy talked with the

passengers. They sure enough described a man like you."

"I'll bet they did . . . after Quinn had described me to them first. Did it ever strike you that this was wished on me and Dusty too sudden? That someone was mighty eager to elect us by unanimous consent with a hurrah?"

"Got an alibi?"

"We have and we haven't. About the time the stage was being held up we met two old prospectors heading for the Dragoons. Dusty was acquainted with 'em. One he called Toughfoot Bozeman and the other Hassayampa Pete."

"Where was this?"

"A few miles this side of Sugarloaf Peak."

"What time of day, did you say?"

"About ten o'clock, I reckon."

"That sure lets you out if they back what you say. I'll send someone out after the old donkers."

Boone, in his soft drawl, raised a point. "Talking about alibis, I wonder what kind of a one Curt French and Sing Elder would offer."

The sheriff's eyes clamped to his. "Meaning just what?"

"I'm interested about how they would explain their little *pasear* if anyone asked them. They left town Tuesday morning half an hour after Dusty and me. French rode a sorrel. Sing Elder was on a bay. Sing is some shorter than his friend."

"Where did they go?"

"That's what I'm wondering. Your guess is as good as mine."

"Got any proof of this?"

"Mack Riley. He's swamping at the Buffalo Corral. Mack says French had been drinking and had a bottle with him. French said they were deputies of Bob Hardy on official business and for Riley not to say anything about them leaving town."

"French had the measles," Doc Peters added. "I was attending him. He sent word to me that morning not to come to see him as he wanted to sleep. Bob Hardy brought me the message and asked if I would call after supper, instead. Quinn came to me long after French and Sing Elder had left town . . . that is, if it is true what Riley says."

"Looks right queer." The sheriff's eyes narrowed. "When did they get back to town?"

"We don't know," Doc Peters replied. "Not till after Riley was off duty. He went off about four in the afternoon."

Brady muddled it over in his mind. If the Quinn outfit had done this and had used him to further their plans, if they were laughing up their sleeves at him for a chuckle-headed rabbit, he would show them a thing or two before he got through. Anger simmered in him. Whip Quinn had flattered him for his prompt action in issuing the reward. Why had he taken the trouble to do this? What did he care whether the bandits were caught?

Unless he had a personal interest in it. Come to think of it, the stage was never held up when Russ Quinn was the shotgun messenger. Nor was it robbed unless there was a gold shipment aboard. It looked as though there was a leak of information some-where. In that case, the robbers must live in Tough Nut and must be close to the company. Whip was a boon companion of Dugan, the local manager of the express company. Very likely Dugan was not in on the robberies. He was a vain little man who took much pride in being the friend of the great Whip Quinn. It would be easy enough for Whip to get out of him, casually, what he wanted to know, especially since Russ was employed in a confidential capacity by the company.

The longer Brady thought about it the more convinced he became that the Quinns or some of their friends were at the bottom of the robberies. His anger against them mounted. They had chosen him as their monkey, had they, to draw the chestnut out of the fire for them? He would show them whether they could make a fool of him. But he must go slow. He must not take it for granted that this Texan was innocent.

"Since you claim you're innocent, why didn't you surrender peaceable at Galeyville?" Brady asked.

"They began shooting at me, first off. Later, I wouldn't surrender to Russ Quinn because I figured I would never reach town alive."

"You wouldn't have, either . . . not if what you say about the bandits being fellows close to the Quinns is true. But folks are all het up about you shooting Buck Galway and then that cowboy Barkalow."

"Is Barkalow dead?"

"No, sir. He's got better than an even break to live, I hear. But that isn't your fault."

"Nor his," the Texan added. "I can prove he fired at me while Quinn was talking to me under a flag of truce."

"Maybeso. Point is that folks ain't in a mood to listen to any of your explanations. You're a regular Billy the Kid. So they think. Their notion is that the sooner you're bumped off the better it will be for all concerned. I'll have to arrest you, Mister Sibley."

"I've ridden fifty or sixty miles to give you a chance, Mister Sheriff," the young man answered, a faint ironical drawl in his voice.

"I reckon I'll play my hand close to my belly till I find where we're at. No use telling the Quinns where you are. I'm arresting you for stealing a horse up at Prescott. Your name is Jack Blayney, if anyone asks you."

"I'll remember that."

"Now, I'll take your guns, Mister Sibley, if you please."

The Texan handed over his six-shooters. "Mister Blayney, you mean," he corrected with a smile.

194

XVII

Tough Nut buzzed like a beehive with whispered comment. Women gossiped and men hazarded surmises as to future developments. The *Gold Pocket* had come out editorially in defense of the accused men, Sibley and Rhodes. Its story of the battle at Galeyville did not carry the slant hitherto given the affair. According to the newspaper account, the two men had been fired upon without warning and Rhodes wounded. The Texan had defended himself, one against fifty. He had shot Barkalow only after the cowboy had violated a flag of truce by firing at him. Eventually he had escaped only because a young woman, who he had rescued from a band of Mexicans a day or two earlier, had risked her life to save him.

As to the attack upon the stage, the editor of the *Gold Pocket* said the accused men, so at least one of them claimed, could establish an alibi, if given time. The paper advocated patience on the part of the citizens of the town and county. Facts were likely to develop within a day or two that would entirely change the present outlook. Precipitate action of any kind, such as had occurred at Galeyville, was to be deplored.

Those who had inside information saw, both in story and in editorial, a challenge to the Quinns.

Deputy U.S. Marshal Bob Hardy had, with Whip Quinn, taken charge of the hunt for the bandits. They had followed the trail into the hills and lost it. They had interviewed passengers on the stagecoach and obtained descriptions of the robbers. On their advice a reward had been offered for Sibley and Rhodes. Whip's brother Russ had taken command of the cowboys in the Galeyville attack.

"It's a Quinn proposition from start to finish," a miner at Dolan's Palace said to another. "They've got it hung on Dusty an' this Sibley. Prob'ly they've got the right guys. Where did this Texas man hail from, anyhow? Nobody knows. But we're sure he's a tough son-of-a-gun. That's been proved aplenty. Turley had ought to know the Quinns ain't gonna be pleased for him to try to give 'em the laugh by claimin' they don't know what they're doin'."

"Turley is too biggity. He wants to run this 'ere town like a Sunday school," responded another. "Then, when we have a cold-blooded murder, he sticks up for the guy because the fellow done him a good turn. Or maybe he's hired to, I dunno."

These represented fairly enough the casual opinion of Tough Nut, but there were those who believed the Quinns had a much more urgent reason for resenting the articles in the *Gold Pocket*. One of the latter was Sheriff Brady, now riding doggedly toward Bisbee after a rather active night spent not at poker. Another was a young man in jail charged with stealing a horse at Prescott. Doc Peters and Mobeetie Bill were two others. And Mack Riley, at the Buffalo Corral, began to be uncomfortably aware that something serious was in the air and to wonder if he had talked too much with his mouth.

It was observable that at Jefford's, at the Last Chance, at the Occidental, and at other gambling houses men began to gather in knots to discuss the affair. In each group was one positive individual who sawed the air with forceful gestures. It might be Curt French. It might be a Quinn. It might be some one of their hangers-on. But the purport of the argument was always the same. The time had come to show Turley where to get off at. He was standing up for criminals and cold-blooded murderers, and he ought to be tarred and feathered and ridden out of town on a rail. The more excited the orators became, the more necessary it was to wet the throat with another drink all around. Each drink called for more heated vituperation.

Meanwhile, Whip and Russ Quinn walked down to the newspaper office. An itinerant printer who was cleaning type told them that the boss was out. Perhaps he was at his house. The Quinns went to Turley's home and found him there. But not alone.

Two visitors from the hills were also present. "I think you know Mister and Miss McLennon," the editor said. The editor's heart melted within him. Had the Quinns come to exact vengeance upon him for his defiance of their warning?

"Yes, we know 'em," Russ said harshly, his eyes fastened to those of Tilatha. "Be glad to smoke 'em out right here and find where they're at. Do you claim you're friends? Or ain't you?"

Hugh McLennon spoke evenly. "Just as friendly as we ever were, Russ."

"Don't look like it, the way this fool girl acted at Galeyville."

"What would you expect?" asked Hugh, a suggestion of the grating of steel in his voice. "Sibley saved Tilatha from those Mexicans. Wouldn't you figure she'd do him a good turn if the chance came?"

Whip took the answer quickly out of his brother's mouth. "Of course. Russ is sure sore the fellow got away. Can't blame him. But we don't aim to have any trouble with you because Miss McLennon was some too impulsive. We're here to ask Mister Turley some questions."

"G-glad to answer any," the editor said in a fading voice.

"First off, what d'you mean by claimin' this Sibley was in the right at Galeyville?" The voice of the older Quinn stung like a whip lash.

"Why, my information . . . if I'm wrong I'll be

glad to correct what I wrote . . . but Miss McLennon was there . . . and . . ."

"Does she say there wasn't a reward out for this killer, dead or alive?"

"She can speak for herself," Tilatha answered. "She says they never gave him or Dusty a chance to surrender before they began firing at them."

"Didn't Russ give him a chance afterward?"

"Yes, and while they were talking, Jim Barkalow fired at Mister Sibley. He was afraid they'd kill him if he did surrender."

"He was thinkin' about what he did to Buck Galway. That's why he didn't surrender," Russ broke in savagely.

"My notion, too," his brother agreed. "But pass that. Another question, Mister Turley. Is it Dusty or this other killer that claims they've got an alibi? And when did he claim it?"

"Miss McLennon says . . ."

"Passin' the buck again," Whip interrupted grimly. "Well, what does Miss McLennon say this time?"

"Dusty told me, Mister Quinn," Tilatha replied, "that they met two old prospectors in the desert just about the time the stage was robbed."

"And who were these prospectors?"

The hill girl caught the flash of warning in the editor's eye. "He didn't *give* their names. They were going into the Dragoons, they said," was her answer.

"About like I expected. He had to claim something, didn't he?"

The girl's spirit flashed to expression. "I don't care. I believe every word he says. They didn't do it."

She thought Whip Quinn's smile hateful. It implied much more than it said, more than he would have dared say in words. Beneath the tan, color flamed into her cheeks. Yet there was no answer she could make, not without giving him more excuse to believe his unspoken accusation.

He turned again to the editor. "What facts are likely to develop that will change the present situation as regards this killer Sibley? Just what did you mean by your editorial?"

Turley. tugged at his mustache helplessly. He dared not let Whip think for a moment that the Quinns or their followers were suspected. A moment of inspiration saved him. "Why . . . about the alibi . . . it's likely to be established when word reaches the prospectors, don't you think?"

"No, by God, I don't." Whip brought his big fist down on the table like the blow of a hammer. "I think you've thrown in with those road agents. That's what I think. This fellow Sibley, and Dusty Rhodes, too, was at your house the night of his run-in with Curt French. Did you fix it up then that, if they didn't make a clean getaway after they robbed the stage, you was to claim in your paper they were innocent?"

"You don't mean that . . . seriously?" the newspaper man gasped.

"It's ridiculous . . . and hateful . . . to say that about Mister Turley!" Tilatha cried, her eyes flashing fire. "As though . . . as though he were a robber!"

"He's tryin' to protect one . . . a robber and a murderer both," the younger Quinn answered.

"That's not true, Russ Quinn," Tilatha flung back at him. "He's neither one nor the other. What are you-all so anxious to condemn Boone Sibley without giving him a chance? What harm did he ever do you?" Her stormy eyes challenged the angry ones of Russ.

"Looks that-a-way to me, too, boys," Hugh said amiably enough. He had no wish to quarrel with the Quinn crowd. That would be both dangerous and unprofitable. "You're sure enough barking up the wrong tree. I reckon Sibley has lit out for good. But Dusty is still with us. Fact is, he's at the ranch now. Give him a chance to prove his alibi. Won't do any harm, will it?"

"Nor any good," Whip retorted. "I worked up this case myself, me and Bob Hardy. Real thorough, too. D'you think we're fools, McLennon?" Abruptly he turned to Turley. "Look out for yourself. We've protected you up to date. But no more. If the citizens of this town through a law-and-order committee take action, don't blame us."

He turned on his heel and strode out of the room. Russ frowned at Tilatha. He hesitated, as though he were about to say something, then closed his mouth like a steel trap and followed his brother.

"What did they mean about a law-and-order committee?" Turley asked McLennon.

The ranchman shook his head. "No idea what he meant. Maybe just trying to scare you."

Turley thought that if that was what Quinn wanted, he had certainly succeeded. If any law-and-order committee waited on him, he knew that Whip Quinn would be back of it. They would do what he told them to do, yet he would not be responsible for their actions in the eyes of the community. What did law-and-order committees do to their victims? Did they hang them? Or did they merely beat them with whips till they wished they were dead?

XVIII

Sheriff Brady's trip to Bisbee did not unearth any important evidence, but it had the effect of disturbing some conclusions regarded as already established. The passengers could give no accurate description of the robbers. Buck Galway had been killed almost before the stage stopped. The effect of this had been to terrorize those on board. The big bandit—the noisy one who did the talking—handled his six-shooters so recklessly that they had been too frightened to make accurate observations. Moreover, most of the time they had been lined up with their backs to the road agents.

Before leaving for Bisbee the sheriff had made a discovery of interest. The day after the hold-up, Curt French had bought at the leading jewelry shop in Tough Nut a diamond pendant, presumably for a sporting lady named Faro Kate in whom he was interested. He had paid for it with greenbacks. The significance of this lay in the scarcity of paper money on the frontier. It was practically never used in Tough Nut. A strange coincidence was that one of the passengers on the stage, a New Yorker, had been relieved of $600 in bills.

In the jail yard Brady hitched his horse and

knocked the dust from his hat. He bowlegged into his office. Two old-timers were making themselves at home there. Both were smoking corncob pipes. One was laboriously reading a newspaper to the other.

"The king at present on the thorn sits in-se-cure-ly. No, Frank, I reckon it ain't 'thorn' . . . must be 'throne', don't you reckon?"

Brady guessed what they were doing here, but he did not give them a lead. "Thought you old vinegaroons were out prospecting in the Dragoons," he said.

"We was headed that-a-way, but seems like one thing an' another is always comin' up," Hassayampa Pete complained.

"Fellow told us how Dusty Rhodes an' another gazebo held up the Bisbee stage Tuesday," Toughfoot Bozeman explained querulously.

"That's what they say, about ten in the morning."

"Well, they didn't. We met 'em out on the desert about that time up somewheres near Sugarloaf."

"Would you know the fellow with Dusty?"

"I ain't plumb blind, be I?" demanded Bozeman.

Five minutes later they confronted Boone Sibley.

"That's him . . . the fellow with Dusty," Pete snapped.

"Y'betcha!" corroborated his partner. "An'

someone has sure got to pay us for the time an' trouble we've took to come to town."

"Reckon Mister Sibley will be willing to foot that bill," the sheriff said. "First off, though, we'll git your story on paper and witnessed. I'll ask you both to stick around town for a couple days."

"*Humph!* Mister Sibley payin' for that, too?"

"I'll see you're paid," the sheriff promised.

After the prospectors had gone, the sheriff summarized the situation. "Well, Sibley, it looks like we haven't got a thing on you. Soon as you like, you can walk out of that door."

"About that horse I stole up at Prescott," Boone drawled.

Brady grinned. "Mistaken identity. Turns out you ain't Blayney. Still and all, I'd advise you to stay right here or light out *pronto*. Some up-and-coming lad might bump you off before I can get that reward withdrawn. Then there's the Quinns and Curt French."

"That's good medicine, Sheriff. Since you're so hospitable, I'll sleep in your hotel tonight, anyhow. I'd hate to be shot for a reward that isn't."

"Make yourself comfortable. I'll tell Hank you're your own boss now."

The jailor, Hank Jacobs, offered his guest a cot downstairs in exchange for the cell he had been occupying.

"Glad you proved you wasn't the man," he said. "Horse stealin' in Arizona ain't no game for amachoors to buck."

"No business for a quiet, timid man like me," Boone agreed. "By the way, Sheriff, do I get my six-shooters back? Might run across a rattle-snake."

Brady handed the guns to him. "You be right careful how you use these, young fellow. Don't you go firing them off promiscuous in this town. Well, I got to go home and meet the wife. She claims she's a widow since I took this job. My own kids don't hardly know me."

Boone sat in an armchair in the sheriff's office and read the newspaper. The jailor excused himself, retired to a back room, and prepared to make up arrears of sleep.

The young Texan read the advertisement offering a reward for him dead or alive. In a parallel column was the story of the Galeyville battle. It was written without color or bias, but so vividly that he lived again the half hour before he was astride Billy galloping for the chaparral. On the inside was the editorial pleading for fair play.

Dusty was right, Boone thought to himself. *Turley has got guts. He's sure the nerviest scared man I ever met. He's got no business in this town with the Quinns rampaging around.*

An hour passed. Boone had read even the

patent medicine advertisements. He dropped the newspaper on the desk, leaned back, stretched his arms, and yawned to the bottom of his lungs. Time to turn in. He chopped the yawn off unfinished, arms still extended. What was that noise? It sounded like the roar of surf. Then he knew. The night had become vocal with the growl of many voices drowning each other out. Boone rose, walked to the door, opened it, and stepped out.

Down the street, three hundred yards away, the road was filled with men. Others were pouring out from saloons and gambling houses. They were like busy ants swarming about. Something was afoot.

A man hurried past. Boone called to him: "What's up?"

"They're running Turley outta town . . . gonna tar and feather him first."

Boone asked no more questions. He knew why, just as he knew that the better element— nine-tenths of the citizens of the town—would disapprove of such a lawless high-handed proceeding. The riff-raff and the ignorant were doing this, instigated by the Quinns, who very likely would stay in the background and laugh up their sleeves.

Already Boone was striding down the street. This was his business. It had been for espousing his cause that Turley became the object of their wrath. He began to run.

XIX

During the day Turley had heard rumbles of the coming storm. He was as uneasy as a man sitting on the edge of a volcano due to erupt any minute. Just before supper Doc Peters came to him.

"I don't like the way things look, Thomas," he told his friend. "I don't want to alarm you, but there is trouble brewing. The sober people of the town will back your policy, but there are a lot of hoodlums and some thick-headed honest men ready for mischief. The whole gambling element is lined up against you. If I were you, I'd leave town at once, and stay away until the excitement has died down."

Turley shook his head. "Can't do that, Joel," he said, his voice heavy with gloom. "I've done nothing wrong. I won't run away like a cur."

"I would. Don't be obstinate, Thomas. It's the Quinns' work. Why oblige them by staying here and becoming a victim of it?"

"No. I won't go. Probably the whole thing will blow over, anyhow. I've put my hand to the plow. I'll stay."

Dr. Peters knew it was no use to argue with him. Besides, it was likely he was overestimating the danger. Perhaps the best way was to stay and face it down.

"I wish you had a bodyguard . . . someone like that Boone Sibley," he said.

The editor's answering smile held no mirth. "Do you know anyone looking for a job like that, with French and the Quinns and Sing Elder as my chief enemies? Not to mention that eminent peace officer, Bob Hardy. If you meet such a man, please send him around. I'd like to see him, though I won't promise to hire him."

"At any rate, go armed."

"Why? I can't hit a barn door. It is known I don't carry weapons. That serves me as a protection."

"Did it help you when Curt French shot you?" the doctor asked bluntly, and left.

Turley found it difficult to eat his supper. Food stuck in his throat and choked him. He could hardly get it down. His mind was full of alarms. He found himself listening intently. For what?

A knock! Perspiration burst from his brow. His body shook as the housekeeper, a Mexican woman, went to the door.

Turley heaved a sigh of relief. It was Tilatha McLennon. She read instantly the fear and alarm on the editor's features in his nervous movements. She had known that he would be this way, and it was to help him, to steady his nerves by her encouraging presence, that she had come. But she pretended not to know what might be troubling him so much.

In a tone of casual surprise she asked: "Aren't you feeling well? You seem upset. What is it?"

"Nothing. I expect I'm a little nervous. I've been under some strain. Afraid I'm not very good company."

"I don't wonder you're nervous after all you've been through. It's horrid of those ruffians, but I wouldn't worry about them."

He sat down after supper and tried to read while Tilatha busied herself with some sewing that she had brought along. The Mexican woman had cleared off the table and was doing the dishes.

The book he had picked up was one of Herbert Spencer's. He found it impossible to concentrate. His mind hopped back, whenever he would let it alone, to the immediate problem of his life. How was it possible to cope with such ruffians as these who were his enemies, strong, unscrupulous men striding to their end without jumpy nerves to hamper them? One ought either to get out of their way or knuckle down, unless he were like this Sibley, as game and harsh and forceful as they were. And the odds were that these wolves would drag down and devour Sibley, too, if he stayed in their vicinity, in spite of his scornful confidence and his uncanny skill at self-defense.

Someone hammered on the door of the house. Turley leaped from his chair as though released by a spring. His legs shook as he moved forward.

Tilatha reached the door first to let in this imperious visitor. Mobeetie Bill turned the key in the lock after he had entered the hall and came into the room. His faded old eyes were shining with excitement.

"They're after you, Turley. Right damn now. Headin' this-a-way already. Light out. *Pronto.*"

The heart of the editor died within him. It had come, the hour he had dreaded. "Where shall I go?" he faltered.

"Anywheres but here. Slip out the back way. Circle round an' head for my shack. We'll git you a horse."

"And . . . Miss McLennon?"

"They won't hurt her none. She'll be in my care. Don't worry about her. Move lively."

Turley forgot his resolution not to be driven away. Already he could hear the low ominous voice of the mob. Anything was better than to stay and face it.

Tilatha urged him to speed. "Hurry . . . hurry!" she cried, and clung to the trembling man as she pushed him toward the back door.

They passed through the kitchen. He opened the door. A revolver barked. There was a spatter of adobe dirt from the wall three feet from his head. Hurriedly he closed the door and drew back

His face was ashen. "God," he murmured.

"Too late," the ex-buffalo hunter said. He bolted

the door and blew out the kitchen lamp. "It wasn't aimed to hit you, Turley. Jes' meant as a warnin' to stay here."

"What'll I do?" By sheer willpower Turley dragged himself back from panic. "I can't stay here and endanger Miss McLennon." There flashed to his mind a picture of the Galeyville battle as he had imagined it, scores of guns pouring lead into a building where one man crouched like a trapped wolf. In such a mêlée this girl might be shot down before the mob dragged him out. He could not risk that. He must give himself up.

"Don't push on your reins," the old-timer urged. "We'll play for time. Hear what they got to say. Talk 'em out of it if we can."

Mobeetie Bill had no confidence in his own program. But they were in no position to choose. The cards were stacked and had to be played that way. Strangely enough, his old blood warmed to the danger. It had been years since peril had jumped at him in this stark fashion. He remembered the yell of Morgan's raiders. It was in his throat ready to leap out. Back of that, in his early youth, he had ridden on that disastrous filibustering expedition when gallant Ewan Cameron lost his life. He had seen George Crittenden draw the white bean that meant life and then hand it to a married comrade with the remark that he could afford to take another chance. Brave days those, when life and death hung on the color of a bean drawn from a box. It thrilled him to renew for an hour the old daily association with danger. Better, far better, than to sit nodding in the sun waiting for his days to draw out.

They could hear outside the tramp of feet, the sound of many voices. Mobeetie Bill blew out the lamp in the sitting room.

"Let 'em guess where we're at," he added.

The mob murmur died down. A heavy voice called: "Come outta there, Turley! We want to see you."

It was Mobeetie Bill who answered. He stepped to the window, which was open, and looked out into the moonlit street.

" 'Evenin', Mister French. Who was it you said you wanted?"

"Tom Turley . . . and quick, too."

"What do you want with him?"

"None of your business. Who are you, anyhow? It's Turley we're after."

"Me, why I'm only an old donker, a stove-up pilgrim from Texas. You know Mobeetie Bill, don't you, Curt?"

French moved forward. "Tell Turley if he doesn't come outta there, we'll drag him by the neck. No use hidin'. We know he's there."

"Now, looky here, Mister French," the old-timer protested. "I 'low you don't mean any good to

Turley. Let's talk this over, friendly-like. Prob'ly we can fix up a reasonable compromise."

"Don't argue with me, you old fool!" French roared. "I'm comin' to drag him out immediate!"

Later Tilatha never could explain the impulse that urged her to swift, rash action. Tilatha had known what to do when the life of her lover was in danger. Tilatha had not stood and wrung her hands despairingly. So she now stepped into character and did an amazing thing when the life of an innocent and righteous friend was in danger.

Without a word, she slipped into the hall and unlocked the door. In another moment she had whipped it open, stepped outside, and closed it behind her. She stood, drenched in the moonlight, facing that hungry wild-beast mob.

It was appalling to look down on all those harsh faces—unshaven, savage, inflamed by the strange lust of the pack for the kill. They were normal human beings, most of them, moved by the common emotions of mankind, by tenderness, by generosity, by greed, by sudden unaccountable hates and loves. None of this she saw now. They were not individuals, but the pack. Only one stood out among them. He was bearded, heavy, full-bodied. His eyes were bloodshot, face gross and sullen. He moved slowly toward her, as far as the bottom step.

There he stood staring at this fearless girl, who

confronted him and his followers. It could have been no more astonishing if a winged angel from heaven had descended from the sky, so alien was she to the spirit of their purpose. What was she doing here? From where had she come?

"Where in Mexico did you come from?" demanded French hoarsely.

She found her voice. "That doesn't matter. You stay where you are!" she cried, the fire dashing from her eyes in the moonlight.

XX

The effect of Tilatha's sudden appearance, of her command, was startling. The wild frontier always respected good women. They were as safe as though they were in God's pocket. The worst outlaw, if there was any basis of manhood in him, would go far to aid and succor any of them in need. This girl's youth, her charming heroism, enhanced by the simple white dress she wore, touched by the magic of moonlight, reached them as though they had been well-calculated stage devices.

Even Curt French was taken aback. He glared sullenly at her, while his slow brain groped with the problem. A bully and ruffian, a killer never deterred by moral distinctions as to fair play, his impulse was to crush her and push on to his purpose. But he knew that would not do. Vaguely he was aware that the men behind him were sentimentalizing the situation. She was not just a fool girl to them; she was for the moment the embodiment of an ideal they had been cherishing in their hearts through the sodden years.

"Now, missie, you-all better run along some-wheres. We 'low to have a li'l' talk with your friend," he wheedled. "Jest a li'l' talk about business, y'understand."

"No . . . stand back!" Her refusal went past him to the men behind. It was as though she knew that she might win them, if not their leader.

"We know he's backin' up this killer Sibley," someone flung back.

"But he just asked you to wait, not to make up your minds too soon. I'm only a girl. I don't know anything about it." Her voice broke in a little wail. She was doing a little play-acting now—aware that sometimes a woman's weakness is her greatest strength.

"This here is a he-man town," another man growled. "We don't aim to let him run it like a kids' school an' then renig when he feels like it."

"Cripes, no!" French flung out an oath. "Nor can he hide behind a woman's skirt. Outta the way, girl. We won't hurt you none, but we aim to get Turley."

He took two steps forward, then stopped. Someone had come around the corner of the building, vaulted lightly to the porch, and was standing beside Tilatha.

The killer's jaw dropped. Never in his turbulent life had he met such a surprise as this. The man who had joined the girl was Boone Sibley.

It was a murmur to begin with, the sound that swept the crowd, then, as the name passed from one to another, it became a roar. Before the harsh menace of it Tilatha shrank back, appalled. But not the Texan. He faced the rising storm of rage silently, his eyes undaunted, poised figure motionless. He made no gesture toward a weapon.

The house door opened. Mobeetie Bill came out, caught Tilatha by the shoulders, whirled her bodily, and pushed her into the passage. He grinned at Boone. "Looks like a pleasant time was gonna be had by all," he drawled.

"What are you doing here?" demanded Boone.

"Or you, comin' down to cases?" the old man retorted. His faded blue eyes were blazing with excitement.

There was an upheaval in the mob, a shrill outcry, and from it broke two men. They ran past French to the porch.

"Not the right fellow!" one screamed, while the other shouted: "We're alibi-in' this bird." They were the two old prospectors, Hassayampa Pete and Toughfoot Bozeman.

French threw a wild shot from the holster—a second—a third. In the moonlight his distorted shadow was like some malignant creature conjured from hell.

Mobeetie Bill tried to steady himself, caught at the wall, began to slide down. With incredible swiftness Boone's Colt was out and booming. He fired twice, then stopped.

French had dropped his six-shooter and was clutching at his elbow, face distorted with pain.

A voice shouted. "Stop shootin'! Listen! Listen to me, you damn' fools!" It was Sheriff Brady pushing through the crowd, his hands raised. "Listen! Listen!"

Hassayampa Pete had snatched up the fallen gun of the killer. Boone dropped the barrel of his revolver toward the floor and stood waiting. French cursed bitterly, savagely.

"Listen, you wooden heads!" the sheriff ordered, his words carrying to everyone present. "He's not the man that killed Buck . . . this Sibley here. Not the guy that held up the stage. Him nor Dusty, neither. They were forty miles away at the time . . . in the desert near Sugarloaf, talking to Pete and Bozeman at their camp when the stage was stopped. Step up, Bozeman. You tell 'em."

Bozeman told them, and after him Hassayampa Pete. Sibley's alibi was established beyond doubt.

"Who did it, then," someone demanded sullenly, "since you know so doggone' much, Brady?"

"I'll tell you tomorrow," the sheriff answered. Then abruptly he added: "Don't you, Curt. Don't you! I'll sure drop you in your tracks." Brady had snatched out his gun and was covering French. The bad man had drawn a long-barreled .45 from under his shoulder. He had done it with his left hand, awkwardly and slowly, because his right was disabled.

"Take that gun from him, someone," the sheriff ordered. "You . . . with the brown hat . . . take it. And bring it here."

"I'll sure fix you for this, Brady," the bad man swore, "if it's the last thing I ever do."

The sheriff did not answer him. He addressed the crowd. "You better drift, boys, don't you reckon? You're doing yourselves no good here. Turley was right. He told the truth, but you were hell-bent on believing Sibley guilty. So you had to get all het up and go off half-cocked. I sure hope you-all are proud of yourselves. Me, I'd say you ought to be put to bed and spanked real thorough."

Someone laughed and broke the tension. From that moment the danger was past. The crowd began to thin away. French went, nursing his elbow and threatening vengeance.

Already Boone was on his knees, supporting the old buffalo hunter. "Hit bad, old-timer?" he asked in a low voice.

Mobeetie Bill's cracked laugh answered: "Not bad, Texas man, but good . . . good an' thorough. I got aplenty."

Boone picked him up, carried him into the house. Gently he put the old man down on the bed. Tilatha administered first aid.

"Has someone gone for a doctor?" Turley asked.

"No use," the old fellow answered. "I'm headin' fast for the divide. You stay with me, Texas man. The trail's gettin' steep . . . an' it's dark. I got to find the way home." Already his mind was beginning to wander.

"I'll go get Doc," Sheriff Brady said.

"My bronc' must've piled me," the wounded man murmured, his hand against his side. "I'm right bad hurt, seems like . . . all stove up inside. . . . The greasers are crowdin' us, boys. Look out." Vaguely his mind was in the past. "Dark tonight, sure enough . . . but . . . right clost to home." His feeble voice rang firmer. "I drew a black bean, boys. Suits me fine. So long. Well, I'm ready, you damn' greasers." Presently he tried to raise himself without success. He waved a weak arm. The old Rebel yell quavered in his throat.

Ten minutes later he passed away.

Tilatha looked up at Boone. "Has he . . . gone?"

The Texan looked at her and nodded. Her eyes misted. "Don't you feel bad," he said in a murmur. "He wouldn't've had it different, not if he could have chosen for himself."

Turley looked at the old wrinkled face lying on the pillow, and he was greatly moved. "He died on my account . . . came to warn me what they were going to do."

The Texan smoothed back gently the old-timer's scant gray hair. "He'd say it was all right, if he was alive to tell you. No kick coming from him. He took his fighting chance, like any man has got to do. Maybe he knows how we feel."

"It's terrible." The girl shook.

The young man differed. "No, it's not terrible.

He had to die soon, and this was the way it was coming to him . . . the one way he would have wanted it to be. He wouldn't have asked a better break. You see, miss, he was one of the old Lone Star State fighting crowd, and you can't say better than that of anyone. You tell 'em in your paper tomorrow, Mister Turley, that he knew Travis and Bowie and Crockett and fought with 'em. Tell 'em the story of the black bean."

The Adam's apple in Turley's throat shot up and down spasmodically. "I'll do just that," he promised.

They moved toward the other room, the lamp in the editor's hand. The Mexican woman drew Turley to one side to discuss arrangements with him. The two went into the kitchen, leaving Boone and Tilatha together in the moonlit bedroom.

The girl looked up at the young Texan, gifts of admiration and gratitude in her eyes. Boone wanted to thank her for her act at Galeyville.

The door of the room opened. Doc Peters walked in, followed by Hugh McLennon.

The doctor moved to the bed the instant he came into the room. Now he spoke, very quietly: "My patient is past needing me, Miss McLennon."

Tilatha turned to him with a nod. "Yes, I know," she said.

XXI

Alive, Mobeetie Bill had been of no importance in the community, nothing but a garrulous old-timer who filled a chair on the sidewalk in front of the Dallas House and told cheerful reminiscences of the good old days. He had been a bullwhacker and a muleskinner, a buffalo hunter and a soldier. His life had been an adventurous one, but the younger generation often was in too much of a hurry to listen to his comments on the passing show as illustrated by experience.

Dead, he had been for a day the most important figure in Tough Nut. The circumstances of his going might not have occasioned much discussion if Turley had not dramatized the event in the *Gold Pocket*.

Old Mobeetie Bill would have been much embarrassed if he could have read what was there said about him. He would have called it "guff". It would have seemed to him like boasting, even though another man had written the account.

There was a sketchy story of his life, pieced together from information dropped by him at various times. This followed the lead covering his death. On the editorial page was a black-bordered box enclosing a tribute to him headed MOBEETIE BILL DRAWS A BLACK BEAN. The editorial ran:

We called him Mobeetie Bill because he came to us from the Panhandle. He was a Texan and proud of it. We never knew him by his real name William Blake until after his death. Nor did we know that in the days when Travis and Bowie and Crockett fought for the freedom of the Lone Star State, they hailed him comrade. He lived an adventurous life, and as he lived, he died. So he would have had it. Pioneer, soldier, buffalo hunter, freighter, he played always a man's part.

Nearly fifty years ago William Blake rode with Ewan Cameron when his expedition crossed the border in pursuit of marauding thieves. The story of that unfortunate raid, filled with highlights of tragedy and heroism, deserves to rank in some ways with that of the Alamo. The invaders were captured and ordered flung into dungeons with the lowest criminals. They overcame their armed guard and escaped to the mountains. Some few reached the border, but most of them were recaptured after desperate resistance.

General Santa Anna, in reprisal, ordered the Texans decimated. Their individual fate was determined by lottery. Each man drew a bean from a sack. If the bean was white, he lived; if it was black, he died.

The story is that the Texans went to that fatal lottery as though it had been a game. They jested as they drew the beans that meant life or death. One of them, George Bibb Crittenden, later a Confederate general in our Civil War, gave the white bean he had drawn to a comrade who had wife and children, with the remark that since he was unmarried he could afford to take another chance. William Blake was fortunate enough to get one of the white beans that meant life. Years later he was freed from a Mexican dungeon.

The last words of Mobeetie Bill were that he had drawn a black bean. He smiled when he said it. Never a man passed into the unknown with soul less troubled. God rest our gallant old friend. He died to help a girl and an unarmed man.

Tough Nut read the story and the editorial, and the effect was immediate. Drunkards wept maudlin tears over their rum. Miners agreed that he sure was a good old donker and it was a damned shame. Women grew sentimental and busied themselves about the funeral. Citizens affirmed, not too loudly, that something ought to be done about the killing.

Almost everybody in town, with the exception of Curt French, attended the funeral. The Quinns,

225

their cousin Elder, Bob Hardy, and Brad Prouty were there in a body. In an attempt to stem the tide of public opinion, Whip had announced that he would pay all expenses of the interment. This gesture cost him nothing, since Sibley, Peters, and Turley, all present as pallbearers, had already settled with the undertaker.

Whatever the intentions of the Quinns might have been as to Sibley, these had temporarily to be postponed. It would not do just now to precipitate trouble. The town was in no mood to permit it.

"Right soon folks will be over this sentimental jag," Whip told his brother and French. "Then we'll talk turkey to this pilgrim."

"And what if he talks turkey to us first?" Curt wanted to know from the bed on which he lay. "They say Brady has done made him a deputy. What in Mexico does that mean if not trouble?"

Whip looked down at him blackly. "There wouldn't have been any trouble if you and Sing hadn't robbed the stage, or if you hadn't got drunk and killed Buck. Or even then, if you hadn't bought that fool pendant for Faro Kate with the greenbacks. And if that ain't enough, you've got to get drunk again and bump off old Mobeetie Bill, instead of Sibley. By God, Curt, you sure wear your welcome out amongst your friends."

"Don't pull your picket pin, Whip, and go to snortin'," answered French, scowling sulkily. "I had bad luck. I ain't denyin' it, am I?"

226

"You made your own bad luck, and ours, too. Now we've got to back your fool plays and bluff our way through. This last week you've done nothing but get us in bad. Right now we're mighty unpopular, and you especial. It's got to stop, Curt, unless you want to go it alone without us."

"Was it me fixed up to tar and feather Turley and run him outta town?"

"No, but it was you got drunk and killed old Bill," Whip answered curtly.

"I noticed none of you Quinns was on the job that night," French jeered. "Not a one of you."

"You needn't have been, either. I told you to stay out of it and let the crowd do the work for us, but, no! You were hell-bent on being in it. Consequence was, you kill Mobeetie Bill, and Sibley shows you up like a busted flush."

"Me! Me! Shows me up?" roared the bully. "Goddlemighty, Whip, you can't talk that-a-way to me."

Quinn's bleak eyes met the furious ones of the wounded man. "What you mean I can't, Curt? I'm tellin' you what this whole town is sayin'. Make your choice, and make it quick. Do like I tell you from right damn' now, or play a lone hand."

"Me afraid of that pilgrim, by . . ."

"I didn't say that. I said that so far he'd taken every trick . . . and he has. It'll be your turn later . . . maybe. Question is, are you quittin' all this foolishness, or ain't you?"

"I'll sure make that bird climb a tree when my arm gets right," French bragged. "If anyone thinks different . . ."

"Not the point right now, Curt. Answer my question. Are you gonna let me play the hand from now on? If you trail with our outfit, you've got to take orders."

"Take orders! Where do you get that talk from, Whip? I never have took orders. I never will. Far as this stage hold-up goes, Sing is in deep as I am. Don't you forget that for a minute, Whip. If they hang it on me, they're gonna hang it on him, too. You can bet your boots on that."

Whip looked at him with a steady, unfathomable gaze. Something about it made the wounded man uncomfortable. Yet all Quinn said in a quiet low voice was: "Suits me if it does you, Curt."

"'Course, I don't aim to make any trouble," French added by way of concession. "But if you try to make me the goat, I'll squeal sure."

"I'll see you don't," Quinn returned quietly.

The other man, meeting those cold black eyes, felt a chill run down his spine. He did not know that he had just condemned himself to death.

What French had said was true. After the funeral Sheriff Brady had offered Boone a position as deputy, and the Texan had accepted it.

"I'm gonna call for a showdown," Brady said.

"We'll arrest Curt for killing old Bill, then we'll spring it that he shot Buck Galway, too. I want a deputy back of me who'll stay put."

"Have you figured how you're gonna arrest him without the Quinns taking a hand?" Boone asked. "Don't forget their cousin Sing was in it. I'll say that for the Quinns . . . they back their friends."

"My notion is to drive up to the Widow Slater's, where he's got a room, right after suppertime. You'll stay outside with the buckboard and I'll bring French out. Then we'll take a back street to the jail. It'll be kinda dark, anyhow."

"We may have to hog-tie him if he's obstinate."

"That'll be up to him. If he acts up, he'll get what any other bummer would. I'm through kowtowing to him and his friends," the sheriff said.

It was growing dark when two men in a buckboard left the Buffalo Corral, drove up Howard Street, turned to the left at Piñon, and drew up in front of the Widow Slater's house. The taller one of the two waited outside, while the shorter one went into the front yard and knocked on the front door.

Mrs. Slater opened to the knock.

"Good evening, ma'am," the visitor said. "I'm Sheriff Brady. I'd like to talk to Curt. . . . No, you needn't tell him I'm here. I'll just drop in on him. . . . This room? Much obliged, ma'am."

French was playing, awkwardly and slowly, a one-handed game of solitaire, using the bed quilt for a table. He looked up when the sheriff entered. His jaw dropped. He cursed as his left hand dived under the pillow.

The sheriff had him covered. "Empty, Curt, empty. Bring your hand out empty. I don't want to plug you. . . . That's the idea."

"Whatchawant?" the bad man growled, in one word.

"You, Curt. I'm arresting you for killing old Bill."

"Had his gun out, hadn't he?"

"Not so I could notice it . . . till after you began to shoot."

"Well, he had . . . him and that Sibley, too."

"You'll get a chance to tell the judge that, Curt. Lucky you're dressed. We got a rig out front for you."

"I'm not gonna stand for that, Brady. You can't get biggity with me. I've killed guys for less."

"That's why I'm arresting you. No use belly-aching, Curt. You're going with me."

French hesitated, then admitted defeat in a fury of anger. "Oncet I get out, Brady, I'll kill you on sight."

"You're not out yet. You're just going in. Here's your hat."

Sullenly the killer moved to the door, passed into the other room, and out of the house. He drew back when he caught sight of the driver on the buckboard.

"So you're in this," he snarled. "It's a frame-up to gun me whilst you've got the dead wood on me."

"Get in that buckboard and don't be a fool, Curt," the sheriff ordered. "You'll get a fair run for your money and that's a lot more than you'd give either one of us."

By back streets Boone drove the buckboard to the jail. Once, French shouted to a man he knew: "Tell Whip Quinn this . . . sheriff slipped up whilst I was sleepin' and is takin' me to jail."

Brady took his prisoner upstairs and locked him in a cell. All the time the vitriolic tongue of the bad man flung blistering epithets at him. The officer paid not the least attention. Presently he rejoined Sibley downstairs in the office.

"I reckon now we can begin to look for trouble," he said to his new deputy.

"Trouble on our trail, sure enough. Question is, what kind? I hardly think the Quinns are ripe for shooting yet, not in public, anyhow. Whip's too smart for that. He knows the town wouldn't like it, and he's not ready to ride roughshod over public opinion. Not for a while, anyhow."

"My notion, too, but you never can tell. It'll be some kind of law move first, don't you reckon? Bly eats outta the Quinns' hands. He's the J.P."

"Maybeso."

"Unless Russ or Sing hear we've arrested

231

Curt before Whip does. They're liable to come a-shooting, either one or both."

Within the hour Whip Quinn and Bob Hardy, accompanied by Justice of the Peace Bly and Dugan of the express company, were in the office of the sheriff.

"What's this grand-stand play, Brady?" demanded Whip harshly. "You know you can't make it stick."

The officer ignored the curtness of Quinn's voice and manner. "I'm sheriff, Whip. The boys elected me to enforce the law. I aim to do it. So I had to arrest Curt for killing Mobeetie Bill. That's reasonable, ain't it?"

"Did you have to sneak up on him when he was alone and asleep? Why not arrest him open and aboveboard, if it was a straight game?"

"I arrested him open enough, and he wasn't asleep, either."

For the first time since he had come into the room, Whip let his black eyes rest on Boone. "If you didn't aim this at us, Brady, why for did you get this Texas warrior to help you?"

"I know a good man when I see him, Whip."

"You know a man who is our enemy, and you pick him for your deputy . . . a man accused of murder and robbery. What am I to think of that?" Beneath the heavy black brows Whip's dark sunken eyes blazed. The fingers of his left hand nursed the imperial below the tight thin lips.

"You've always been against us, Brady. You're showin' your hand now because you think we're in a jam."

"Nothing to that, Whip," the sheriff denied. "Live and let live. That's my motto. As to what you say about Sibley, he's been cleared of the stage hold-up. If he's your enemy, I don't know it. I made him my deputy because he'll do to take along, if you want to know."

"Cleared by a coupla old desert rats you could buy for a pint of red-eye," Whip flung back bitterly. "We've not come to the end of that road yet. What's your play, Brady? Why are you standin' in with this Texas killer? That's the question folks are askin'."

Brady had been brought up on the fighting frontier. He was a quiet man, one who preferred always to side-step trouble when he could. But he was no coward. Now anger burned in his face. "They're asking another question, Whip," he retorted hardily. "They're asking where Curt French got the ten marked twenty-dollar bills that fellow Lacy lost when the stage was robbed?"

Whip glared at him. For a moment an explosion seemed imminent.

Then Dugan cut in suavely: "One moment, gentlemen. Do you claim, Sheriff, that Curt French was one of the stage hold-ups?"

"I claim the evidence points to him."

233

Dugan had no more to say. He looked at Bob Hardy, a triumphant little smile twitching at his lips.

Hardy was a smaller man than the Quinns. He had come from a city of the Middle West, and he lacked the brawn and sinew that an outdoor life had given his friends. But his skim-milk shallow eyes were cold and hard. Now he stepped forward and took the stage. "I want Curt, Sheriff, for robbing the United States mail. This is a federal case, and it takes precedence of any claim you may have on him."

Brady stared at the deputy marshal, taken aback by the audacity of the demand. Yet he was not sure that he could deny the legality of Hardy's position. As a representative of the United States government he had a right to take French in charge, very likely had a prior right to his own. He played for time.

"Kinda sudden this, Bob. But look at it this-a-way. Murder is a more serious offense than robbing the mails. Couldn't that come first?" His perplexed doubt was offered to the company at large, but his eyes turned to Sibley to learn what he thought of it.

"Looks so to me, but I'm no lawyer," Boone answered.

"Fellow, you're not in this," the marshal said to Sibley insolently. "Brady, use your head. The government has a murder charge, too. This hold-up killed Buck Galway, didn't he? And Buck was guarding the mails."

"Do you claim you're arresting French for that?" the sheriff asked skeptically.

"I'm arresting him because you say you've got evidence against him. Have you? Or are you four-flushing?"

"I have. Considerable of it."

"Then that's enough. I want my prisoner."

The sheriff looked down at the table as though he could gather wisdom from it. Doggedly he said: "I got to have some kind of legal paper, even if you're right."

Hardy handed to Brady a document demanding the body of French.

The county officer read it, still uncertain whether it was effective in law. He grinned a little, to palliate the effect of his words. "'Course, you may be running a shenanigan on me, Whip. Looks like you got the dead wood on me right now, if you got a right to serve this paper on me."

"Ask Bly," Whip said scornfully. "He drew it up, and it's gonna stick."

"It'll stick if I'm convinced it's OK," Brady said stoutly.

"Then I'd advise you to be convinced," Quinn flung back.

"Don't get on the prod, boys," the justice of the peace advised. "It's a perfectly good order of the court, Brady. You got no option but to honor it."

Again the sheriff looked toward his deputy, found no suggestion in Sibley's wooden countenance, and decided to give way.

"All right, Bob. You can have him. Want to keep him in the jail here?"

"No, sir."

Brady looked at Boone. "Bring him down, Sibley."

Five minutes later the small group of Quinn adherents went away jubilantly, French in their midst. The prisoner left some threats for the sheriff and his deputy to ponder over. He swore either to run them out of town, or see them planted in Boot Hill.

Boone observed that Whip Quinn did not echo any of his henchman's wild talk. In fact, he made one sharp criticism. "That's plumb foolish talk, Curt. You're shootin' off your mouth a heap much when it's not necessary."

Later Boone wondered why Whip had declared himself thus publicly. Was he getting ready an alibi against the day when he might need one?

XXII

With a caution not in the least obvious, Boone walked the streets of Tough Nut. His bearing, his strong stride, held the easy confidence of one at peace with the world. Yet he knew that at any moment a bullet might come whistling from door or window at him. French had been released on bond given by Whip Quinn and his man, Bly, and he was breathing vengeance threats at every gambling house. Probably he would wait until his shooting arm was healed, but his impatience might outweigh his discretion. The man's vanity had been affronted. The Texan guessed that he would be simmering with rage until he had wiped the slate clean.

The Quinns and their other adherents, too, had to be reckoned with as enemies, though Boone did not expect any of them to pot him from ambush. They were too arrogant and self-confident for that. They would set the scene for a battle, take whatever odds they could, but they would fight in the open.

In front of Jefford's, Boone met the two old prospectors who had come to town to testify in his behalf. He stopped and shook hands. "I haven't told you-all yet how much obliged I am for your good word the other night in front of Turley's place," he said.

"*Humph!* Nothin' to that, fellow," snorted Hassayampa Pete. "You hadn't paid us yet for our time an' expense stickin' around town. If you'd got shot up, we'd've been out what all is comin' to us."

"Y'betcha!" agreed his partner. "An' what I can hear . . . you ain't any too damn' good a risk now. Don't you reckon you better settle with us immediate before anything happens?"

Boone smiled. These gnarled old desert rats would hate to admit they had helped him out of friendliness. "Suits me. What's the damage?"

"Oh, well, we don't aim to break you," Pete said, and named a sum astonishingly low.

Boone paid it, thanked them, and went on his way. They were good old scouts even though they harshly denied it.

At the post office Boone saw Tilatha McLennon. An underlying glow of carmine streamed into her cheeks. She knew this, and it annoyed her. In answer to his greeting she bowed stiffly.

Boone got his mail and returned to the doorway. He ripped open a letter from his mother, but his eyes followed the figure that moved down the street with such light grace and supple movement. She walked as though she loved the air and the sunshine, as though she were kin to all wild free things.

He put the letter back in his pocket, stepped out,

and presently was beside her. She turned, a hard, lively light in the eyes beneath the finely arched brows.

"Like to say a few words to you, Miss McLennon," he said, lifting his wide hat.

"There's nothing preventing you, is there?"

Unfortunately he smiled. She was so uncompromisingly hostile. At once he knew that smile had been a mistake. The stab of her eyes, which had in them little tawny flecks matching the hair of lustrous copper, dared him to be amused at her. He did not say at once what he had come to say. Instead he asked her a question.

"Why do you hate me so?"

"Hate you! I don't hate you. But it's just like you to flatter yourself that I do. You're so . . . so important, aren't you?" She flung it at him insultingly, with a flare of feminine ferocity.

Her manner puzzled him. He did not see any justification for it. Why did she always clash with him whenever they came together? Was it for his own good that she . . . ?

"Am I?" He smiled again. For the life of him he couldn't help it. She was so direct and uncompromising.

"I suppose you think . . . because people talk about you . . . that you're a great man and can strut around. . . ."

"So I strut, too, do I?" He strangled a desire to shout with laughter.

She understood his reaction, and it irritated her the more, drove her on to a further exhibition of temper that later she would lash herself for. "You're hateful," she told him.

"I see. I'm hateful, but you don't hate me," he drawled.

Two defiant stars flashed at him. "I never knew a man so . . . so . . ." She stopped, for sheer inadequacy of expression.

"All right, Miss McLennon, I'm conceited and I strut and I'm hateful. We'll let it go at that, unless you'd like to free your mind real thorough. But I'm not ungrateful. I haven't had a chance yet to thank you for what you did for me at Galeyville. I'm thanking you now. Hadn't been for you, I'd never have reached the roof in time, and if I had, I'd never have made a getaway without your pony."

Under the direct look of his steady gray eyes she felt her blood flutter. Somehow he had disarmed her anger at once.

"Billy got back," she said irrelevantly, not knowing what else to say.

"I never saw the like of it . . . you coming across the roofs to pull me outta the tightest hole I was ever in. Twice I'd told you I didn't want your help. But I took it, and mighty glad to get it. So no matter how hateful I am, you'll know that once I wasn't strutting."

This time she did not mind his smile. She liked

it. There was something warm and winning in it that went straight to her hammering heart. This cold, hard man had never offered her friendship before, if he was really offering that now.

Her eyes fell. "I don't think you're hateful always," she said.

"That's something." He laughed. "Anyhow, I got it said, what I've been wanting to tell you."

"There's something I wanted to tell you, that first night we met, but I didn't say it. You wouldn't let me . . . at least, I thought you wouldn't. It hurt my feelings because you acted as though it didn't much matter whether you had rescued me or not. And first thing I knew I was mad at you."

"There seems almost always to be a breeze when you and I are in the same neighborhood," he commented.

"I don't know how to say thank you nicely, the way some girls do. I'm too independent, maybe."

"You're criticizing, Miss McLennon, I'm not."

"And I fly off the handle so. I've always had my own way too much, I reckon."

He had nothing to say about that. Tilatha took his silence as condemnation. Boone was about to leave her.

They had walked to the end of a side street that looked down into the valley and across to the mountains beyond. He lifted his hat and turned to go.

Out of the last house on the street came Russ Quinn. He stopped in his stride to stare at them, in the middle of the road, directly in the path of Boone. There was in his attitude the menace of a hesitation that might in an instant leap to action.

Boone moved forward evenly, eyes fixed on the face of his foe.

"Russ!" the girl cried in warning.

Already Quinn had read the meaning of the girl's stormy face. They had been quarreling, these two. He moved aside and swept his hat off in a bow to the Texan. "Not yet, Mister Sibley," he jeered. "It'll be some other day for you and me."

"You'll find me waiting at the gate, sir," Boone said quietly.

"Any time, any place, Texas warrior."

Boone did not look back, but he knew Russ Quinn had joined Tilatha.

XXIII

Sheriff Brady took the stage and train to Tucson. Casually he mentioned at the Last Chance that he was going to run down a tip he had been given as to the whereabouts of a horse thief wanted in Cochise. His real purpose was to consult a lawyer in whom he had confidence as to his status in the Curt French case. It would be strange, he thought, if the law was so written that a man could walk the streets undisturbed with two separate murder charges hanging over his head.

The sheriff was back in Tough Nut next day, his mind made up as to what he could and could not do.

"Matlock says if Curt is free, we can arrest him," Brady told Boone. "If the government wants to sit in, it will have to bring charges against him in the proper legal way. Bob Hardy hasn't done that. He doesn't aim to put any charges on record at all. Well, we'll arrest Curt again and make the Quinns show their hand. They'll have to put chips in the pot, if they want to draw cards."

"Sounds reasonable."

"Anything happen while I was away?"

"Not much. Quiet all along the Potomac. Oh, one little thing, which may or may not be important.

Sing Elder had words with Curt French at the Occidental. Don't know what the row was about."

"You can guess, can't you?"

"If I was guessing, I'd say Sing was some sore at Curt for balling up that little business they were on the other day. I'll lay a two-bit bet with you, Sheriff, Curt ain't going to lie down in brotherly love with the Quinns much longer."

"No takers present. Now, about this arrest. The sooner, the quicker. Why not now?"

"You're boss of this roundup, Sheriff. Now it is."

They made what preparations were necessary and started on their way.

"He'd ought to be getting around to the gambling houses about this time of night," Brady said.

They did not find him at Dolan's Palace, but Boone saw there a man he had met in the hills, Tom Tracy. His arm was in a sling from the wound he had received during the attack on the Mexicans.

"How's Dusty Rhodes getting along?" the Texan asked him.

"I'm not keeping cases on Dusty," the man answered sourly. "Ask Tilatha McLennon, if you're anxious to know. I hear she nursed him real tender."

"Better look cheerful when you talk about Miss McLennon," Boone advised him coldly. "Some of her friends might misunderstand your manner."

"Do you claim to be one of them?" Tracy asked insolently. "She has some right ornery ones."

"We'll not discuss Miss McLennon here, Tracy."

The cowboy looked at him and started to say something, then changed his mind. He wanted to be ugly, but the steely eyes daunted him. This Sibley was no kind of pilgrim to work off his temper on. Moreover, at that precise moment he heard the sheriff put a question to the bartender. In a low voice, Brady asked if Curt French had been around that evening.

Tracy glanced at the sheriff and back at the deputy, murmured an indistinct defiance, and withdrew from talk. A moment later he departed by the back door.

"That fellow Tracy has gone to warn French we're out after him, looks to me," Boone said to his chief as the cowboy slipped out. "We better get right busy."

They tried Jefford's and the Last Chance. French had not been in either place. "Liable to be at home yet," one faro dealer said to Boone, a gleam of malice in his eye. "He don't get around so much since . . . since his accident."

The officers walked to the house where French roomed.

"Better wait here and get him as he comes out," the sheriff decided. "He won't be surprised in his room a second time."

Boone did not answer. He was listening. Voices

from within the house came to them, harsh, menacing voices. A shot rang out, two more almost together, then a fourth. There came the sound of running feet—and silence. For a moment they could see shadowy figures vanishing into the darkness.

"Went out the back door, whoever they were," the sheriff said.

"In a sure enough hurry, too. Not waiting for the neighbors to gather."

Brady drew his Colt .45 and trod softly toward the house.

"Won't need that, I reckon," Boone said in his ear. "Still, might as well play it safe."

"You figure he's gone," the sheriff whispered.

The Texan looked at him queerly. "Yes, gone."

"If Tracy was here to warn him, what was the shooting about?"

"Tracy wasn't here."

Boone tried the front door, turned the knob gently, and tiptoed in. From under the door of the bad man's bedroom came a gleam of lamplight. The officers moved gingerly across the floor. One of the boards squeaked. Brady motioned to his deputy to give him right of way. The sheriff felt for the latch, raised it slowly, and flung the door open.

He stood in the doorway, crouched, wary, revolver in hand. "We've got you, French. Don't . . ." The words died in his mouth.

Boone looked over his shoulder. A man lay face down, half on the bed and half on the floor. The fingers of the left hand still clutched a six-shooter. His legs were sprawled out awkwardly. The bandaged right arm hung lax. In the supine body was no sign of life. Neither of the officers needed to turn over the bearded face to know that this was Curt French.

"They got him right," Brady said.

Boone examined the weapon. "He fired once. A bullet struck the floor over there, probably his, after he was hit, likely. . . . See, they hit him three times . . . here and here and once in the throat."

The sheriff agreed. "The last shot after he was down. They intended to make sure."

"They were thorough . . . figured that a dead man couldn't do 'em any more harm and that a live one might upset their apple cart."

"The Quinns did it, you think?"

"Heard from Tracy we were gonna arrest French and beat us to it. Maybe they didn't intend to kill him, only to make sure he'd keep still, but when he acted ugly they let him have it. You can't tell. Might have been that way."

"Which of the Quinns?"

"When we find out which ones Tracy met when he reached the Occidental . . ."

"How do you know he went to the Occidental?"

"He'd head straight for there, wouldn't he? Since he scouted up the alley, he wouldn't meet any of 'em before he reached there, chances are."

"It had got to where the Quinns had to kill him, you figure."

"Don't it look that-a-way? Maybe not the Quinns, but some of their friends. He got 'em into this jam . . . first by getting drunk and killing Buck Galway, next by buying the jewelry with the marked bills, then by shooting Mobeetie Bill. He'd gone wild. They couldn't control him any longer, and they didn't know what he would do or say. They had to get rid of him or light out themselves. Naturally they bumped him off."

"Well, he was a bad citizen. He was after your scalp and mine. I won't mourn him any."

"Nor I. He was a killer of the worst kind . . . irresponsible. He killed when there wasn't any need of it. You could never tell when he would break loose. I expect he would have got me if the Quinns hadn't held him back."

"He died with a gun in his hand. We can't prove he didn't fire the first shot."

"No, I don't reckon he did, but we can't prove it."

For some moments they had heard voices outside. Now someone called to them, asking what the trouble was.

The sheriff went to the door. "You can come in, boys, far as the inner room. Curt French has been killed by parties unknown. Don't come any closer. I want the coroner to look things over first."

The men in the doorway stared at the figure lying on the edge of the bed.

"Who killed him?" someone asked presently.

"Your guess is as good as ours, Hartley," the sheriff answered. "We found him dead when we got here. We had come to arrest him."

"Missus Slater had gone to prayer meeting. She always does Wednesday evenings," a neighbor contributed.

"Too bad she wasn't here. She would have known who was with Curt," Brady said.

One man rubbed his chin and sidled a look at him, another at Boone. There was suspicion in those furtive glances. "Doncha reckon they chose a time when they knew she'd be out?" he asked.

"Don't know a thing about that, Hartley. Would you mind bringing Meade up?" Meade was coroner and undertaker. "Now I'll have to ask you boys to get out for a while."

"Just a moment, Hartley," demurred Boone in his low even voice. "Might as well take a look at our guns before you go . . . the sheriff's and mine."

Brady looked at him, surprised. He had not caught, as the Texan had, those looks of veiled suspicion. "What for?" he asked bluntly.

"Some folks might claim we did it, Sheriff, as

the easiest way to get rid of him. Better set all minds at rest about that right now."

Boone handed his revolver to Hartley. The man examined it. The hammer rested on an unloaded chamber. The other five held cartridges.

"Not been fired recently," Hartley reported, showing the six-shooter to the others present.

Then the weapon of the sheriff was passed from one to another.

"Now make sure we're not carrying any other concealed guns," Boone said.

Hartley patted the bodies of both the sheriff and the deputy.

"Curt had been making his threats everywhere about what all he was aimin' to do to both of you," someone said. "If you'd killed him, any jury would have said self-defense, and there wouldn't have been any complaints from decent citizens."

"Only we didn't kill him," Boone replied. "That's the point we're making clear."

"Who did, d'you reckon?" blurted out a little fat man, one whose curiosity and instinct for gossip outran discretion.

The sheriff, face immobile, eyes cold and blank, looked at him. "You tell us," he suggested.

XXIV

Tom Tracy stepped out from the Bohemian Theatre and turned his steps down Apache Street. It was nothing to him that the sky was full of stars and that a lovers' moon rode the heavens, that a faint breath of wind carried with it the low murmur of pines. What he wanted to hear was the rattle of poker chips; what he wanted to see was an ace full pinched closely in his hands.

Light swift footsteps sounded behind him. A voice drawled in his ear. " 'Evenin', Mister Tracy. Walk with you, if you don't mind."

Tracy's hangdog look took in Boone Sibley. "I'm particular who I walk with," he blustered.

The Texan laughed. "So am I . . . sometimes, and since we're both . . ."

"I'm not lookin' for your company, sir."

"Well, I'm looking for yours," Boone told him.

The cowboy stopped. "Meanin' what?"

"Like to have a few moments' conversation with you at the sheriff's office."

"You arrestin' me? What for?"

"I didn't say so. Want to ask some questions, that's all," Boone told him.

"Ask 'em here," Tracy said belligerently.

"I mentioned the sheriff's office."

251

"You got another mention comin', fellow. I ain't goin' there. You got no right to take me."

"I reckon I have. Anyhow, that's the way it'll be."

Stormily Tracy glared at him. Surges of rage swept him but did not reach the point of explosion. There was something about this long Texan that daunted him. He dared not call for a showdown. "You can't take me without a warrant," he protested.

"Turn to the left here," Boone said in an even, matter-of-fact voice that had compulsion back of it.

Tracy hesitated, then with an oath did as directed.

The sheriff was reading the evening paper in his office. He took his feet down from the desk and nodded amiably at Tracy.

"'Lo, Tom. How's your arm coming?"

"Bring me here to ask me that?" growled the cowboy.

"Other things, too." The sheriff put his arms on the desk, leaned forward, and looked hard at the cowboy. "After you left Dolan's a while ago and went to the Occidental, you met Sing Elder and Brad Prouty. The three of you went outside together. Where did you go?"

"Say, what's it to you, Brady?" bristled the hill man. "Do we have to ask you where all we can go?"

"We know what you told 'em. That's not important. Point is, where did you leave 'em and when?"

"I ain't said I was with 'em a-tall. None of your business whether I was or wasn't. I choose my own friends, Mister Sheriff."

Brady nodded to himself, apparently as though this confirmed something he had in mind. "We'll lock this fellow up in a cell, Sibley."

"What for?" demanded the cowboy.

"For the murder of Curt French."

Tracy's jaw dropped. He stared at Brady, eyes wide with astonishment. "Curt French . . . dead?" he got out incredulously.

"Where have you been the last hour and a half, Tom?" the sheriff asked.

"Why, I been in a box at the Bohemian, drinkin' beer with one of the house girls."

Boone said: "All OK. I've checked up on that."

"When did you get to the Bohemian?" the sheriff asked Tracy.

"I dunno exactly. Right after I left Sing and Brad."

"And where was that?"

The cowboy grew cautious. He had not meant to make that admission, though he did not know what the sheriff was after. It had been surprised out of him by the impact on his mind of stunning news, that French had been killed and he was charged with the crime.

"What you drivin' at, Brady? Do you claim I killed Curt French . . . if he's dead?"

"The story has been on the streets an hour, Tom. It certainly reached the Bohemian. Funny you hadn't heard it."

"Tell you I was alone in a box with a girl watchin' the show. How would I hear it?"

"You didn't help kill him, then? Didn't you know he was gonna be killed?"

"No sir," Tracy protested, little beads of sweat on his forehead.

"If that's so, all you can get is a penitentiary sentence for concealing facts and helping the murderers escape."

"Me? Why, I got no notion who they are. Didn't know Curt was dead till you told me two minutes ago. I ain't gonna be drug into this, Sheriff."

"Come clean, Tracy," urged Boone. "When did you leave Sing Elder and Brad Prouty?"

The cowboy gulped. He would have liked to talk with his friends before he did any explaining. As it stood now, he was quite in the dark. One thing he knew—he had no intention of being dragged into this killing when he had had nothing to do with it.

"What's the idea, Brady? Are you claimin' Sing and Brad did this? That's a fool notion. Ain't they all good friends? Don't they all run together?"

"We're asking the questions, Tom. You don't have to answer them if you don't like. You can stand your fighting chance of acquittal at the trial."

"Trial!" the cowboy repeated, his voice raised. "Hells hinges, you can't try me for something I didn't do. Send for Whip Quinn. I want to talk to him."

Brady shook his head. "No, Tom, you're going into a cell, and you'll do no talking to anyone . . . not yet. We'll find out what we want to know without your help. Don't blame us later when you're in a jam. You've had your chance to talk."

"I left 'em right outside the Occidental," Tracy blurted out. "Right away."

"When you told them we were looking for Curt French, what did they say?" asked Boone.

"Why, I dunno. I don't recollect hardly what they said." The cowboy's manner was sullen and reluctant.

"Said they were going to warn Curt, didn't they?"

"Maybeso."

"They did or they didn't. Which?"

"Why, yes, I guess they did."

For half an hour they grilled the harassed man. They got out of him all he knew, which was not very much. Then, in the presence of Hank Jacobs, the jailer, Tracy signed a statement covering the facts.

"Can I go now?" he asked.

"Sorry, Tom, but we'll have to hold you for the present," Brady said after a low-voiced consultation with Boone. "Don't worry. I reckon you're not in this."

"If I ain't in it, why can't I go?"

Brady did not tell him the real reason, which was that he would run at once to Whip Quinn with the story of what had occurred. Indignant and ill at ease, Tracy found himself locked in a cell for the night. It was, he felt, a high-handed outrage. He would sure tell Whip and have him bring these fellows to account.

XXV

Hugh McLennon had gone back to the ranch, but his sister stayed in town as a guest of Mr. Turley. Tilatha did not herself quite know why she was remaining. She felt that he would need the companionship of a strong-willed woman. He was not a man's man. And the presence of the Mexican housekeeper made it all quite within propriety.

Tilatha could not bring herself to go home yet because she felt, too, that the struggle of which Boone Sibley had become the central figure was moving to a swift and tragic climax. No longer did she deny to herself that he held her heart in that strong brown hand of his. He could crush it if he wished. Hourly he walked his light-footed way in great danger. Soon now the blow would fall, and when it struck him down she, too, would be stricken. She would, of course, go on living, but she would carry always in her bosom the dull ache that is close to despair.

The news of the death of Curt French came to her at first as a shock of relief. He had spread his threats broadcast. Now he was powerless to execute them. One great danger no longer confronted the man she loved.

She wondered how French had come to his death. There was some mystery about it.

Apparently the sheriff and his deputy had cleared themselves, though there had reached her rumors that they knew more than they were telling. Logically, as far as she could see, they were the men who benefited most from his death. Perhaps they had tried to arrest him and had been forced to shoot when he resisted.

She called on her dressmaker for a fitting the morning after the bad man had been killed and she met Russ Quinn in front of Blum's photograph gallery.

At sight of Tilatha the man's dark eyes lighted. He had supposed she had left town with her brother.

"Glad to meet up with you," he told her. "Thought you'd gone home. This is a pleasure."

Tilatha changed the subject. She did not want to discuss even in badinage Russ Quinn's feeling for her. He was out of the running, definitely, finally. She did not understand now how she could ever have considered him as a husband. From that point of view Boone Sibley filled her horizon.

"Have you heard anything more about Curt French . . . who killed him, I mean?" she asked.

The muscles in his dark face tightened. "I don't need to know any more. Sibley and Brady killed him."

"But they showed their revolvers to everybody in the room. They hadn't been fired."

"What leads you to think this Texas warrior ain't a two-gun man?" he demanded. "Brady, too, for that matter."

"They were searched by Mister Hartley."

Quinn laughed unpleasantly. "So they were, after they had got rid of their second guns. That's an old dodge. And tell me why this Texas man mentioned looking at his gun if he wasn't fixing up an alibi."

"He knew he would be accused, since Curt French had been threatening him and Mister Brady. They did not leave the house. What became of the other guns, if they had two each?"

"Gimme a harder one," Quinn returned scornfully. "Why, they shoved 'em in a bureau . . . or under the bed . . . or beneath the mattress . . . till they shooed the crowd out. I notice they wouldn't let the boys come into the room and look around."

"They couldn't do that till the coroner had seen the body," Tilatha protested. "You're unfair to them, Russ. You twist around everything they did."

"Bet your boots they couldn't, not without someone finding the six-shooters. So they didn't take any chances. They herded the crowd out and fixed things to suit themselves."

"I don't believe it, not for a minute. Why should they? Curt French had threatened them

259

both repeatedly. If he resisted arrest, they had a perfect right. . . ."

"And if he didn't resist arrest? If he never got a chance to resist?"

Tilatha flung up her head and looked straight at him. "That wasn't the way of it. They're not that kind of men, either of 'em."

His black eyes narrowed. "You mean Sibley ain't that kind of a man," he challenged.

"I said both of 'em. I say it again. Why do you stick up for Curt French when you know what he was, Russ Quinn?" she asked indignantly.

"I know what this Sibley is, too. Up to date, he's sure had a lot of luck. First that business of Buck Galway and the stagecoach robbery, then Jim Barkalow,"

"Jim Barkalow isn't dead, and he isn't going to die."

"Then Curt French."

"That's not proved."

"If he gets by with that, too, he's certainly a good one. Listen, girl. He's struck twelve o'clock. He's through."

"I should think you'd be ashamed to mention Jim Barkalow . . . fifty of you against one."

"Against two," he corrected darkly. "I've not forgot that."

There had been the sound of footsteps clicking down the walk. Boone Sibley was striding directly

260

toward them. Tilatha and Russ Quinn looked up and became aware of his approach.

The shotgun messenger spoke first, his voice harsh and insolent. "I've been tellin' Tilatha McLennon that you and Brady murdered Curt French!" he called out.

Tilatha noticed for the first time how like a bird of prey this black Quinn was. He had the rapacious nose and the glittering eyes of a hawk. He seemed, at this instant, about to swoop down on his victim. The eyes of the men actually seemed to clash, so hard and steely was the meeting of them.

"Then you've been telling her what's not true," the Texan countered. "And I reckon you know it."

"Meanin' what, Sibley?" asked Russ, his body dangerously tense and motionless. "That I'm a liar?"

"Meaning that we've got the killers locked up in jail."

Quinn forgot, in his astonishment, the anger that had been simmering to the boiling point. "Got 'em locked up! Who?"

"The men who killed Curt French. You notice I choose my words, Quinn. I don't know whether they murdered him or not."

"I asked you who you're talkin' about."

"So you did. Sing Elder and Brad Prouty."

"You've got 'em in your jail . . . Sing and

Brad?" the express messenger demanded. Quinn was amazed. He could hardly believe it. Yet he knew it was true if the Texan said so.

"How come they're there? Who took 'em?"

"I did."

"When?"

"This morning. Half an hour ago."

"And they didn't shoot you full of holes . . . either one of 'em?"

"Not so I noticed it. They were right sensible and peaceable, once they had time to think it over."

"By God, I don't believe it."

"That's your privilege, Mister Quinn."

Russ glared at his enemy savagely. He wanted to break loose now and have it over with. He had no fear. He was game and hardy and self-reliant. If he reached for his six-shooter, he or this Texan who he hated would be dead within a few seconds. But something held his hand. Was it the presence of Tilatha? Was it his wish to consult Whip before he struck? He never knew. Abruptly he turned on his heel and strode away.

Tilatha, white to the lips, stared at Boone. "I thought . . . I thought . . ."

She did not finish the sentence. Tilatha knew what gun play meant. Her imagination had heard the roar of guns, had seen the flash of fire, had felt the stab of bullets. She leaned sickly against an adobe wall, limbs and body lax. For the first time in her life she felt as though she were going to faint.

Boone looked at Tilatha. What he saw in her face made his voice gentle. "It's all right," he told her.

"It's all wrong," she cried brokenly. "He nearly . . ."

"He was some annoyed," the man told her. "Can't blame him for being disturbed at bad news."

"Did they do it . . . Sing Elder and Brad Prouty?" Tilatha asked. Her impulse was to divert him from her agitation.

"We think so. Looks that-a-way. A woman saw them going into the house where French roomed. That was five minutes before the shooting began."

"But why should they kill him? He was one of their crowd, wasn't he?"

"Yes, but he was running wild on them. They couldn't trust him, the way I figure it out. They had just got news that the sheriff was looking for French to arrest him again. Sing was in the stage hold-up with him. We know Sing had had trouble with the fellow at the Occidental. I'd guess French was making threats to spill the beans if he couldn't have things his way. Prouty and Elder are thick as thieves. Maybe they called on French to make sure he'd keep his mouth shut, and a quarrel flared up. We can't prove they went to kill him or that they fired the first shot. We do know the only shot French fired went wild, as it might have done if he was badly wounded when he pulled the trigger. But there's an answer to that guess. He was using his left hand and wasn't used to handling his six-shooter so."

"And might have been trying to beat them to the draw," the hill girl added.

"Just that, and in his hurry turned loose before he was ready."

"But if you think that, why arrest them and make them and the Quinns mad?"

"I didn't say I thought so. I said it might be like that. It's up to Elder and Prouty to show self-defense if they can."

Tilatha shook her head. "I don't see why you couldn't let them alone. They can't be convicted. You know that. Why make trouble for yourself?"

"We're law officers, Brady and I. We've made up our minds to clean up this town, if we can. What kind of sheriffs would we be to let these fellows get away with this and never even call for a showdown?"

"You don't have to go looking for trouble, do you?"

"We have to meet it when it looks for us. No use beating about the bush, Miss McLennon. We've served notice to the Quinn outfit that law has come to this town to stay."

They had turned and were walking back to the Turley house.

"Tell me how you captured them," Tilatha said. "They're so . . . so lawless, both of them."

"Got the drop on both. I knew they were up till two, three o'clock at the Occidental and would sleep late. So I dropped in and waked 'em. Sing hadn't even bolted his door. He hadn't a chance to resist. The other fellow, Prouty, came, and opened the door when I called. I gave the name of your friend, Russ Quinn, to him. He was sleepy and yawning, so I had him, too. For a moment he had notions, but he changed his mind and saw reason."

Tilatha made a little gesture of impatient despair. "If it would do any good, but they'll be out again soon, walking the streets and looking for you. Don't you know that? But of course you do."

"I know, too, that there's a change in the sentiment of this town," he told her. "Most folks here always were honest and law-abiding, but they didn't dare protest. Turley played almost a lone hand. Now it's different. Men meet me on the street and wish more power to us. The time has passed when the Quinns can run the town by high-handed methods."

"The time hasn't passed when they can shoot you down in the streets," Tilatha replied. "What's the use of saying that law is here when it is no such thing?"

"It's on the way. Don't you worry, Miss McLennon. The day of the Quinns is pretty near past, and nobody knows it better than Whip Quinn. He won't give up without a fight. But he's fixed so he loses if he wins. Say he wipes me and Brady out. Public opinion . . ."

She looked directly at him. He noticed for the first time the tawny flecks in the big brown eyes. "Will public opinion bring you back to life after they have killed you?" she flung fiercely at him.

He was surprised at the passion in her voice. No reason was apparent to him for so much ferocity. The thing he was doing was only what had to be done. Even she must realize that, untamed and wilful though she was.

"They haven't killed me yet," he told her grimly.

"No, but they will. Why do you come here and mix up in this? It's not your fight . . . but you hadn't got clear into town with your mule team before you had started it."

"Strutting around, I reckon," he murmured with a smile. "Me thinking myself a big man and wanting folks to talk about me."

She brushed aside his drawling quotation of her frank appraisal of him made at their latest meeting. "How you can stand there and joke about it when you know, just as well as I do, that . . ." The hill girl broke off her sentence. Unexpectedly her throat had filled with a sob.

Boone looked at her in swift surprise. He saw the stormy rise and fall of her bosom. A flag of color fluttered in her cheeks. Tilatha bit her lip, turned, and walked swiftly into the house. His amazed gaze followed her.

XXVI

To Tilatha came a grinning little colored boy
with a note. It was coached in phraseology con-
ventional to time and place. It ran:

> My Dear Miss Tilatha: May I have the
> pleasure of accompanying you to church
> tomorrow evening?
>
> Your friend,
Russell Quinn

"He never called me Miss Tilatha in his life,"
said the young woman who bore that name. "But
I suppose, since I'm in town, he wanted to do
this the way it ought to be done." She showed
the message to Mr. Turley.

"Shall you go?" asked the editor.

"Yes, I'll go. I don't want to, and it won't do any
good, but I can't afford to offend him," the hill
girl said wearily.

Turley did not need to ask her why she could
not afford to offend him. He understood that
Tilatha's fear was for the man she loved; she did
not want to inflame Quinn's passion against him
by anything she might do.

So Tilatha sat down and wrote a staid little
note in reply, to the effect that she would be very

pleased to have Mr. Quinn escort her to church tomorrow evening, then gave it with a dime to the shiny-faced black boy.

"What do you s'pose he wants?" Turley asked. "'Course, I know he wants *you*. But church! He doesn't *look* like a nice, quiet, church-going person. He isn't a deacon."

Tilatha laughed. "Not exactly. Church is the only place to take a young woman in this town. It's the proper thing to do for a young man who likes a girl. When he has been seen with her several times, he has served notice that his intentions are serious."

During the night, contrary to custom, Tilatha wakened several times, her thoughts full of apprehension. She knew Russ Quinn, and to a lesser extent she knew his associates. They were stark, ruthless men. When they struck, it would be certainly and finally. They might take their time, let days pass before they brought the quarrel to issue, but even if they did, she could gather no hope from that.

And there was nothing she could do—nothing at all. She could only wait for the blow to fall. No law officers could be appealed to, since the contending factions represented what established order there was in town. Boone Sibley was as immovable as a great rock to any prayer she might make. He would go his own way, alert and fearless and apparently unperturbed, until the Quinns called him to account.

At noon, when Turley came home for dinner, he brought with him news. There had been a jail break when Hank Jacobs had gone to the cells of the prisoners in the morning. One of them had struck him over the head and knocked him senseless. Just how it had been done was not clear, but the keys had been taken from him and all prisoners released. Among these were two Mexicans, an ore thief, Tom Tracy, and Elder and Prouty. The last three had obtained horses and ridden out of town.

"They think Prouty did it," Turley went on. "Old Jacobs has been out of his head most of the time since, but he mentioned that name once."

"Is he badly hurt . . . Mister Jacobs?" Tilatha asked.

"Yes. Doc Peters can't tell how badly yet. He thinks there is a chance for him."

"Sheriff Brady and Mister Sibley weren't at the jail when it took place?" the hill girl asked, her eyes aflame with interest.

"No. They didn't hear of it for an hour. They have taken the trail after the escaped men."

"After Elder and the other two, you mean?"

"Yes. I saw Brady for a moment. He was not very sanguine about finding them. It is easy to lose one's self in the desert. The chase may last several days."

Tilatha drew a breath of relief. To pursue outlaws who might at any time turn on them and fire from ambush was not the safest occupation in the world, but it was less dangerous than to be in town with the Quinns on the warpath.

The editor talked during dinner about the jail break and its effect on the citizens of Tough Nut.

"A week or two ago there would have been no outspoken criticism of the Quinn crowd," he said. "It would have been taken for granted that they would do as they pleased. But there has been a change. Men are beginning to speak out and say we have had enough of the whole crew. Sibley is responsible for this, and he alone. His stand has showed people that the Quinns and their friends are not invincible."

That evening Russ Quinn could not keep his somber eyes from Tilatha. She was in a sprigged taffeta that billowed with ruffles below the waist. It was a new dress, and it suited the long supple lines of the girl from the Chiricahuas.

Tilatha slipped her arm under that of her escort and stepped into the gathering darkness. As Quinn turned to the left instead of the right at the next cross street, she glanced at him in surprise.

"We're not going to church," he said.

"Oh, aren't we?" she said docilely. "Where are we going?"

"For a walk. I've got something to say to you."

"We'd better not go far. If we go wandering

about and don't show up at church, people might talk."

"Let 'em talk."

"Easy for you to say that, Mister Russ Quinn," she answered lightly. "It's not you they'd talk about, but me. I'll go a little way with you, though."

"You're gettin' right fussy, Tilatha. If we were at the ranch, you'd ride twenty miles with me after dark any time you'd a mind to."

"We're not at the ranch," she told him. "When we are at Tough Nut, we must do as Tough Nutters do."

"Most generally I do like I want to, and I've noticed you do the same," he told her carelessly.

"Yes, and I've been wondering about that, Russ . . . whether we're right or not, I mean. Ever since I was a teeny little girl, I've been set on having my own way. Mostly I've had it. Well, what good has it done me? I've overridden everybody that stood in my way, as though nobody but me had any rights. The consequence is that folks dislike me . . . at least they think . . ."

"The consequence is that you're a fine high-steppin' girl. . . ."

"Which is only a polite way of saying that I've got a bad temper."

He laughed at that, pressing her arm against his side as they walked. "You're tempery, redhead. I wouldn't have you any other kind, since I aim to have the taming of that bad disposition. You be as ornery as you like to other folks, and you and me will step in harness together right friendly at a good fast clip."

Tilatha hurried on. She had not yet said all that was in her mind. Probably there was no use in saying it, but at least she would have done her best to let him know how she felt and to bring him to a reasonable consideration of their problems.

"That's just it, Russ. We've got no more right to click our heels and hold our heads high than other folks. I've always acted as though I had, but I know that's just a form of conceit. We've always got to respect others' rights if we play fair, don't you reckon?" She asked it impetuously, with a kind of desperate seriousness. It was a prelude to an appeal that she felt she had to make.

"We're sure havin' the sermon whether we went to church or not," he told the girl, smiling down at her a little derisively, but still amiably.

"No, but really, Russ, isn't it true?" she pleaded. "I know I'm not the one to talk. I've always ram-stammed through, as my father used to say. But things look different to me now. It's not the way to do."

He thought he knew why things looked different to her now. Another man had come into the equation of her life. The voice with which he answered her was harsh, the manner abrupt. "Listen, girl. You'll find both brush rabbits and panthers out there." His arm swept out toward the darkness to indicate the desert and the mountains. "If you're a brush rabbit, you play the game that-a-way . . . if you're a wolf or a panther, why that's different. All the little laws, they're for the rabbit tribe. You'll find lots of 'em right here in Tough Nut. But if you're strong enough and game enough, you make your own laws. Question is, do you want to be a rabbit or don't you?"

"I don't want to be a wolf, Russ. But that doesn't force me to be a rabbit. There are all sorts of lovely creatures that are neither wolves nor rabbits."

"You can't buck the facts, girl. We're in the desert here, not back in Boston, if that's where your sassy editor friend comes from. There's one law out here. The strong get there, the weak go under. It's written over every arid acre between here and your ranch. There's nothin' but fight to it. Every bunch of greasewood, every shoot of ocotillo fights for water and goes halfway to China for it. Every saguaro and catclaw has got its spines and barbs. Why, the very foxes are made different, leaner and tougher than others so they can live longer without moisture. Animals are at war one with another. They got to be to live. It's the same with us humans. We've got to play the cards the way they're dealt us. Me, I'm not allowin' to slink about and sneak and be on the dodge like most of the scurryin' tribe out there. When I'm challenged, I fight."

"Yes, but you don't always have to carry a chip, do you?"

He frowned. "Spit it out, girl. Get down to brass tacks."

"I think we've got to change our way of looking at life, you and me both, Russ." She put her hand on his arm with a friendly little gesture that begged him to meet her halfway. "We've got to learn to respect laws and sometimes give way to the other fellow's point of view. It's kind of stupid to claim that we're above the laws that are made to help folks get along with each other."

He seized on one word of her argument and let the rest go. "The other fellow! That means Sibley. You're askin' me to give way to that Texas warrior. No, by God! He never saw the day when I'd give him a foot of the road, that bird." His voice was hoarse with anger. He strode up the footpath they were following, pushing forward so fast that she almost had to run to keep pace with him.

When he stopped, he was at the edge of an old prospect hole, one that had been deserted years before. It was in a district little frequented. Prospectors had tried their luck on the ridge and given it up, since all the pay mines lay in the opposite direction from town. The lights of Tough Nut lay below them, to the west. Apache Street seemed to open up from the very foot of the hill where they stood. Yet Tilatha knew the near end of it was more than half a mile distant. Seen in the moonlight, the noise of its revelry blotted out, the place looked peaceful as old age.

He turned fiercely on her. "Tilatha, you're makin' a fool of yourself over that Sibley. I'm through. I won't put up with it. It stops right now."

The color poured into the girl's tanned face. "If I am, that's my business," she flung at him.

"Anyone can see it. The way you're throwin' yourself at him is plumb ridiculous."

She tried to hold in leash her temper. "How long have you been running a young ladies' finishing school and teachin' deportment, Miss Quinn?" she taunted.

"If you had any self-respect . . ."

Her brown hands clenched. "Russ Quinn, if you dare say . . ."

"Don't try to bully me!" he cried, moving a step nearer and looking straight into her furious eyes.

"Bully! That's a nice word for you to use," she panted, almost as though she had been running. "What else are you ever but a bully? You glory in it. You think that . . . that if you look at a woman, she should come running to you like a whipped cur. Bully, indeed!"

What she said did not trouble him. She could have made charges that would have stung, but this was not one of them. He knew that if he was a bully, he had the courage to back his domineering manner. Indeed, he hardly heard what she was saying. But the challenge of her manner stirred the rapacious instincts of his predatory nature. The rise and fall of her stormy bosom, the breathing color driven into the cheeks by strong emotion, the healthy vigor of her wild young beauty, all went to his head like strong drink. The blood drummed through his veins. His woman! In spite of hell and high water, he would have her, regardless of her rebellious will. As he had conquered fractious horses by spur and whip, so he would subdue this defiant young spirit. She needed a master. He would be the man. Those eyes flashing fire at him would offer instead gifts of adoring love. The vital courage of her must be beaten down. Until she came to him with hands outstretched, he felt he would never know a moment's peace. She was to be his. She was to know herself to be his, body and soul.

Quinn caught her wrists in his sinewy fingers and held them fast, his eyes burning into hers. She did not try to free herself but faced him with a kind of fierce disdain, head up, gaze locked to his. His arms went around her and he snatched her close, kissing cheeks and lips and throat with an unleashed savagery.

Not even then did she resist. Her strength was powerless against his, and to oppose him would be to give him the satisfaction of a sort of victory. She held her body stiff and inert, gave no response whatever to his flaming passion.

So, for lack of fuel, the man's ardor died down. His arms relaxed, though he still held her and looked hungrily down into her face. When he spoke his voice was rough with feeling.

"You're mine, girl. You're wearin' the Russ Quinn brand. I'll kill any man that comes between me and you."

She made no motion to free herself. Her arms hung by her sides. When he looked at her and heard her voice, he knew she had never been more remote, never had he known her to be less his.

"If there wasn't another man in the world, I'd never be yours," she told him.

His heart felt as though drenched with ice water. This was not the hot-headed impulsive girl he knew. There was a cold finality in her voice. She looked at him like a strange judge who condemns a criminal without emotion. It came to him that he had lost her, that all his strength could not tear aside the barriers between them. And he thought of the man who he held responsible for this.

"I'll kill him soon as we meet . . . tonight, if he's back," he said.

"Do you think you're God . . . or Satan?" she asked him.

"Him or me . . . right away," he said, his voice

law. He was staring at her but he did not seem to see her. Behind the girl, in the shadows of the night somewhere, was the man he had doomed.

She knew she had lost. No use to talk to him about the sacredness of life, no use to plead for this one man who was dearer to her than breathing. He would go his own tragic way, no matter what it might involve. Then in a surge of feeling, she knew she could not bear to be with him another moment.

Quinn was standing with his back to the prospect hole scarce a yard from the edge. A cactus barred her way, and she had to pass close to him. He stepped back. The moon shone on his harsh, strong face. One moment he was there, an imminent threat to all the joy of her life, the next he had vanished, swallowed by the earth.

She gasped, starting back. The ground on the edge of the deserted mine had caved in and taken him down to the bottom of the hole with it.

XXVII

The fugitives had no more than an hour's start on the sheriff and his deputy, but sixty minutes was as good as a week. They had taken the Benson road, which was pretty fair evidence that they were not going to Benson, since all three of the escaped prisoners had been on the dodge often enough not to leave a straight plain trail behind them.

A muleskinner freighting to Tough Nut had passed them, "ridin' hell for leather" as he put it. A covered wagon outfit a mile farther on the road had seen nothing of them. Evidently the outlaws had taken to the chaparral at some point between the two.

The officers backtracked slowly, checking up on the road. They picked up the trail again, but after the loss of a precious hour. It led east.

"Looks like the boys are heading for the Chiricahuas," Brady said. "They'll find friends there, I shouldn't wonder. But not so many as they would have done a few weeks back. The cowboys feel kinda sore about Sing Elder killing Buck Galway and then trying to lay it on Dusty. Buck come from that-a-way and was popular with the hill folks."

They rode cautiously, eyes and ears open, for

they did not want to run into an ambush. At present this was not likely, since the men they were after did not know their trail had been picked up.

Presently the sheriff and his deputy lost the trail in heavy brush.

"Just as well," Boone said. "We'll make better time without it. They're heading straight for Galeyville, looks like."

The two men plodded on through the sun and the dust. Their throats were caked before they reached Galeyville, and their clothes were covered with white powder. Lather streaked the flanks of their mounts.

Stiffly they dismounted and bowlegged into the Silver Dollar saloon. They strolled in with apparent carelessness but with a very real wariness. Four cowboys were playing a game of stud. No others were present except the bartender, who nodded in a friendly way to the sheriff and stared with frank interest at Sibley. One of the cowboys ambled forward, the game suspended for a minute, and offered his hand to Boone with a grin.

" 'Member me . . . Sandy Joe. Glad to meet up with you again, Mister Sibley."

Boone shook hands. "Heard you'd been hurt . . . falling from a horse or something. You all right now?"

"Yep. False alarm. One of the greasers creased

me. No harm done. I was needin' a haircut anyhow. Bullet didn't hardly break the skin."

"Good enough. Heard how Dusty's getting along?"

"Fine. Fine as the wheat. He was a right patient invalid for a spell, but his nurse has done gone to town and the boy's rarin' to go again. He's still up at the McLennon Ranch. Why don't you drop in and see him? He'd be real pleased to see you."

"Here on business," Boone said in a low voice. "Under the sheriff's orders. Seen anything of Tom Tracy, Sing Elder, or Brad Prouty?"

Sandy Joe looked shrewdly at him. "They been up to some mischief . . . something new, I mean?"

"Charged with killing Curt French, two of 'em."

"That sure must hurt your feelin's, if what all they say is true."

"My feelings don't figure in it. But that's not all. They broke jail this morning and left old Hank Jacobs for dead."

"Killed him?" Sandy Joe asked eagerly.

"Not dead yet when we left. You know what we want, Joe. We think the three men came to Galeyville. Seen anything of 'em?"

The cowboy took a swift glance at the bartender and another at the card players. "Why, no. No, I haven't."

Boone understood that he was not getting the truth and that the cowboy might be willing to talk if they were alone. The sheriff was engaged in conversation with the bartender.

"We need fresh horses, Joe," he said, moving toward the bar. "Know where we can raise some *pronto*?"

They drank, discussing mounts. Sandy Joe suggested Pete Andrews as a possible source of supply.

"Store's closed," he added. "Show you his house."

They moved to the front of the saloon and passed out. Boone asked a question, not changing his tone of voice or his indolent manner. "How long ago?"

"Three hours. Stayed half an hour, got fresh horses, and lit out."

"Went which way?"

"No idea. Find out for you. Be at Sanford's store in fifteen minutes. If they went north, I'll buy chewing . . . if south, I'll be smoking. Watch the way my right hand points when I yawn. . . . No, I don't know how much Andrews will want for 'em. He'll be reasonable, I'd say." This last for the benefit of a couple of men passing into the saloon.

"How is Barkalow getting along . . . the man I had to shoot?"

"Got nine lives, that fellow has, like a cat. Doc

says he never did see a man get well so fast. He'll be out in two or three weeks more. Well, so long."

Boone went into the saloon again and joined the sheriff. Presently the two returned to their horses, and Boone told Brady what he had learned.

"Good. Didn't get a thing from the barkeep. Afraid to talk, I expect, especially with so many present. Well, let's drift over to Sanford's."

At the store they bought a few supplies. Sanford watched Boone for a few moments from the homemade desk where he was sitting, then moved forward to the counter, where the sheriff and his deputy were looking at a spur.

"I've been wondering, Mister Sibley, who's paying for my stock in the store damaged the other day," the merchant said.

Boone showed surprise. "Why, didn't the boys fix that up with you, Mister Sanford?"

"No, they didn't. They took up a collection and paid for new windows. But I'm not talking about the windows. Two good suits of clothes had bullet holes shot in them. Several sacks of flour and grain were practically ruined. Do you think it right for me to have to stand the loss?"

"No, sir," Boone answered promptly. "The fellows that shot up your stock ought to make the loss good. Maybe Russ Quinn would like to send in a contribution to the cause. I'd write to him about it."

"Here's my point, Mister Sibley. I'm not rambunctious about this, y'understand. It won't break me if I have to make good the loss myself. But if you hadn't run into the store, the stuff wouldn't have been spoiled. Isn't that so?"

The Texan considered. "Tell you what I'll do. Call in three of the boys. Say the first three that pass the store. We'll put it to 'em, and I'll abide by their decision if you will. Is that reasonable?"

Sanford agreed.

Three cowboys passed a moment later. They were the ones who had been playing stud at the Silver Dollar. The merchant stated the case. Boone added a word or two. The jury retired to a corner of the store and consulted.

They presently came forward. "Verdict in," said one of them. "Jury finds Mister Sibley not guilty but Sanford had orta get damages. Wherefore jury agrees to raise the amount by unpopular subscription among the gents participating in the fireworks."

Boone smiled. "I participated to a certain extent, so I'll shell out ten dollars as my share," he offered, and at once tossed over a piece of gold to the chairman of the committee on restoration.

Into the store came Sandy Joe. "Glad you ain't closed yet, Sanford. Gimmie a plug of the old reliable and charge to yours truly," he said. The cowboy yawned, throwing wide his arms in a gesture of abandon. "The fingers of his right hand pointed northwest. "That poker game has sure been runnin' steady last two, three days. I aim to get caught up on my sleep tonight for sure."

The foreman of the jury disagreed. "You think so. Different here. Betcha a dollar you're sittin' in before twelve o'clock midnight this very p.m. Either at the Silver Dollar or some other place."

"Take you, fellow. I can use that dollar."

The officers left the store and returned to their horses.

"Sandy Joe was pointing right straight to the McLennon place," Brady said.

"In that direction, sure. What say we ride over there? We can get fresh horses at the ranch," Boone suggested.

"Might as well. Hard to tell where those fellows have holed up. I don't hardly reckon they'll be at the McLennon place."

"No, but Hugh may know something, or in the course of a day or so may hear where they're at. You know how news travels up here."

They took the road to the ranch, jogging along easily to rest their tired horses. The stars were out before they dropped into the mountain park where the ranch was set. They could see the lights gleaming from the house windows as they splashed through the creek. A young hound barked furiously at them and the Chinese cook came to the kitchen door.

"Hello the house!" the sheriff called. "Reckon we'll light, Charlie, if you can fix us up some grub."

"Me fixum," the yellow man promised.

A man flung open the front door. The man was Dusty Rhodes. "Don't shoot, whoever you are!" he called cheerfully to them.

"Any other guests here except us, Dusty?" asked Brady.

"None, unless I'm one. Why? Are you allowin' to give Hugh and me a surprise party? Dog my cats, if it ain't the Texas warrior!" He fell upon Boone and pounded him with both fists. His boyish face was alight with pleasure. "We was plumb low for excitement. Hugh and me was debatin' whether I'd better massacre him or him me to stir things up."

"Come in, boys," invited Hugh. "Had any supper yet?"

"No. Charlie's gonna fix us up some. When did you get toney and set up a yellow boy for a cook, Hugh?" the sheriff asked.

"Tilatha found him stranded in Galeyville and brought him home. He was plumb down to the blanket. She was tight busy, and, anyhow, she wanted to get away for a while. Charlie ain't permanent."

Hugh did not ask them why they had come or what they wanted. That was their own business. If they wanted to tell him, they would do so in due time. Meanwhile, they were welcome to the best he had. Hospitality on the frontier is not a virtue but a matter of course.

They chatted in a casual fashion, mentioning to one another such news as might be of interest.

"I reckon you heard about Curt French getting shot," the sheriff said during a pause.

"Yep. Hugh was in town, you know. Good work, Texas man. Would suit me down to the ground if you'd have sent him to Boot Hill."

"Not referring to that. I reckon you're suited, Dusty. You haven't heard about him getting killed, then?"

"No. Who shot him," Dusty asked quickly.

"We don't rightly know," the sheriff answered nonchalantly. "Evidence points to Sing Elder and Brad Prouty. So we arrested 'em on suspicion."

"But great ginger mills, what in Mexico would they bump Curt off for?" demanded the cowboy.

"Seems they had had a quarrel," Brady said. "Curt got right troublesome to his friends, I shouldn't wonder."

"So you've got Sing and Brad in your calaboose," Hugh made comment. "I expect that will rile 'em some."

"My teacher usta tell me I got my tenses all mixed, Hugh," the lawman aired. "You're that-a-way, too. We had 'em, but we haven't got 'em now. There was a jail break this morning and,

288

right now, the county doesn't have to feed any of its guests."

"A jail break!"

"Hank Jacobs got careless, and they hit him over the head with a piece of iron pipe. Fractured his skull, looks like."

"Bad medicine," said Hugh. "And the prisoners lit out?"

"Three got horses," the sheriff said. "Sing and Brad and Tom Tracy."

"Tom. Was he in the Curt French killin'?" asked Dusty.

"Not in it. A material witness."

There was a moment of silence while Hugh and Dusty digested the news. They did not need to wonder any longer what Brady and his deputy were doing here. The officers were after the escaped prisoners.

XXVIII

None of those present said instantly and frankly what was in his mind. The subject was a delicate one and recognized as such.

McLennon approached it indirectly. "So, they made their getaway. Wonder which way they headed."

"They were in Galeyville three, four hours ago," the sheriff said, rolling a cigarette. "Our information is they were moving kinda toward Cochise Head. How about fresh mounts, Hugh? Ours are played out."

The eyes of the sheriff and the rancher met. Brady was asking a good deal, and he knew it. McLennon was surrounded by rustlers at outs with the law. To supply horses to officers on the trail of criminals would be regarded by many as an unfriendly act, even though the men wanted had not been engaged in cattle or horse stealing. Hugh knew this. If he did what the sheriff asked, he would be aligning himself squarely with the law against those who went their own wilful way. But he realized that the present conditions could not endure. Law must come to the mesquite. Long ago he had made up his mind to help bring this about at the proper time.

"I can let you have horses," he said.

"Good." Brady smiled wryly. "I ain't sure they'll do us any good. Be like finding a needle in a haystack to run these fellows down in the hill pockets around the Head."

Dusty looked at McLennon. His eyes asked a question.

"Go ahead, Dusty," his host said. "Shoot your wad. It's a free country. I'm not covering for these scalawags. Time honest men showed their colors."

"They're makin' for the Clear Spring cache, looks like," Dusty told the officers.

"My guess, too," agreed Hugh.

"Could a fellow find this cache?" the sheriff asked casually.

"Not unless someone took you there. It's hidden in the hills."

"Think we could get a guide?" Hugh spoke with studied indifference.

"Maybe so. When you want to go?"

"Right damn' now. Soon as we've eaten, anyhow."

"Are you asking for a posse man or for a guide to the hole-up?"

"All we want is a guide. Soon as we reach the cache he can cut his stick."

"I reckon I might find you one," the ranchman said.

No promise of secrecy was given or asked, but

all those present understood it was implied. Hugh lived in the country and expected to continue to do so. He could not afford needlessly to make enemies.

After supper horses were roped and saddled. Hugh had not said who the guide was to be, but he swung on the third horse and led the way over the hills.

The country they traversed was rough and broken. It was seamed with gulches and scarred by rock slides. The riders went up breakneck hills and slithered down pitches covered with loose rubble. They wound in and out through arroyos running in all directions. But Boone noticed that McLennon never hesitated. He knew exactly where he was going.

They climbed steadily, after the first two miles, coming at last to a ridge looking down a wooded slope. Along this ridge the ranchman led them. For perhaps a half mile they followed it before he stopped.

"See those two rock spires ahead," he said. "Go between 'em and dip sharply to the right. You'll find yourselves in the cache."

"We'll not forget this, Hugh," the sheriff promised. "*Adiós.*"

The officers went on alone. They passed between the spires as directed, swung down a precipitous slope, and found themselves entering a gateway to a small park. In the moonlight a corral could be seen, and presently a lit cabin nestling on the edge of timber.

"We'll tie here," the sheriff said, swinging from his horse,

The officers crept forward on foot. They approached the cabin from the timber in the rear.

Boone reached the window first, raised himself, and looked inside. Three men were in the room—Elder, Prouty, and Tracy. They were playing cards by the light of a tallow candle stuck in a beer bottle. Even as Boone looked, Tracy dealt a hand, rose, and walked to the door.

The Texan did not stop to discuss with the sheriff what must be done. He ran swiftly around the house, jerking out his six-shooter on the way. Tracy was standing in front of the house, his back to it, a few yards from the door, which was partially closed.

At the sound of footsteps, he turned lazily. Evidently he thought one of his friends had come out of the house, started to speak, then stopped, mouth open and eyes bulging. A revolver in the hands of Boone was pressed against his stomach. The cowboy swallowed hard. This was the last thing in the world he had expected.

"Don't speak . . . or move," the Texan advised in a whisper.

The sheriff came around the corner of the house and in one glance took in the situation.

Boone held up two fingers and pointed to the

house. Brady nodded, stepped to the door, and walked inside. His six-shooter was in his hand.

One of the men at the table had his back to him, the other sat in profile.

Elder spoke. "We're waitin' for you, Tom." Then he looked up and made a motion to rise.

"Stick 'em up," the sheriff ordered. "Both of you."

Both men stared at him stupidly, as though their brains had not yet functioned clearly enough to understand what had taken place. Neither of them put up his hands, neither made any gesture toward any offensive.

Brady watched them closely. He did not expect any trouble now, since he had the drop on them. They were too old at the game for that. But he knew that the least wavering of the eye might be fatal.

"Reach for the roof, boys," the officer said sharply. "No foolishness."

Elder found his voice first—"This some of Tracy's work?"—he asked with an oath.

"Get your hands up! *Pronto*!" Brady's voice had a whiplash sting.

Four hands went up reluctantly.

Tracy came into the house, followed by the deputy.

Prouty looked venomously at the Texan. "So you're in this," he snarled.

"Collect the hardware, Sibley," the chief officer

said. "Throw the guns on the bed for the present."

Boone did as directed.

"Put on the cuffs," Brady continued. "Look out, fellows. Don't make any break, or you'll sleep in smoke."

The three men submitted to be handcuffed.

Sing Elder turned on Tracy. "You claimed this was so safe . . . nobody knew your hole-up but friends. If you've sold us out, fellow . . ."

"Don't get on the prod, Sing. I dunno how they come here any more'n you," Tracy protested sulkily.

"You'd better not," growled Prouty.

Neither of the officers volunteered any information. If their prisoners got to quarrelling among themselves, they were likely to tell more than they should. There might be mutual recriminations and accusations, out of which might come the discovery of which one had struck down the jailer.

Elder, the shrewdest of the prisoners, realized this and changed his manner. "Might as well make the best of it, boys. I don't reckon Tom has had anything to do with this. Fact is, I don't see how he could, since he's been with us all day, Brad."

"Any fool could see that," Tracy said bitterly. "You got no more right to blame me than I have you. Come to business, not as much, because . . ."

The cowboy cut his sentence off without saying what was in his mind. But Boone could have made a pretty good guess as to the unspoken part of it. The man had been about to say that he was not as much to blame for the trouble they were in because he had not slugged Hank Jacobs.

"No need going into that," Elder admonished. "Far as that goes, I'd as lief go back to town as not. Like to get this thing cleared up for good."

"What thing?" asked Brady.

Elder turned his cold, wary eyes on the sheriff. "Why, whatever you claim to have against us. We know you, Brady. You've thrown in with our enemies, and you're trumpin' up whatever you can against us."

"Nothing to that, Sing," the sheriff denied amiably. "No sense in blaming me because your own bull-headedness gets you-all into trouble. You know dog-gone' well I've got to make these arrests."

"We know you're runnin' with this Texas killer. You two and Turley are tryin' to get control of Tough Nut. Because we won't stand for it, you're abusin' your position of sheriff to hound us."

"Have it your own way, Sing. I don't aim to start any debating society here. Now, we'll have to fix up some way to sleep our little family. How about blankets, boys?"

The sheriff and Boone took turns sleeping. Their prisoners were handcuffed, but they had to be watched. A moment of relaxed vigilance might give one of them the chance he was looking for.

The night wore away. Light sifted into the sky. The sleeping men woke, three of them stiff and cramped from the constrained position in which they had been forced to lie. Boone lit a fire in the stove and started to prepare breakfast.

"You better step out and look up mounts, Sibley," the sheriff said. "Guess you better rope and saddle while I fix up some grub."

Prouty had got out an old greasy deck of cards, and the three prisoners were sitting at the table, still handcuffed, playing seven-up.

"Got to have that table in a minute, boys," Brady said. "Finish your game, though. I'll mix up a batch of flapjacks first."

The sheriff's six-shooter was in his way as he worked. He took it from where it hung by his side and thrust the barrel into the leg of his boot.

Boone hesitated a moment. It was in his mind to tell Brady to be careful while he was away. But why? The sheriff presumably knew his business and did not want any advice from a young deputy of not one fifth his experience. Anyhow, the prisoners were handcuffed. Apparently they were intent on their game. The deputy left the house and started for the corral.

"I'm against that fellow every turn of the road, Brady," said Elder harshly. "Don't see why you cotton to him. . . . High, low, and game. Tom gets jack."

"He's all right," Brady said cheerfully. "Wouldn't want a better man with me, Sing." He was pouring flour into a tin pan. "I reckon you boys have got good healthy appetites."

"Yep." Sing was dealing the cards awkwardly on account of his bound wrists.

Presently Brady had his pancakes mixed and moved to the stove.

The cabin was small, and the table where the players sat was to the right of the stove, about three feet from it. Brady dropped the dough into two frying pans sputtering with grease. He kept an eye on the prisoners, never turning his back on them. The cuffs jingled as they gathered and played their cards. He was glad to see that they appeared in a more amiable frame of mind than last night. Sing Elder especially seemed to be taking the arrest philosophically.

"Makes game, boys," he said to the others. "That's a dollar six bits you owe me, Tom. You and me are square, Brad."

"No such a thing," Prouty protested. "You owe me four bits, Sing. There was six bits comin' to me from the other game, and now . . ."

Elder, shuffling the cards carelessly dropped one and stooped to pick it up. He fumbled awkwardly for it. With his shackled hands he could not easily reach it and pushed his chair back toward the stove. Swiftly his hands lunged out and snatched at the butt of the .45 sticking from the sheriff's boot leg.

Brady was not a quick man. His brain and muscles co-ordinated one instant too late. Elder had the six-shooter in his grip before he woke to action. The sheriff dived for his wrist and closed on it. They struggled, Brady to keep the barrel pointed down, and the outlaw to raise and fire it.

Prouty rose heavily, flinging down the bench upon which he sat. He and Tracy closed with the officer. A shot rang out and a bullet crashed into a wall of the cabin. Prouty raised his arms and brought down his wrists upon the temple of the sheriff. Struck by the heavy iron, Brady swayed on his feet, fell against Elder, and slid to the floor.

"Gimme the six-shooter!" Prouty called to Elder. "Quick. I'll finish his business."

"No need of that," Elder answered. "Find his keys, Tom. In that right-hand pocket. We got to get these cuffs off."

Tracy stooped, fumbling for the keys. It took him several seconds to find and drag them out.

"Here they are, Sing. We got to hustle."

The door was flung violently open. Boone Sibley burst into the room.

XXIX

Boone walked out to the corral and got his rope. He stepped inside the fence and adjusted the loop. The wary horses had already edged over to the farther side of the enclosure. Boone moved slowly forward, the rope snaked out and the loop fell true over the head of a sorrel gelding. Not knowing which outlaw owned the horse, he chose the first saddle that came to hand.

The animals began to circle the corral once more as soon as he stepped toward them, lariat in hand. Boone missed his next cast, arranged rope and loop, and caught a round-bellied bay. This, too, he saddled. He had just finished tightening the cinch when a shot sounded.

The sound had come from the cabin. His reaction was instantaneous. As he ran toward the house, he dragged out a revolver. The chances were ten to one that Brady had not fired the shot, and even if he had, it was because trouble had started. He had been careless. One of the prisoners had found the opportunity for which he was looking, had perhaps got his fingers on some gun hidden in the bedding. Or Brady, taken by surprise, had been forced to defend himself.

The Texan had no time for strategy or finesse. He plunged at the door and flung it open. A bullet struck the jamb close to his shoulder. Sing Elder, hands still shackled, had fired at him. Almost without breaking his stride, the deputy charged him. In that fraction of a second he had seen that the sheriff was down, that the prisoners were still handcuffed, and two of them unarmed. He might have played it safer by killing. He chose, if he could, to take his men alive.

The barrel of his Colt struck Elder's forearm, but not before another bullet had crashed into the wall. The gambler's weapon fell. With a side sweep of a foot, Boone kicked it under the stove as he braced himself to meet Prouty's rush.

The fellow was powerful and heavy set. His drive was intended to fling the deputy back upon the stove. Boone dodged the full force of it by side-stepping and clinching with Elder. Prouty plunged into the stove, and the pipe came clattering down.

By this time Tracy, too, was lumbering into action. His arms were raised to use the handcuffs for a weapon. Past the shoulder of Elder the Texan drove a hard left into the man's unprotected face. For the moment it stopped him completely.

Elder had seized Boone's right wrist. The deputy struggled to free it, for Prouty was gathering himself from his frustrated assault. Elder was big and strong. His grip was like living steel. The deputy's left hand went to the man's face. The heel of the palm caught under the chin and thrust upward and back. The finger searched for the eyes. With a howl of pain Elder fell away from the torture, releasing the wrist. Boone's right arm rose and fell. The heavy barrel crashed against the man's forehead. Elder swayed against a bunk and collapsed upon it.

Just in time Boone got out from the corner where he was. With a roar of anger Prouty flung himself at the young officer. Still Boone did not fire. Without looking down, he felt an overturned stool brushing against his leg. He gave ground, inching the stool into Prouty's path. The man stumbled, caught at Boone's waist with his bound hands, almost dragged the deputy down with him. Boone was flung against a wall.

The Texan hung there, breathless and shaken. But the day was won. Elder rolled over, trying to rise. Prouty had fallen hard, his head under a bunk. In cuffs, he found it difficult to get out and rise. Tracy had backed away, his hands up.

Brady was sitting up, his hand to his head. He looked at the red stains that covered it, then at Boone, with an odd chagrined humility. "I got careless, Texas man," he said.

Boone spoke sharply to Prouty and not to his chief. The man was awkwardly getting to his feet. "Line up beside Tracy. Don't you even look like fight or I'll shoot you down."

Prouty glared at the young Texan. His mouth was a thin, cruel line below the drooping moustache. The sullen eyes burned with hatred. But he knew when he was beaten. He slouched across the room and joined the cowboy.

"No breakfast here now," Boone said, glancing at the smoking stove. "What say we go to the McLennon Ranch and get a hand-out, Sheriff?"

"Just as you say, Sibley." The sheriff recovered his weapon. "I sure played a good hand mighty bad. Hadn't been for you, I'd have had to go sneaking back without my prisoners. Well, a fellow lives and learns. I'm an old dog, but that was sure a new trick I picked up from Sing."

Elder was sitting on the bed, nursing his head. "We was all shackled. Hadn't been for that, it would have been different." He looked at Boone sulkily. "I'd like to meet you on even terms somewhere, Texas man. Gimme a chance and I'll show you up."

"We'd better all go out and finish saddling," Boone suggested to his chief, "after you've tied up your head."

"I reckon," Brady agreed. He was quite dispirited. What had just taken place was a reflection upon his capacity as an officer. He had just missed disgrace by a hair's breadth, and by no merit whatever of his own. He rose from the stool on which he was sitting and moved toward the water pail.

"Need any repairs, Sing? I'll fix you up if you do," Boone said curtly.

"You touch me and I'll beat your brains out," Elder promised viciously.

"Which is a polite way of saying no thank you, I reckon," Boone said. "Well, it's your head and not mine. Have it your own way."

He tied up the sheriff's wound, a watchful eye on the prisoners. This done, the party adjourned to the corral. Fifteen minutes later they were riding up the slope that led to the spires.

It was a sorry-looking party that forded the creek and rode up to the McLennon ranch house. That active five minutes in the shack had damaged the appearance of several of its members. His wound still unwashed and unbound, Elder looked much worse than he actually was. Prouty had cut open his cheek when, in falling, he had struck the edge of the bunk. The sheriff's bandaged head was frank admission that he had been through battle.

Dusty followed Hugh to the porch. He took one sweeping glance at the riders. "Meet a cyclone on the way, boys, or anything?" he asked.

"No, Dusty," the Texan answered. "Some of us had a few ideas, but we've got over 'em now. The sheriff and I persuaded them to play our way. . . . Can we get some breakfast here, McLennon?"

"Sure. I'll speak to Charlie."

"We been through with ours for two hours. Wasn't there any grub where you-all come from?" asked Dusty.

"We kinda kicked the apple cart over amongst us," Brady said. "We spent the night in a shack up a ways in the hills, but I noticed about breakfast time we didn't seem hungry. Too busy. Still, at that, don't forget we're full-grown men when you turn that order in to Charlie, Hugh."

They dismounted. The sheriff ranged his prisoners in a row on the porch and watched them while Boone and Dusty took care of the horses. While breakfast was being prepared, Hugh McLennon gave first aid to Elder. This done, he turned toward Prouty.

"How about you, Brad?"

Prouty looked angrily at him. "All I want from you is water. I'll tend to this cut. If anyone asks you, I tripped up. That's how I got it. That ain't all, Mister Hugh McLennon. You claim to be our friend. Well, I see what I see. These fellows come right to our hang-out, straight as a crow flies. They're on horses wearin' your brand. Someone brought 'em there. By God, I can guess who."

Hugh McLennon was no faint heart. He had put up more than one gunfight when forced to it. It was known all over the country that he had sand in his craw. Now he looked grimly at Prouty, eyes steady and cold. When he spoke it was after he had come to an important decision. "What do you mean I claim to be your friend, Prouty?" he asked. "I know you by sight. I know the name you go by. Does that make me your friend? If you want to know, I'm particular who my friends are."

"I've heard about rats and a sinkin' ship, Hugh," Elder jeered.

The poet Joaquin Miller once said about the Forty-Niners: "The cowards never started, and all the weak died on the road." This was not literally true of the Argonauts any more than it was of the early Arizonans, but it held more than a kernel of truth. These pioneers were men and women who had fought Indians, drought, hunger, and the lawless depredations of their own race. Most of them were hard and weather-beaten and virile. Hugh McLennon was a leader among those with whom he had cast his lot, and he had won preëminence by the strength in him.

His bleak look met Elder's sneer steadily. "You're beginning to hear about the law, too, Sing," he said. "It's come into this country, and it's come to stay. I'd advise you to think about that. I'm on that side. I'm against skulduggery and promiscuous killings and stage robberies. When the sheriff of this county comes to me and asks for horses to go about his business of running down men wanted for crime, as a decent citizen I give him mounts to help him on his way. When he asks me to guide him through this country with which I am acquainted, I guide him. I'm not concerned whether that suits you or not."

"You talk mighty big. Get down to cases. Do you claim I've done any promiscuous killin' or robbed any stages?" Elder demanded.

"I don't know a thing about that," came Hugh's prompt retort. "All I know is that the law charges you with crime. That's enough for me. You'll have chance enough to prove yourself innocent."

The pig-tailed head of the Chinese cook appeared at the kitchen window. "Bleakfast all leady," he announced.

Recrimination ceased. The men filed into the house, sat down, and began to stow away cornbread, bacon, eggs, and coffee.

XXX

Tilatha looked down into that black hole, standing as near the edge as she dared. She had no idea how deep it was, no assurance as to whether Russ Quinn was dead or alive.

In a faint voice she called down: "Russ . . . Russ . . ."

There was a sound, as though of something stirring. Then an answer to her call, if it might be called an answer, for what she heard was a deep-throated curse.

"You're not hurt?" she cried.

"No. Shaken up. Go get help to haul me out."

"Yes," she promised. "I'll not be long."

She turned and ran down the ridge toward the road. But she did not run more than a hundred yards. There had come to her the memory of his threat to kill Boone Sibley this very night if the Texan had returned to town. She could not rescue him without condition, knowing what he meant to do. She stood, thinking, then walked slowly back to the prospect hole.

"Russ!" she called down.

"Meet someone to send to town?" he shouted up.

"No. Listen. I want you to promise not to hurt

Mister Sibley. He's not looking for any trouble with you. Let him alone."

His voice was hoarse with anger. "You go down to the Occidental and tell Whip what's happened to me. Dirt's tricklin' in here right along. And hurry, too."

"No . . . but, Russ, listen! You're all wrong about him if you think he's interested in me. He's not. He never looks at any woman. Hates them all, or at least doesn't know they're on earth. If you'd be reasonable, if you'd understand . . ."

"Don't stand there arguin' with me, girl. You light out *pronto* and get Whip. No use tryin' to bully me into any promises. I'm intendin' to get that Texan right away."

She pleaded with him, eagerly and forlornly and at times passionately. The only effect was to increase his rage.

"How can I have you brought up from there when you tell me that you want to get out to kill a man . . . one who saved me from a bunch of Mexican raiders? Don't you see I can't, Russ? It would be like me being a party to it. If you'd only be human . . . like other folks." Her voice broke a little.

"Can't you ever learn to mind your own business?" he burst out. "I never saw such a girl. Always got to run things. If you were mine, I'd lay a horsewhip across your shoulders. By thunder, I would. You're the most aggravatin'

309

little fool. . . ." He stopped from sheer exasperated inadequacy of expression.

"Not the least bit reasonable," she said hopelessly. "Can't you see my position, Russ? If I had you hauled up while you're in that state of mind, it would be just like turning a raving maniac loose with a six-shooter. I can't do it . . . I can't."

"You do like I say, and do it right away. Don't you stand there dictatin' to me what I'm to do." He ripped out a sudden furious imprecation.

There was no use talking further with him. Tilatha turned away and walked slowly back to town. She did not know what to do. There seemed no way out of the situation, none that had any promise of hope. Very likely he might stay there days without being discovered, or, on the other hand, someone might hear his shouts before the night was out. She could take food and water to him, but she could not tell that there would not be another cave-in of loose earth that would bury him completely.

Mr. Turley was in the parlor reading. At Tilatha's entrance he wheeled to face her. "Must have been a short sermon," Turley said.

"We didn't go to church," Tilatha answered. "We took a walk instead."

The editor flashed a quick look at her. Tilatha looked depressed and worried. That the situation had been threshed out, and to a conclusion not satisfactory to his guest, Turley knew without having to be told in so many words.

"Where did you go?" he asked to make conversation.

"Oh . . . around," the girl said warily. She took off her hat and sat down on the sofa.

There came a knock at the door. Turley opened it to let in Doc Peters.

He sat down in a rocking chair. "How is poor Mister Jacobs?" Tilatha asked.

"Doing very well. The skull isn't fractured. He isn't out of the woods yet, but unless complications arise, he should continue to improve."

"I'm very glad to hear it. I suppose we'll not see anything more of the ruffians that did it for some time," the editor said.

"You think not?" The doctor looked at him, a humorous gleam in his eye. "Haven't you any confidence in our sheriff?"

"They'll hide out in the chaparral," Turley replied. "Very little chance of finding them, unless Brady settles down to make a long hunt of it."

"If that is an editorial opinion, I'm glad you haven't put it into print yet," the doctor mocked. "Brady and Sibley reached town twenty minutes since, with three prisoners."

Turley sat up. "What prisoners?"

"Some outlaws by the name of Prouty and Elder and Tracy."

"Where did they find them?"

311

"In the hills somewhere near Cochise Head."

"And these men surrendered without a fight?"

"I took a look at a couple of broken heads. Brady has one of them . . . Elder the other."

"Boone Sibley?" asked Tilatha. The words came as though almost without her own volition.

"Oh, that young man bears a charmed life. But I dressed his wounded hand again. He used it in the scrimmage."

"I've got to go to him . . . at once," Tilatha said, rising from the sofa. "It's very important."

The doctor looked at her and read the agitation she was suppressing. He judged that if Miss McLennon said her business was important, it was likely to prove so. She was not a young woman given to hysteria.

"I don't know where he is, but we can find him," Doc Peters answered. "Very likely he is at a restaurant or at the Dallas House. Let me be your escort, young lady."

"If you will, Doctor, please," Tilatha responded. "I . . . I must see him, just as soon as I can."

They found Boone at the Dallas House. He was washing up for supper, but he came down to the hotel parlor as soon as he had finished. Dr. Peters withdrew to the porch.

"I had to see you . . . to tell you something," Tilatha explained as soon as the two were alone.

Her heart was behaving queerly, as it always did nowadays when she was with this quiet

312

brown man. She felt love pouring through her strong young body. His steady eyes seemed to plunge deep into her, to set fluttering pulses of quivering emotion. He said nothing, waiting for her to define her errand. That was like him, she thought, characteristic of his reticent force.

"About Russ Quinn," she went on. "He wants to kill you . . . tonight . . . as soon as you meet."

"Where is he?"

"He has fallen in a prospect hole. I thought . . . before we let him out . . ."

"How did he fall in?"

"I was with him. We took a walk there. He wanted to talk. Then he told me he was going to kill you . . . and he fell in."

"Is he hurt?"

"No. I tried to get him to promise not to hurt you." The color beat through her skin in a rich tide. "But he's gone crazy about it. I had to tell you. What will you do?"

"Defend myself," he said quietly. "Have you sent anyone to get him out?"

"I wanted to see you first . . . to tell you what he's threatening."

His immobile face told nothing. She did not know how much he had thought of her these last few days, how in the watches of the night he had seen her, stormy, gallant, aglow with life, or perhaps shining with a soft and gentle warmth. She did not guess how he admired her fine, healthy,

313

vigorous body, built up by years in the open.

"That's right good of you," he said gently.

"You won't go away?" she asked without much hope.

"No, I won't go away."

"But you're not a killer like they say you are. You don't want to kill or be killed. Surely you don't."

"No."

"Then go away. Just for a while. It's awful to stay . . . and wait for him."

He smiled grimly. "Tell *him* to go. I'm making no threats. I'm going about my business, looking for no trouble. He's the one you'd better argue with, don't you reckon?"

She caught her hands together for a moment. "Oh, I have. But he . . . he won't listen."

"Then you've done all you can, Miss McLennon. And I thank you for your kindness."

"My kindness!" She cried the word bitterly. "I could wish that the sides of the hole would cave in and bury him. What right has he got to talk about killing another human being? God gives life. I think . . ."

"Is the hole caving in on him, or likely to?"

"I don't know. It's loose around the edges. If it does . . ."

He interrupted again. "We'll get a rope and some men. Maybe there's no time to lose. Meet you at Turley's in fifteen minutes."

314

"You're not going yourself?"

"Yes. Why not?"

"No. You don't know what he'll do when he sees you. I won't have it!" She spoke a little wildly.

"First thing is to get him out. Probably that will be easy enough. After that . . . oh, well." He shrugged his broad shoulders.

Tilatha found herself walking beside him along the sidewalk. A tumult stirred in her mood as she kept step. He moved like a young Greek god come back to earth. Instinctively matching his pace, her legs reached out resiliently, with an untamed joyous freedom born of muscles perfectly co-ordinated. She begged no more, surrendered her will to his. What must be must be. A lift of the spirit glowed in her. After all, the future was in God's hands. In spite of all his pride and arrogance, Russ Quinn sat in the bottom of a hole, helpless as a child, waiting for someone to come and rescue him, while she walked beside the man she loved—the clean, brown, straight man who passed through life so fearlessly without regard to those who, like wild beasts, were ready to pounce for the kill.

He left her at the corner, and she went alone to the house. It had been in despair that she had gone to him, the threat of what was to come hanging heavily over her soul, but some quality in his strength had blown away her fears, as a breath of wind does the morning mists. Now she moved eagerly, deep-bosomed and supple-limbed, no longer afraid. What was it about him that made everybody so sure of him?

His eyes, maybe? They were so level and steady, flinging out no flags of flurry. Out of them looked the man's character. They promised, if he was your friend, to go all the way with you, to ride hard and risk much, to see you through your trouble, never to give up as long as there was life. But there was more than that. Her brother Hugh's blue eyes said all that. So did those of a dozen cattlemen she knew. Dusty Rhodes, for instance. But when she thought of Dusty, she did not walk a feather-footed trail. She did not know that of all the men she had ever met, Boone Sibley was the king, her heart did not yet sing a song of rapture.

Tilatha laughed a little breathlessly. She whispered to herself, without words, "I love him . . . I love him." With a fine rapture her shining eyes looked up at the stars. For the first time she knew the ecstatic shock of a maiden's plunge into the wonderful pool of love.

XXXI

"Is he going to pull that man out of the hole to let him shoot him?" asked Turley.

"I don't know. He's going to pull him out," Tilatha answered.

"But . . . if the man says he's going to kill him . . . ?"

"Boone doesn't pay any attention to that. He never does. He acts as though he couldn't be killed, as though these men who threaten him were children."

"This Russ Quinn is dangerous," Turley said. "He doesn't think right. I don't understand such men. They are cold and deadly, like a rattlesnake. It's not as though he and Mister Sibley were going to fight fair and square, though heaven knows that would be bad enough."

"I've told myself all that," said Tilatha wearily. "But what can we do? Nothing. Nothing at all." She looked at her watch. Fifteen minutes since she had left Boone.

A knock sounded on the door. Boone was there, two men with him. They had a coil of rope, a pick, a shovel, and some lamps and candles. Tilatha joined them. She and Boone led the way. They turned from the street and followed the trail she and Russ Quinn had taken.

"Not far from here," the girl said. "Over this way."

"Must be old Jim Bleam's hole," one of the men said.

"Better not crowd too close," Boone said once they arrived at the hole. "More ground may be ready to cave in." He dropped the slip noose of the rope over his head and tightened it around his waist. This done, he moved cautiously forward. The other end of the rope was in the hands of the men. Near the edge of the pit he stopped. "Everything all right, Quinn?" he called.

There was no answer. He shouted a second time. Still no reply came to him.

"Is he . . . has something happened?" Tilatha asked.

"There's been another cave-in, looks like," Boone told her. "He doesn't answer. Nothing to do but for me to go down and find out what's wrong."

Her heart seemed to drop into her stomach. If there had been two earth slips, there might very easily be a third, especially if the soil was disturbed by the pressure of a man's weight upon it. But she said nothing.

"Gimme some slack, but not too much," Boone said to the men. "The ground looks firmer on the other side. Circle around that-a-way. Correct. Now, pay out rope as I call for it."

Close to the edge of the pit, he lay face down

and wriggled backward till his toes kicked into space. Very cautiously he worked himself over. He could see the trickling of rubble, could feel the ground softening and cracking beneath his weight.

"Now, then . . . slowly," he ordered. "The whole thing is ready to give if we're not careful. That's right. Easy now."

Foot by foot they lowered him. Little splashes of dirt struck his upturned face now and again. The stretch of starry sky above contracted as he went jerkily down. He guessed he must be twenty-five or thirty feet below the surface when his foot struck something solid.

This proved to be a timber jammed across the pit. An examination showed him that it was one of several. Either they had fallen or been flung in from above. He had not yet lit the miner's lamp or candles, and in the darkness of the pit he had to feel rather than see the problem before him. There was dirt piled up on the timbers. How far below them the excavation went he could not tell. Quinn must be still lower, probably at the bottom of the shaft. Boone called to him.

A voice answered: " 'Lo! Who's that?"

The Texan did not give the information. "Come down after you," he said. "You hurt?"

"No. I backed down and in a bit farther, and then another load of dirt fell right where I'd been before. Some timbers, too. Reckon there's some diggin' to do . . . this passage is almost closed up."

Anxiously Boone lit a candle and made an inspection of the bottom of the shaft. Russ was shut off by a bit of planking, the end of which stuck out from a mass of earth that covered the rest of it. With great caution Boone slipped down through a narrow opening. He took the shovel with him. As he raised the candle to see what was the best way of getting to work, Quinn recognized him.

"You!" he exclaimed.

The Texan nodded, only to say: "A bad business. We've got to go mighty carefully about this." He stuck the candle on an outcropping ledge and began to shift the lose earth toward the other side of the shaft.

"Get outta here," Quinn said bitterly. "Send someone else."

"Like to oblige you if I could, but I reckon we got to play the cards the way they are dealt."

"I don't want you here, Texas man. Get out."

Boone continued to shift the earth. It was possible that he might get enough of it away to remove the plank without having to send any up in a bucket. "No use you or me either bucking about this, Quinn," he said in a matter-of-fact voice. "We're here, you and me both. You can cuss me out after we get back above . . . if we ever do. No sense in us acting like children, especially when we've got to pull together to make the grade."

Russ said no more. What was there to say? He knew that this quiet, imperturbable man would pay no attention to him.

"We're digging out," the Texan answered queries from above. "Takes time, but we're making progress. Looks like we won't have to send any dirt up if we're lucky."

He shoveled industriously but cautiously. He did not want to shift the dirt below in such a way as to bring down that which was resting on the timbers. Again he laid aside the shovel. With both hands he lifted, very slowly, the end of the broken plank. Inch by inch Quinn edged forward. Boone's muscles grew taut under the strain of the weight, but he did not lower the timber until the other man was free. Then, again with the greatest care, he released his hold. The two men stood face to face. Dirt had been trickling down from above in little spurts ever since Boone had begun to work. Now a small rivulet of it poured upon them.

"Make ready up there!" Boone shouted.

"Got him out?" someone asked.

"Yes. Wait till I give the word." Boone undid the rope from himself and tied it around the waist of Russ Quinn.

The man looked at him defiantly. "You first. I'm not going up first." His voice was low.

Boone Sibley decided not to argue the point. "How many are there of you up there?" he shouted upward. He knew by voices that more men had arrived.

" 'Most twenty," came an answer.

"Let down another rope."

A second length of rope came slithering down. Boone tied it about himself. "All right!" he shouted. "Pull up both ropes at the same time. Go easy . . . the dirt's coming down on us."

XXXII

The sight that greeted Russ Quinn's eyes as he emerged over the edge of the pit, was not one to pacify his turbulent spirit. He scrambled to his feet under the scrutiny of a score of spectators. At his side stood Boone Sibley, slapping dust out of collar, chaps, and sleeves. To be openly indebted to Boone Sibley, before this crowd, was something that the Quinn ilk could not stomach. Gratitude to an avowed enemy was harder even to feel than to express, and Russ Quinn was equal to neither. Quick resentment surged into his flaming eyes. And if the presence of so many spectators were not enough to enrage him, the appearance of his brother lent the sole required spark to his passions.

Whip Quinn came striding up to the scene with anger carved deep in his every feature. Word had come to him that Boone Sibley was down in a pit digging out Russ at the risk of his own life. No greater humiliation could be visited on a Quinn than to be rescued by an enemy—particularly when that enemy was Boone Sibley, the very man whose intentions were to stir a tidal wave of public sentiment that should engulf and destroy the Quinns.

Russ quickly caught the sign in Whip Quinn's

face. He turned savagely on Boone. "Texas hero"—the latter word dripped in a long, contemptuous sneer from his mouth—"you've made another play to the grandstand. Any man could have gone down in there. You made sure to be first, didn't you? What for did you do it?"

Boone Sibley shook out his neckerchief and wiped dirt from the corners of his eyes.

"Just strutting," he replied calmly. "I like applause."

Whatever might have been Russ's retort, it did not come then. For Whip Quinn cut in sharply: "Now *I'll* tell you where we stand, fellow," he grated. "I'd made up my mind to call for a showdown, to sleep on your trail till we got you. You're a meddler. Texas warriors can't crowd us. You poor fool, the boys would have got you long ago if I hadn't held them back. You wouldn't be warned. You kept pushin' in, crowdin' your luck, and headin' straight for Boot Hill. Fellow, your hour was set."

The steady, watchful gaze of Boone did not relax. He said nothing. As yet he did not want to commit himself, for Quinn's remarks seemed to be only by way of preliminary. He had not come to the meat of his message.

"You're the big auger here now, Texas man, by your way of it," Whip Quinn went on bitterly. "You whopped a bunch of fools like Curt French and Brad Prouty, so you got all het up with the idea that you'd beat the Quinns. Why, we hadn't lifted a hand . . . hadn't begun to fight."

"Why should you fight now?" Boone asked quietly. "I'm not looking for trouble with you. I've never done anything against you, unless you claim partnership with the killers and bad men we've had to round up."

"Are you makin' any charges against me, sir?" Quinn asked, his voice ominously low.

"No, I'm not . . . you are. I'm merely asking a simple question. I never told you the road to Tucson was good. I never described the stage hold-ups to look like you, or to be riding horses like yours. I never had a three thousand dollar dead-or-alive poster nailed up for you . . . and no brother of mine ever headed a mob of fifty armed men against one of you, at Galeyville. I'm repeating . . . I merely ask a simple question . . . why should you fight me, unless you're all tied up in one parcel with hold-ups and murderers like Curt French and your cousin Sing Elder, and with killers like Brad Prouty?"

The crowd edged back. They sensed a quick, unexpectedly early termination to the battle for supremacy at Tough Nut. They knew that the drama, long in the making, was about to be enacted. They knew that sometimes bullets go astray—and for that reason they edged backward, to give free play to dancing guns. The silent Texan had broken his silence.

To Tilatha McLennon there came a weird, unearthly fear. Something was happening, something was taking place beyond her powers of control. And the tragic thing was coming in a form a thousand times worse than her worst anticipations. Bad enough that Boone had tempted one of the Quinns at a time. But now both Quinns were here, firmly set for a killing, both of them—and Boone was alone. Sheriff Brady was not even in sight.

The fear that was in her gripped her heart. She must not give way—she must not, she must not! It was up to her to put a stop to this tragedy in the offing. Boone would die without a chance. She felt that she would either faint, or give' way to hysteria—but she must do neither.

On a sudden impulse she rushed forward. "Stop," she cried, "stop . . . you . . . !"

A hand reached out of the crowd and grasped her by a wrist. "Stay back outta that," a voice commanded her.

Whip Quinn did not bat an eye. The hatred within him for this quiet, fighting man from Texas rose into his eyes and made them twin balls of black-flecked flame. Before this crowd he meant to scorch the Texan with his eyes, burn him down till the Texas man's gaze should waver and fall. But it was his own lids that asked to flicker first. Whip felt called on to speak before he lost the battle of the eyes.

"Sibley," he hissed, "there's only one thing keeps my hand off my gun right now. You tied it up by goin' down in that hole and pullin' a Quinn out. You showed yourself to be handy with your fists when you first came to town . . . now you showed yourself to be handy with a shovel. But my hands ain't goin' to be tied long. It's you or me, Sibley. One of us has got to get out and stay out. I'm givin' you till tomorrow mornin', sunrise. If you ain't on your way where nobody from Tough Nut can ever see you again, by sunrise in the mornin', you'll be havin' to show you're as handy with guns as you are with fists and shovels!"

It might have been settled in that manner, if not for the effect created on Russ Quinn by Tilatha McLennon. That Tilatha should be witness to his humiliation was too much to bear. It seemed that at sight of her, at hearing her voice, all the evil in him that he had never let out rose to the surface. The desire to explode hell in the faces of all these people and drench the Texan in its fires gouged out the last bit of restraint in a man of powerful passions.

"Wait a minute," Russ Quinn forced in a throaty hoarseness. "Not so easy! My hands ain't tied. He came down there after me . . . and I told him to get out! He didn't. I made a promise to Miss McLennon just before it happened. I promised her I was goin' to shoot this Texas meddler full of holes the first time we crossed. I aim to keep that promise . . . *now,* not sunrise!"

The hush that had fallen on the crowd deepened. Tilatha stood petrified for a moment, then suddenly made an attempt to twist herself out of a man's grasp. He held her fast.

"Russ!" she cried. "You can't . . . he risked his life for you . . . that whole shaft might have caved in on both of you! You can't . . . ."

"I'm drawin', Texas man!" came Russ Quinn's inflamed challenge. Tilatha McLennon's voice only maddened him to the bursting point.

Whip Quinn, never lowering his eyes, stepped away. Russ and Boone were hardly four feet apart, and only a man's length away from them was the yawning pit out of which they had emerged. Deathly silence prevailed.

Russ Quinn made the first move. His right hand darted to his holster. The metal of his gun flashed in an eerie, reflected light. The light came from the explosion at the tip of Boone Sibley's roaring gun. For Boone Sibley had waited only for a sign of hostile motion by Russ Quinn. No sooner had the Quinn hand moved, when the Texas man's wrist flipped, leaving an empty holster beneath it.

Russ had not pulled a trigger. His gun fell to the dry earth. He spun about, his right hand shattered. The impact of the bullet whirled him sidewise. For a moment he tottered at the brink of the pit. The caked dirt cracked, gave way beneath his feet. A two foot square of treacherous black earth slid away, and with it toppled Russ Quinn into the abyss of darkness.

"Look out!"

The warning cry came from a dozen husky throats. Boone Sibley's eyes were now riveted on Whip Quinn, in anticipation of an ugly move from that quarter. He heard a slithering sound, and leaped suddenly sideways. A moment later a huge block broke away, a crackling sound issued, and a great mass of earth slithered over the edge of the pit and into the chasm.

Instantly the crowd retreated in a body. A roar of rushing wind, dirt flying high from air pressure shooting upward, a thunderous *whack* from the belly of the pit, and the great movement was on. Timbers loosened, leaned over, and fell. Earth, stones, rock, wood, metal clumped and clattered and skidded mercilessly down on the doomed man. For two whole minutes the break-up and filling continued, while Boone Sibley never took his eyes off the brother of the luckless Russ.

At last it was over. The shower of flying dust settled or rode away on the billowing back of a west breeze. The air cleared.

"He shot Russ in the hand," someone exclaimed.

"He shot Russ into hell!" came another exclamation.

"He shot 'im where he belongs!" came another.

The tension was lifted. Nowhere, among that crowd, could be seen a sympathetic face. It was as though a great weight had been lifted, and bowed shoulders could straighten. There was no cheer. Only sunlight seemed to dance out of darkness and brighten faces long drawn in fears of uncertainty. There flashed across the minds of men that Curt French was dead, Sing Elder and Brad Prouty were in jail awaiting trial for murder, Russ Quinn was buried with his evil forever—and only Whip Quinn remained.

Had the power of Whip been lesser than it was, nobody could have foretold what might have happened at this moment. There might have been discovered the limb of a convenient tree. And certainly there was enough length of rope at hand. But Whip Quinn held them, held them almost as of old.

But his power of command was broken, and he knew it. With his dead brother Russ, it lay shattered to bits under that avalanche of earth and débris in the black pit. Gun play was now more than futile. Whip knew that even if he'd win, he would lose. Whip Quinn knew when he was beaten. He knew also how to keep his colors flying in the fate of defeat. He took his eyes off Boone and glanced into the chasm of defeat. All his plans, all his hopes, all his future lay there, buried.

He turned on his heel and walked away. At the edge of the crowd he once more faced Sibley. "You crowned your luck once more, Texas warrior," he said. "It held again. You won. I never saw a man with so much crazy luck. I reckon it's too much to show you the way out of Tough Nut by dawn. I'll be goin', Texas man. I reckon there's a right plenty of customers for the Occidental."

He turned again. This time his stride held.

Tilatha McLennon spent a night of self-torture. It came to her in all its force while she was alone, that she had given her hand and heart away before the crowd at the hole. True, Boone had escorted her to the Turley house, but it had been almost in silence. Not a word had he said. Not a word, that is, of what was uppermost in her mind. His silence had stifled her, gored her.

The sun rose. She got out of bed, dressed. She meant to be gone before anybody was up and about. Boone must not find her in town. It would be almost as though she were waiting for him to come to her. Her pride was too strong for that!

She packed her new dress and a few articles of clothing. A few minutes later, saddled, she was on her way along the road that led out of town. Suddenly her heart pounded hard. The blood raced through her veins.

"You've kept me waiting almost an hour," said

Boone Sibley. He had appeared unexpectedly from behind the shadows of a row of houses.

"Waiting?" Tilatha repeated.

"Yes. I was expecting you to light out like this. I . . . I was tongue-tied when I took you home."

They rode together. Cochise Head was in front of them as they rode along the hill shoulder, knee brushing against knee. The only sounds were the occasional clip of a horse's hoof striking a stone or the chuffing of the saddle leather. Dawn was radiant.

"Good to be here with you," Boone said at last.

Woman-like, now that the hour she had longed for was at hand, she sought for little barriers to build against it.

"It's such a relief to know that nobody is waiting for a chance to kill you, that all your enemies have ridden away and left you unharmed."

He smiled. "I'm a heap easier in my mind. But I was talking about something else. I was talking about you and me."

She flashed one swift glance at him, and then looked at Cochise Head, resplendent in the bright rays of morning sun.

"Are we to travel the long trail together, Tilatha?" he asked simply. "That's what I've been wondering a heap."

She evaded an answer. "I thought you didn't like women."

Boone swung from the saddle, dropped the reins, and came to her. "I'm not saying anything about women, but about a woman. I like her a lot more than I ever expected to like one."

"Are you . . . so sure?" she murmured.

He drew her gently from the saddle into his arms. She rested there, content. Only her heart beat against his.

He drew her soft tanned cheeks toward him, looked into the love-lit eyes, and kissed her lips. Her supple body made a little motion of abandon as her emotion met his.

The sun rose to bathe the crown of Cochise when once more they started on the long trail.

ABOUT THE AUTHOR

William MacLeod Raine, hailed in his later years to be the "greatest living practitioner" of the genre and the "dean of Westerns," was born in London, England in 1871. Upon the death of his mother, Raine immigrated with his father to Arkansas in the United States where he was raised. He attended Sarcey College in Arkansas and received his Bachelor's degree from Oberlin College in 1894. He was troubled in his early years by a lung ailment that was eventually diagnosed as tuberculosis. He moved to Denver, Colorado in hopes that his health would improve, and worked as a reporter and editorial writer for a number of newspapers. He began writing short stories for the magazine market. His first Western novel, *Wyoming* (1908), proved so popular with readers that it was serialized in the first issues of Street & Smith's *Western Story Magazine* when that publication was launched in 1919. During World War I, Raine's Western fiction was so popular among British readers that 500,000 copies of his books were distributed among British troops. By his own admission, Raine concentrated on character in his Westerns. "I'm not very strong on plot. Some of my writing friends say you have to have the plot all laid out before you start. I don't see it that way. If you have it all laid out, your characters can't develop naturally as the story unfolds. Sometimes there's someone you start out as a minor character. By the time you're through, he's the major character of the book. I like to preside over it all, but to let the book do its own growing." It would appear that because of this focus on character Raine's stories have stood the test of time better than those of some of his contemporaries. It was his intimate knowledge of the American West that provides verisimilitude to all of his stories, whether in a large sense such as the booming industries of the West or the cruelties of Nature—a flood in *Ironheart* (1923), blizzards in *Ridgway of Montana* (1909) and *The Yukon Trail* (1917), a fire in *Gunsight Pass* (1921). It is perhaps Raine's love of the West of his youth, the place and the people where there existed the "fine free feeling of man as an individual," glimmering in the pages of his books that will warrant the attention of readers always.

ADDITIONAL COPYRIGHT INFORMATION

Center Point Large Print
600 Brooks Road / PO Box 1
Thorndike, ME 04986-0001 USA

(207) 568-3717

US & Canada:
1 800 929-9108
www.centerpointlargeprint.com